D1172663

The Man Who Killed Shakespeare

THE MAN WHO KILLED SHAKESPEARE

KEN HODGSON

FIVE STAR

An imprint of Thomson Gale, a part of The Thomson Corporation

Detroit • New York • San Francisco • New Haven, Conn. • Waterville, Maine • London

THOMSON
━━━━━✦━━━━━ ™
GALE

LIBRARY OF CONGRESS CATALOGING-IN-PUBLICATION DATA

Hodgson, Ken.
   The man who killed shakespeare / Ken Hodgson. — 1st ed.
    p. cm.
   ISBN-13: 978-1-59414-598-8 (alk. paper)
   ISBN-10: 1-59414-598-9 (alk. paper)
   1. Mines and mineral resources—Fiction. 2. New Mexico—Fiction. 3. Swindlers and swindling—Fiction. I. Title.
   PS3558.O34346M36 2007
   813'.54—dc22
                                     2007022616

First Edition. First Printing: November 2007.

Published in 2007 in conjunction with Tekno Books and Ed Gorman.

Printed in the United States of America on permanent paper
10 9 8 7 6 5 4 3 2 1

Some folks say there ain't no such
thing as Hell,
If they've never lived through a depression
how could they tell?

—Lett Halsy

O, it is excellent
to have a giant's strength; but it is tyrannous
to use it like a giant.
—Shakespeare, *Measure For Measure*, Act II, Scene 2

I can believe anything, provided it is incredible.
—Oscar Wilde, *The Picture of Dorian Gray*

CHAPTER ONE

The bullet went high to the left and slammed into the wall a foot away from the apple setting on top of Elmore Wyman's bushy white head.

"Horse dumplings," Jake Clanton grumbled. "I ain't got a dollar for another shot. How about staking me, Bulldog?" he asked with a slur, his bloodshot eyes focused on a burly, jowl-cheeked man standing at the bar holding a mug of beer.

"Nope," Bulldog answered, "you're drunk as a waltzing pissant. I'd never forgive myself if you plugged old Elmore instead of the apple and I paid for the bullet that done it."

"I ain't never hit him yet," Jake whined.

"Reckon it only takes once," the ponderous bartender, Jason McTavish, interjected. "If you shoot him, I'll lose a paying customer. With this Depression on, I plain can't afford that. Nope, no more playing William Tell this afternoon."

"Horse dumplings," Jake repeated, as he holstered his Colt.

The rotund saloon keeper walked around the end of the long mahogany bar to where the calmly snoring old man was propped up against the wall. He shook his head sadly when he noticed the lace work of bullet holes above and around Elmore's form.

"Gonna have to fix that someday," he mumbled. Then he grabbed the apple from Elmore's head, rubbed it on his apron and ate it, core and all.

"I never saw a man eat everything in sight like McTavish does," Arnold Epp commented standing alongside Bulldog.

"Doc told him to watch his weight," Bulldog grinned and took a sip of beer. "So he put it all out front where he can keep an eye on it."

"You guys are just jealous because I'm in the peak of health," McTavish said, patting his ample belly as he made his way behind the bar. "Besides that, I may be out of work when that new owner shows up."

"Ain't no one has any job security nowadays," Epp grumbled. "Hoover saw to that when he put us in this damn Depression."

"Nope, Hoover just inherited the mess," McTavish said. "Those stock-market crooks are the real cause. When the crash hit back in twenty-nine, J.P. Morgan and his cronies started buying up stocks and companies for pennies on the dollar. No sir, the whole shebang was staged by them so they could take over the country."

Bulldog spun his beer glass worriedly on the bar. "One thing's for sure, there's nothing any of us here in Shakespeare, New Mexico, can do about it. All we can do is hang on and hope. Old Wyman's made more money in the past month letting Clanton try to shoot an apple off his head than I have. If I can't find a job pretty soon reckon I'll need to start letting folks take shots at me. The only thing different will be I'll eat the apple myself."

"Won't work like that," Jason McTavish said firmly. "If a man's not passed out drunk he'll most likely jump right into the bullet. That's why Elmore ain't got shot yet. Besides that, I can't afford to pay fifty dollars to every man who gets lucky enough to hit the apple. Elmore has to be it—long as he lasts."

"This new owner," Bulldog said to change the subject. He got depressed when he thought about how long he'd been out of work. "Do you know anything about him?"

"Only that he's from Colorado," McTavish said, dumping a dead fly out of a beer mug and refilling it. "Our local shyster, Otis Tate, is handling Howard's estate. He told me I could expect him to show up today or tomorrow."

"Too bad ol' Howard up and croaked," Epp lamented. "This place was a lot livelier when he was around."

"The mines was running then," McTavish growled. "Besides that, he didn't just up and croak, he had an accident, plain and simple."

"I didn't know choking to death on an antelope steak was classified as an accident," Jake Clanton said.

"Shouldn't have been," Epp agreed, nodding his head toward the bartender. "McTavish cooked it. Everyone knows how tough anything he fries up is. Taking a bite out of a stove would be more tender than gnawing on one of his antelope steaks. Howard just plain forgot how bad a cook McTavish is. I'd say he died from a bad memory."

"Well, none of you sons of guns have to eat anything I fix again if you don't want to," Jason McTavish spat. "I was surprised as everyone when Howard choked. That steak wasn't tougher than normal—for antelope."

"If you'd stewed up a Hoover hog instead of that stringy antelope, Howard would still be running the place," Bulldog said.

McTavish retorted with a growl, "Howard didn't like jackrabbit, they got no taste. Now antelope might be tougher than leather but it's got body to it, keeps your ribs from rubbin' on your backbone."

Epp clucked his tongue, "Maybe you should've ground that antelope into sausage, Jason, then we wouldn't be worried none about having a new saloon owner that maybe won't run us a tab."

"Well, he shouldn't," the bartender groaned, sticking his thumbs under the sides of his bibbed apron, something he always did when he got nervous or upset. "Delight won't run a tab and I should never have started. Whores know better than to trust the likes of you. I'm just too nice a guy. That's what's gonna get me fired. When the new owner goes over the books of the Roxy Jay Saloon I'm going to be out of here like a dried-up tumbleweed in a windstorm."

"We're all good for our bills here," Bulldog said soothingly. "You know that, McTavish. Once the Last Chance Mine gets going we'll pay up."

Bulldog took a packet of cigarette papers from one front pocket of his khaki shirt and a nearly empty bag of Bull Durham tobacco from the other. He slipped out a paper and creased it into a V with a practiced motion and filled it perfectly level with tobacco in one shake. He wet one side with a flick of his tongue and rolled the cigarette tightly. All the while wondering if he was trying to convince McTavish or himself the new silver mine being promoted in Shakespeare was for real. He sincerely hoped so. His total assets consisted of a Model T with a rattling, smoking engine, three changes of patched and faded clothes and six dollars he'd stashed away in case he had to leave town.

He had heard that some of the mines in Silver City were hiring. If things didn't break here soon—Bulldog didn't think things could possibly be any poorer there. Worst of all, he knew McTavish was right in his assessment of the twenty-dollar tab he had run up. There was no way he could pay it. Skipping on a debt was something he'd never done in his forty years. The thought stuck in his throat like bile.

Epp put a comforting hand on Bulldog's massive shoulder. "Sam Ransom, the fellow that's promoting the Last Chance, has money sticking out of ever pocket he owns. We'll be working and making big money contractin' for him right soon."

McTavish agreed. "Of course you will. All you guys will be working soon. That mountain's full of silver, everyone in Shakespeare knows that's a fact. I just hope the new owner of this joint will have a little faith in things for a while."

"And he brings enough money with him to last until things break," Jake Clanton laughed. "Otherwise I'm gonna have to start robbing trains like my granpappy Ike over in Tombstone used to do."

Bulldog shook his head with a grin. "Jake, even if Ike Clanton was your granpappy you'd just get shot or go to prison. Nobody but an idiot would rob a train these days. Banks are where the money's at, unless we're talking about the bank in Lordsburg. There's not enough cash in the safe there to pay for the dynamite to blow it open."

Jake Clanton slouched his shoulders and plopped down on a bar stool. His real name was Clanton, but no one in his family had ever been related to Ike Clanton of Tombstone fame. He had concocted that story when he first came West from his native Texas. While the mines were running, he had always been able to get free drinks by telling made-up tales of his imaginary grandfather's exploits. Nowadays, he had to buy his own beer. Like all of the hangers-on in Shakespeare, Jake was biding time until big-talking Sam Ransom got the silver mine in operation. The only work he'd been able to find lately was working for Dugan's gas station in Lordsburg. It was only a two-mile walk, so he didn't miss having sold his car. Jake had done a lot of bragging about being a dead shot with a pistol. That was how he had come to bet a dollar a bullet against fifty put up by McTavish that he could shoot an apple off old Elmore's head. By Jake's last count he had spent nearly a hundred dollars taking shots at the apple. He was deathly afraid of killing the old man since in reality he could not hit the side of a barn if he was locked inside it. Every bullet had gone wide by a foot. At least the crazy old prospector received free beer from Jake's betting and thankfully had not been killed.

McTavish began drumming his pudgy fingers on his apron. "Boys, I'd say we're all in the same boat and Sam Ransom's bringing the oar. Even if I don't get fired by the guy from Colorado who inherited this place, there's no question that if that silver mine don't start up soon, Shakespeare will be deader than Jake Clanton's granpappy, whoever the hell he was."

"Sam's supposed to be hitting town tomorrow, or so I heard," Epp ventured. "Maybe McTavish and all of us might have some news purty shortly."

Old Elmore Wyman let out a moan, coughed loudly and bellowed, "Give me a damn beer and will somebody help me up. Ever time I take a little nap I wake up over here propped up agin the wall. Hurts my back somethin' fierce."

McTavish and Bulldog helped the skinny prospector onto a bar stool. Once he had a beer in his hand he took a deep drink and slurred, "You boys will get paid back fer the beers in spades when I make another trip to the Lost Dutchman Mine."

"You'd better do it soon," the bartender said firmly. "We're plumb out of apples."

The old man gave a scowl then quickly focused his attention back on his beer. Elmore Wyman didn't have a clue why McTavish had brought up the subject of apples. It sure had nothing to do with him. That much was for certain.

CHAPTER TWO

Otis Tate stared thoughtfully out the front window of his office as he watched a trash-laden dust devil wind its way east along the railroad tracks. He ran boney fingers through the stubble of gray beard he'd worn since coming to Lordsburg over ten years ago, then turned his attention to the big, obviously nervous man who sat politely at his desk with his hat cradled in his lap like a sleeping pet dog.

"Mister Halsy," the lawyer finally spoke, "I'm afraid the estate your late brother left you may not be exactly what you were expecting."

"Sir," Lett Halsy answered softly, "my brother and me, well we ain't exactly been real close lately. I haven't seen him since I started working up in Cripple Creek, Colorado, back in nineteen-seventeen, that's fifteen years. I know he was in Mexico for a spell and then he wrote us—me—that he'd bought a hotel here in New Mexico. I'd reckon that was nearly three years ago, back before the country fell apart."

"Yes, this Depression has hurt nearly everyone. We were fortunate here to have some large mines running until three months ago. Then the company that owned them shut down and laid everyone off. Right now you couldn't buy a job."

"I know sir, it's the same all over," Lett said blandly. "I was let go by the Cresson Mine just two months ago, fired actually. The mine's still running but I'm forty-five years old. They can get young kids that can do more work than me and hire 'em

13

cheaper, too. My rheumatism started acting up and the boss found out I'd been seeing a doctor, so he just up an' fired me."

"I'm truly sorry, Mister Halsy," Otis Tate said sincerely. "I'm not too sure your brother Howard's estate will offer you much relief. There was very little cash. After expenses, such as the funeral and my modest fees, the balance is just over five hundred dollars."

Lett Halsy couldn't hold back a grin. All he had in this world was twenty-two dollars stuck in his boot and a 1923 Chevy Coupe parked outside the lawyer's office. "And the hotel? He mentioned he owned one?"

Otis folded his hands behind his back and walked to the front window again. "Now *there* is where some problems may arise. Tell me, Mister Halsy, are you a single man?"

Lett swallowed hard. "My wife and son, both of them died of pneumonia within a week of each other just three winters ago."

"I'm very sorry."

"Up there in the high country," Lett continued, "pneumonia kills most who get it. We had a home near the old ghost town of Altman, close to the Cresson Mine so I could walk to work. It's over ten thousand feet high there, and tough enough to breathe even when you're healthy. Mattie and Eddie, well they went fast, sir. To answer your question, yes I'm alone these days."

The lawyer's eyes drifted to the floor. It seemed like all he heard lately were sad stories. He started to say once again how sorry he was, but that very word seemed vapid to him. "The place your brother left you is in the town of Shakespeare, where the mines are. It's only a couple of miles south of here. I'll run you out in my car shortly. First there's a few things you should know."

Lett pursed his lips and fingered the brim of his hat. "Yes sir, I reckon I should know all about the joint."

"Joint is a good word to describe the Roxy Jay Saloon. I'm

afraid the word 'hotel' could never be used accurately. There are five little cabins or cribs out back of the bar, but they were intended only for temporary pleasures of the feminine kind."

"A whorehouse!" Lett blurted out. "My brother ran a whorehouse?"

"That's just part of the Roxy Jay. There's gambling and the best Mexican beer and whiskey you can find with prohibition on. Before the mines closed your brother had a booming business. Nowadays, I believe there's only one lady of the night and a rather surly bartender named Jason McTavish in residence there."

"You mean to tell me I've inherited a whorehouse that runs wide open selling booze and has gambling?"

"I think you're getting the drift of it."

"What about the law, man? Back in Colorado a guy could get his nose wet if he spent five minutes looking for a joint. But there's not a place there with a sign on the door saying so."

"No federal agent wants to leave the comforts of Lordsburg to go to a little town like Shakespeare, especially when our esteemed sheriff, Victor Mayes, goes there constantly to make certain nothing illegal is going on. It only costs the Roxy Jay five dollars a month and all the beer Mayes can drink to stay in blissful compliance with the law."

"You talk like you're against prohibition," Lett ventured.

A small grin crossed the lawyer's face. "I most certainly am. You simply can't legislate morals. All that's accomplished when such a law is enacted are wonderful opportunities for organized crime to give people what the government won't let them get legally along with some terrible inequities. Back East a lady with ten kids was given a life sentence for selling two pints of moonshine. Al Capone made a hundred million dollars a year and the only thing our system did to him was give him a few years in prison for tax evasion. I sincerely believe the Volstead

Act will be repealed shortly. Then the sheriff will take a five-dollar-a-month salary cut. Perhaps you'll be here to see it."

"I—I really don't have anywhere else to go. This desert climate seems to agree with my rheumatism. It's a lot warmer here than in Colorado."

Otis chuckled. "Right now it's only May. There's a joke that a preacher can't make a go of it in Lordsburg because once a person has spent a summer here, Hell is pretty much an empty threat."

Lett couldn't contain a snicker. He wasn't able to remember the last time he'd actually laughed. He was taking a liking to the lawyer. Otis Tate was nothing like he'd expected; slender as a bean pole, wearing a stubble of beard, dressed in work clothes and sporting less hair on top of his head than a lightbulb, the man seemed to have somehow maintained a sense of humor despite the crushing Depression.

"This saloon, the Roxy Jay, it's still running?" Lett asked.

"Jason McTavish has kept it open since your brother's unfortunate demise. In view of the mines having closed I'd wonder as to how well he's doing. Why don't we go ask him?"

"Yes sir, I'd like that," Lett Halsy said respectfully. "If you don't mind I'll follow you in my car. If there's some place to stay there I reckon that would be cheaper than a hotel room here in town."

"Your brother lived in one of the cribs out back. Just a one-room cabin, but he had it fixed up comfortable enough. There's a decent bed and probably fewer cockroaches than you'd find in the hotel here. If you'll come to my office tomorrow morning we'll go to the bank and transfer the money into your account."

The worn motor of Lett's battered Chevy finally started on the second try, then he ground it into gear and followed the lawyer's glistening black Maxwell through town to where a dusty, well-traveled road headed south toward a range of barren-

16

looking hills. It was late afternoon and they were the only cars on the road. He was amused Otis Tate had referred to the craggy mounds they were heading to as mountains. Where he came from there were *real* mountains. What he saw were only bumps rising up from the desert floor.

Strange-looking plants and cactus sprouted everywhere in profusion. Lett had found early on, during some roadside stops to relieve himself, that everything growing in the desert had stickers on it. He did enjoy the dry warmth. His knotted hands and bad back seemed less painful than they had been in the cold of Cripple Creek. When he'd abandoned his house there to come to New Mexico, six-foot-deep snow drifts still lay among the tall spruce trees. The temperature here must be at least in the eighties. Lett doubted it ever got cold enough to snow in the desert.

He kept a good distance from the lawyer's car to let the dust settle. Shortly, they drove past a cemetery. Flowers decorated some grave markers, others had fallen; cactus and greasewood invaded the space of those buried there. Lett felt a lump form in his throat when he wondered who would care for his wife and son's graves in distant Colorado.

After climbing a low rise he saw Otis's Maxwell head toward a rambling row of dilapidated shacks lining the gentle valley ahead. The lump in his throat gave way to a feeling of outright despair when he pulled alongside the Maxwell, shut off his sputtering engine and stared numbly at the Roxy Jay Saloon.

Lett Halsy had seen his share of once-booming mining towns fade away into detritus. Goldfield, Independence and his old home of Altman had become nothing but weathered memories clinging to the side of a wind-blown mountain. Shakespeare looked worse than all of those put together. A few of the more substantial buildings like the one sporting a weathered sign proclaiming it to be the Roxy Jay Hotel were built from crude gray Mexican adobe bricks. Most of the other structures were constructed of ragged, bleached plank boards that hadn't seen paint for untold years. Only a few showed signs of occupancy. The shifting winds had driven piles of brown tumbleweeds into doorways and heaped them alongside what passed for Main Street. The happy, tinny sounds of a honky-tonk piano drifting through the swinging doors of the saloon were an antithesis of the entire town.

Otis Tate climbed from his dusty black Maxwell, stuck his bony hands into his pant pockets and proclaimed happily, "Well Mister Halsy, all this is yours."

Lett shook his head and closed his eyes. When he reopened them, things looked as bad as they were before. He opened the door of his Chevy and stepped out onto the powder-dry dirt street. From nowhere a brown-and-white mongrel dog streaked up behind him and took a painful nip on the calf of his left leg.

"Damn that mutt," Lett swore, kicking at the dog that safely dodged the blow and retreated underneath the boardwalk.

"He's *your* dog. That's old Wesley," the lawyer said with a grin. "He always welcomes folks with a friendly nip until he gets to know them. Your brother got bit every day for quite a spell until Wesley finally figured out who fed him. I'd say that dog's a little touched."

"He may be a whole lot gone," Lett snorted.

"Don't be too hasty," Otis said. "That dog's a real good snaker. One day a while back he killed four rattlers in an hour, one of them was a good six-footer. They like to get under the porches out of the sun. Wesley's either too fast for them or too dumb to care if he gets bit."

Lett sighed. "Well, let's go see what *else* Howard left me."

The pair walked through the swinging saloon doors, then hesitated for a moment while their eyes adjusted from the bright desert sun to the dusky interior. The first thing Lett made out was a huge mahogany bar that ran the full length of the building, possibly eighty feet long. An enormous mirror, the biggest he had ever seen, filled the wall behind the bar. To his right, a player piano rattled out the tinkling music he'd heard outside.

"Welcome to the Roxy," a deep voice boomed from a dark corner of the bar. A huge fat man wearing a gray apron and carrying a bar towel draped over an arm fairly ran to meet them. "I'm Jason McTavish. I've run the place here for Howard Halsy for some time, now. You must be the new owner, Mister—?" He stuck out a pudgy hand.

"Lett—Lett Halsy, Howard was my brother."

McTavish looked shocked. "Well, I'll swan. Howard never let on that he had any kin. Glad to make your acquaintance, sir."

Lett shook the fat man's hand. "I'm still trying to make heads or tails out of just what all my brother left me."

"Why just the biggest and best money-making opportunity in New Mexico," the bartender blared. "Once Sam Ransom gets that big silver mine on the hill running, everyone in Shakespeare will be crappin' in tall cotton."

"I'm afraid Mister Halsy may be more concerned with the here and now, McTavish," the lawyer said crustily, wiping the smile from the bartender's face. "Perhaps you could simply show him around. And leave the promoting to Sam Ransom?"

"Uh, sure thing," McTavish mumbled. He poked his thumbs under his apron straps and headed behind the bar. "Would you gentlemen like something to drink?"

"A beer for me," Otis Tate said quickly.

"I'll have the same," Lett said, looking around with trepidation at the motley few men in residence at the bar.

"Sorry about your brother. He was well liked in these parts," a large older man with a deeply wrinkled round face said. "My name's Paul Talbot, but everyone calls me Bulldog. The man on my right's Arnold Epp. We partner together when we're working." Bulldog nodded down the bar to his left, "This here's Jake Clanton, then Elmore Wyman and at the end is Len Miller, he's the town barber and when we got no doc, like nowadays, he fills in. If a body's likely to get well on their own, he works out okay."

Len scowled at Bulldog and started to say something, but Lett Halsy spoke first.

"Glad to meet you gents," he said pleasantly, shaking everyone's hand in turn. "I reckon you're all wondering what I'm planning to do with the Roxy Jay. As soon as I figure that out myself, I'll let you all know. Right now if Mister McTavish would show me the cabin where my brother lived I'd appreciate it."

"Oh, yes sir," McTavish said fawningly. "If you'll follow me, it's straight through that big oak door and right next to Delight."

"Delight?" Lett questioned.

Bulldog answered, "She's the only whore we got left in Shakespeare these days. Most everything worthwhile fell into the crapper when the mines closed. Delight's getting some years on her, but she's still got her lumps in the right places. There's some Mex gals down in Lordsburg north of the railroad tracks that sells it for four bits. Delight charges two bucks, so her bedsprings don't squeak very often these days, but she won't give you the clap like those Mex girls will."

"Had us a real bevy of cuties when the mines were running," Arnold Epp said sadly. "One of 'em was named Brooke; she couldn't have been over eighteen and she was built like a brick outhouse. Most of us called her Babbling Brooke 'cause she never shut up. She charged five bucks a throw and must have been worth it 'cause there was a line outside her door every payday night. The rest of the time she shacked with Howard—"

Bulldog jabbed an elbow hard into Epp's ribs. "What tha' hell'd you do that for," Epp howled, then he thought for a moment; "Oh, I'm just sayin' they was good friends."

Lett Halsy rolled his eyes, looked at the lawyer and sighed, "So far today I've come to own a whorehouse, got dog bit and found out my brother was a pimp. I reckon I oughtta go on out back and finish off the day right—most likely I'll get nailed by a rattlesnake."

CHAPTER THREE

Sam Ransom loved to drive his snow-white, 1931 Cadillac V-12 very fast. The three-hundred-sixty-eight-cubic-inch motor churned out one hundred thirty-five horsepower and could outrun most any car on the road. Right now this was a real plus to Sam's way of thinking. That bunch of morons on the grand jury had decided to indict him on fraud charges, so he was extremely anxious to get out of the state of California in a hurry.

Over the past year Sam had bilked over a hundred thousand dollars from a group of San Francisco investors (he called them and anyone who believed in his schemes "Guppies") to develop and market a perpetual-motion machine.

Sam had a beautiful working model of his engine constructed by a high-priced and tight-lipped master jeweler. He even had a shiny nameplate embossed on the polished walnut base proclaiming it to be the Eternia Power Engine, a name he'd thought up over a wonderful bottle of expensive French wine. Underneath this nameplate, a skillfully hidden small battery kept the little machine spinning happily along. A slim leather belt could be attached to a miniature generator. The Eternia Engine's flywheel would whirl tirelessly, keeping a small light-bulb lit for days. To the wide-eyed Guppies there was no doubt the little motor could run forever.

None of the Guppies who had invested money in Sam's Eternia Engine Company apparently ever paid attention in school. They certainly had never even heard of Sir Isaac Newton or the principal of entropy; a certain amount of energy is always lost due to friction. Perpetual motion in any form is an absolute impossibility of physics.

Sam Ransom had an artist draw pictures of large versions of his Eternia motor powering railroads, ships, trucks and, in one remarkably imaginative scene, an airplane. Gullible people with far more money than common sense had bought stock on the ground floor for only a dollar a share. They received a beautiful gilt-edged certificate in return for their check, which a smiling Sam Ransom immediately cashed.

Then, one of the more business-like of the investors had borrowed the machine one morning under the guise of showing it to a friend who he said was considering buying some stock. Instead, the man took it to the patent office and attempted to have a U.S. government patent on the Eternia Engine issued in his name. Sam had admired the man's gall, but the results were disastrous. In short order a government engineer had discovered the battery and great piles of excrement hit the fan very quickly after that.

Sam knew the laws of California. They wouldn't pursue him once he was out of the state. He'd been very careful not to use the United States mail for any promotion purposes. Couriers were much more impressive to investors and this also had the wonderful effect of keeping the federal government out of his affairs.

Seven of Sam Ransom's thirty-nine years were spent gaining a higher education for his profession. The California penal system had provided him with access to many learned teachers who freely gave him ideas for new schemes and warned him of the type of pitfalls that had landed them in prison.

It had been five years now, since his release. Sam was making the most of his training. One of the first lessons he'd learned was not to get greedy and stick around too long.

"There's always another cow to be milked in another pasture," wheezing old George Graham had advised. Now Sam was heeding that advice. In the backseat of his Cadillac were boxes of blank stock certificates, carefully chosen to be the most impressive looking he could find: gold-laced borders and lithograph pictures of huge buildings with smoke billowing from tall stacks. One box contained brochures he'd had printed in full color with glistening gold and silver bricks on the cover announcing the untold wealth that waited investors in the Shakespeare Mining and Development Company.

Sam knew nothing of mining, but he'd learned that for only a few dollars a man could file a claim or lease a mine with some history of production for only a small payment. In the town of Shakespeare—a name he felt would sell stock all by itself—Sam had done both. The Last Chance Mine was patented, private property. The starving owner of the long-closed shaft was happy to get five hundred dollars a year for the lease. Sam then engaged the services of a prospector and had him stake more claims on open federal land. He didn't care where the man staked them as long as they were somewhere near the Last Chance. The prospector was no fool himself; it was a lot easier to pile up rocks for claim corners on the level desert floor than up in the rugged hills. After spending another five hundred dollars Sam owned a thousand acres of what the brochure touted as "prime mineral property with the extensions of many known high-grade veins apexing on it." If an imaginative person took a ruler and drew lines from some of the rich mines like the Atwood or Eighty-Five, their veins did point towards the general direction of Sam's claims. The only problem being Sam's property was over a mile away and mostly covered with hundreds of feet of dirt. This didn't matter to him; the last thing he cared to know was whether or not there was actually gold or silver in his claims. Sam Ransom was a seller of dreams.

Affectionately Sam fondled the polished leather briefcase on the seat by his side. It held nearly fifty thousand dollars in cash. That and the boxes of stock certificates, brochures and corporate seals with interchangeable nameplates were all he needed to make his dreams come true. Once he got to Shakespeare he'd make every Guppy in the vicinity think buying stock in his company was a better idea than going to heaven.

CHAPTER FOUR

The whore known as Delight stepped onto the worn plank porch in front of her one-room crib. She flashed a practiced smile at the three men coming out the back door of the bar, quickly sizing them up. The portly bartender and skinny lawyer she recognized right off. The third man she decided must be the new owner. Everyone had been expecting him to show up, and that would also explain the concerned look on McTavish's face and his thumbs tucked under his apron straps.

When the stranger gave her a kindly smile, her spirits soared. At the very least he looked like a man who might be considerate enough to let her stay on for a while until the mines reopened. Also, he could possibly be the source of a few dollars. He was a large man, over six feet tall, but lean and powerful looking, obviously used to hard work. She liked his salt-and-pepper hair he wore collar length and his clean, washed appearance. Sadly, this was something she seldom could say for most of her customers.

She had been born Sara Jane Parker, the oldest of eight daughters to a dirt-poor family of dry land farmers in the Oklahoma Territory in the year 1892. She told all her customers she was thirty-two and tried hard to keep the crop of wrinkles that laced her face well covered with makeup. Lately it seemed like a losing battle. Many coats of paint on an old house still fail to mask its true age.

Sara tried desperately to forget the many bitter years since her father had died from lockjaw after cutting himself with a scythe. She was barely thirteen at the time and her mother had quickly remarried. This time to a drunken mule trader with a fiery temper. Sara knew her mother needed help and a woman with eight kids to feed was no man's idea of a prize catch. His name had been Rufus Thompson, a name she would never forget; he was the only man she had ever killed.

On her mother's wedding night Rufus had gotten whiskey mean. Sara remembered how desperately her mother had fought him when he'd raped Sara on the bed in front of the entire family.

"Yer daughter's tha' one I married ya fer ya ol' hag," Rufus had snarled at her crying, screaming mother, as he viciously ripped off Sara's underwear then forced himself inside her. The shock and shame had been worse than the pain.

Rufus's hot, foul breath blew on her face while he was rutting her, nearly causing her to retch. "Damn, bitch, yer so good an' tight we'll do this every night," he'd gloated after one of his ham-sized fists had sent her mother sprawling.

From some corner of her mind, in spite of the pain and terror, Sara had remembered a pair of scissors laying on the night stand. Somehow she managed to scoot toward them in spite of the huge bulk covering her. When she felt the cold steel in her hand, one quick lucky thrust to his neck sliced open Rufus's jugular vein. After only moments of cursing and threatening, Rufus Thompson had bled to death on the floor beside the bed where he'd taken her. Sara couldn't believe the massive amount of blood the man carried in his body. Her own blood trickled down her shaking legs and mingled with his. Through the haze she remembered her mother sobbing to her that she had to run and run far away, very quickly.

As she had gained composure, the shattered thirteen-year-old realized her mother was correct. Most likely the sheriff would hang her for what she had done. She knew a lot of people had been hung for less than stabbing an unarmed man with a pair of scissors.

Her mother stuffed what few pathetic belongings Sara owned into a gunnysack and tied it shut with a piece of rope long enough to make a sling so she could carry it over her shoulder.

Sara Jane Parker never saw or had any contact with her mother or any of her sisters again after that terrible night. She felt dirty and damaged and was scared so badly she didn't think she would ever stop trembling. Her mother had given her all the money there was: three one-dollar bills, two quarters and five pennies. She never forgot this. Sara had counted that money over a hundred times through her stinging tears, trying to decide what to do and where to go. She only knew one large town. Once, when she was ten, her father had taken her to Tulsa to see a traveling carnival, but Tulsa was too close—someone might recognize her as the killer she was. Then hundreds of men would gloat watching her being hanged.

Scared and desperate, Sara knew now what men wanted. Since she was damaged goods, unfit for decent men and marriage, it took her little time to begin trading the only commodity she had for things she needed. At the railroad station the conductor had given her a one-way ticket to Denver in return for her laying with him in the baggage car. The man had been old and more nervous than she was. It only took him a minute to finish and this time it didn't hurt much.

When she reached Denver, a world away from Oklahoma and pursuing lawmen, Sara luckily found her way to Mattie Silk's bordello on Market Street. The young frail-looking girl with long blond hair and azure eyes who gave her age as eighteen took the name of Delight Jones and became one of Mattie's most sought-after courtesans.

Money rolled in, more money than Sara Jane Parker had ever

thought existed. Delight felt nothing for the faceless succession of men who bedded her. They only wanted a good time. This she provided them. Then they left her company to return home to their wives and families.

A severe case of gonorrhea soon left her fallopian tubes scarred. After that, at least, she no longer had to worry about ever becoming pregnant.

When the police closed Mattie Silk's affluent bordello in 1915, Delight Jones took to the road. Butte, Montana; Tonopah, Nevada; Tucson, Arizona, they were all the same. The years rolled by quickly. Too soon most of the men who came to the houses where she worked chose younger, fresher-looking girls— like she had been not very long ago—to take to the back rooms.

In small, out-of-the-way mining towns like Shakespeare, men were forced to take what they could get. Delight had done fairly well the past year. They chose the young girls when they were available and they had the money to spend. Neither was a common occurrence in Shakespeare. Delight was always available and she only charged two dollars. Delight knew her career was ending. No matter how tight her corsets were laced or how heavy and well applied her makeup was, when she looked into the mirror she saw a forty-year-old woman who was fast losing the battle with time.

Delight envied now—something she had never thought she would—the women who had a husband, a home and family. She thought often of some of her friends in the business who had married customers, and she wondered how they were faring.

Whores, when they got too old to attract men, usually moved to a new town and lived a lonely life. Some took the easy way out. A bottle of sleeping pills or strychnine quickly ended their pain. Others chose the slow way, trading their worn-out bodies for drinks, until finally dying in some dark and trash-littered alley.

With the Depression growing deeper by the day, and the mines—Shakespeare's only source of income—closed, Delight knew her options were fast running out. If she could persuade this new owner of the Roxy Jay to let her stay on until Sam Ransom got the big silver mine running, she might have a year, possibly more, to decide what to do. When she thought of what the future held in store for her, Sara Jane Parker felt scared. As scared as the thirteen-year-old little girl who fled the hangman in Oklahoma had been, a lifetime ago.

While Sara Jane Parker might simply be a frightened girl, Delight Jones was not. She knew how to get what she wanted or needed. For the past twenty-seven years, Delight had successfully charmed thousands of faceless men to do her bidding; this new bar owner would be no different.

Delight unbuttoned the two top buttons of her tight fitting print blouse and threw back her shoulders slightly to accent her jutting breasts. She shook out her waist length blond hair, wet her lips so they would shine, put on her learned smile and went to meet the man who had inherited the Roxy Jay Saloon.

"Why, hello," she purred after coming close enough to the stranger so he was enveloped by the heady aroma of perfume. "My name's Delight, what may I ask is yours, sir?"

"This here's Lett Halsy. He's Howard's brother by damn," the piggish bartender broke in to Delight's annoyance. He was always trying to get a free sample from her for steering customers her way. Delight decided that after this, if he ever wanted to climb into her bed, she would charge him double.

"Pleased to meet you ma'am," the big man said pleasantly, offering up his hand. When Delight took it she felt thick callouses that came from years of hard work. "All my friends call me Lett."

"Then Lett it is," Delight said. "You'll enjoy it here in Shakespeare, I *do* hope you're planning on staying?"

"At least for a spell," Lett answered. "I really don't know what the future holds. Don't reckon many folks do these days. Howard didn't leave much money and I was laid off some while ago—"

"He'll do just fine here, Delight," McTavish blurted in again. "That Sam Ransom feller has got a wampus cat by the tail with that big silver mine. Why he told me he'd have a hundred jobs open up right soon."

"I think Mister Halsy would like to see Howard's cabin now, McTavish," Otis said firmly. "Then, when he gets settled, I'm sure he'll want to go over the books with you."

Color fled the bartender's jowls. He tugged so hard on his apron strings one broke. Lett noticed the apron he'd first thought was gray was only filthy dirty.

"Well I got to get inside and take care of business," McTavish mumbled, as he hurried toward the bar.

"I'd reckon those books are going to read like a bad novel," Otis Tate commented.

"Yes," Delight said sweetly, "things have been slow lately, but this Sam Ransom fellow does have a large mine. He drives a new Cadillac and throws money around like it's water. Before I made any judgments, Lett, I'd give him a little time and see if he does get it going. Right now I'm afraid you couldn't find a buyer for this place at any price, even if you were so inclined. If that mine does open, the Roxy Jay will be valuable property."

"I'd venture the lady's right about not being able to sell the place," the lawyer said. "Lots of folks are just walking away and leaving their homes to the tax man. They load up what they can in the family car and head for California. From what I've heard things aren't a bit better there, but once a rumor gets started that there's jobs someplace, it becomes gospel quicker than if a preacher read it from the Bible."

CHAPTER FIVE

"Desperate times make desperate people," Lett said, trying to focus his attention on the small frame house they had been heading for before Delight showed up.

He was taken aback by the prostitute's demeanor. She was much prettier and seemed more intelligent and refined than any soiled dove he had met on Myers Avenue in Cripple Creek. Only once had Lett ventured there. Just a week after being fired from his job the walls of his companionless house had closed in on him. Loneliness for the company of a woman grated on his soul as incessantly as the icy wind that blasted down from Pike's Peak. Lett had felt like he was cheating on his wife when he had taken five dollars from his meager savings and drove to Myers Avenue in a snowstorm. He knew his guilt was foolish, but he had loved Mattie terribly. Nevertheless she had been gone, along with his beloved son, for three years now. And a man has urges and needs.

Three whores were waiting, wearing nearly nothing when he walked through the door of Jenny Belle's, one of the many establishments offering play for pay in the district. The girls had immediately gotten into a hair-pulling fight over who was to get his money, using viler language than any muleskinner. Lett had run from the place, ignoring the curses shouted after him. Later, he had visited a local bar and wound up getting so drunk he'd run his car off the road on the way home.

While Delight had stirred him, Lett Halsy knew he had to

hold on to every dollar.

"Your brother was quite comfortable here," Delight said, flashing her blue eyes toward the little house and shaking Lett from his reverie. "Let me show you inside." She noticed his uneasy look and smiled. "Howard was strictly a landlord and a gentleman."

Lett doubted her statement, but remained silent. When they started walking onto the tin-roofed porch, the lawyer lagged behind.

"I should be getting back to my office," Otis Tate said. "You never can tell when a mining company's going to get in some tooth-and-nail fight over a mining claim. I love it when that happens."

"I'll see you in the morning," Lett said, giving a slight wave.

Tate smiled. "I'm *sure* you will. If you have any questions about the books bring them along and I'll look them over—no charge. Howard was more than a client; I liked the man."

With that statement the lawyer turned and headed through the back door leaving Lett and Delight alone.

The blonde spun and opened the unlocked door with a swish that bathed Lett with her intoxicating perfume.

"I believe you'll find the pantry fairly well stocked. I just hope the mice and bugs have left things alone," Delight said matter-of-factly, as she began opening cabinet doors and pulling out drawers. "Howard generally ate his meals over in the bar. If he'd fixed more meals at home he'd still be among the living. McTavish can't cook a pancake and have it turn out flat."

"All I heard was that he choked on a piece of meat."

"It was a hunk of McTavish's antelope steak that did him in. The only way to prepare antelope is to cook it like a kidney."

"And how's that?" Lett asked.

Delight chuckled, "You boil the piss out of it!"

Lett's own booming laugh surprised him. The last thing he had expected from a whore was a sense of humor. After a moment the thought hit him that she was simply softening him up—shortly she would ask for money.

"It looks like you've got plenty of canned goods, and the flour and corn meal's fine," Delight said. "There's running water that's gravity fed from a tank on the hill. Howard had two more outhouses built, so there's six of those. I'm sure McTavish's cooking is the reason there's so many."

"You talk like you don't care for him."

"Oh, Jason's not too bad as far as bartenders go. He's cantankerous as a grizzly bear, fairly honest and a hard worker. Every month or so he takes a bath and washes his clothes. Like I said, just a typical bartender. He thinks he's a cook from the Waldorf to hear him tell it. There's no way I'd eat anything he cooked. Howard's dog, old Wesley, prefers to eat rattlesnakes rather than anything McTavish leaves out for him. Even the coyotes leave it be."

Lett remembered the still hurting spot on his calf where the dog had bitten him. "Wesley and I've met already."

"Isn't he the sweetest dog?" Delight cooed. "The poor thing just can't get enough pets."

Lady, we're not talking about the same dog here, Lett thought. Then his attention was drawn to several thick gunnysacks tied and rolled up over the windows. "What are those for?"

"They're a little trick folks use here in the desert to stay cool. In the summer time folks drop them down. You'll notice a little water line on top. Open the valve just enough to keep them wet. The breeze always blows out here and you'll stay nice and cool."

"Well, I'll be. Where I'm from in Colorado a person never has to worry much about getting too warm. I've never seen anything like that before."

"Believe me, in a few weeks things will be plenty hot

hereabouts. They call this the desert for good reason."

"I suppose I'll drive my car around and unload it," Lett said. "It'll take me a few days to figure out what I'm going to do." Delight's close presence was making him very uncomfortable.

"I'm sorry, of course you're worn out from that long trip down here. Before I go, there's one thing I'd like to ask."

Here it comes. She's a fine-looking woman but I'm not giving her any money. "And what might that be?" he asked cautiously.

"Howard charged me ten dollars a week rent. Since the mines closed there simply hasn't been any business. Do you think I could stay on until things get going again? Then I'll pay up to date."

Lett was totally surprised that was all she wanted. His mind had been on the five hundred dollars the lawyer had mentioned. Running a business like the Roxy Jay was completely foreign to him. Mining was all he knew. He had made his living blasting and shoveling rock since he was fourteen. Only now his back hurt him so bad there was no way he could work underground much longer. He felt lost and, as much as he hated to admit it, he also was afraid. Lett really didn't know what to do except that he couldn't part with what little money he had. Allowing Delight to stay on at least wouldn't cost anything.

"Sure, I reckon that would be fine," Lett said agreeably.

Delight grabbed him quickly and planted a kiss on his cheek. It was just a friendly peck, but it sent goose pimples running down his arms. Lett hadn't been kissed by a woman since—

"You're a sweetheart," she said happily, turning to leave.

Lett Halsy stood staring out the open doorway long after Delight had gone. "Lord, what have I gotten myself into?" he asked aloud.

CHAPTER SIX

Sam Ransom had thought for certain he was a dead man earlier that morning. While he had been in a terrible hurry to leave California, he'd decided it would be safer not to take the direct route from San Francisco to Nevada over Donner Pass. If anyone happened to be looking for him, that is where they would likely lie in wait.

The law didn't concern Sam nearly as much as some overly upset investor. And he had several of those to worry about. All the law would do, if they caught him, would be to send him away for a few short years of vacation—all expenses paid.

One investor in particular, Al Casey, worried him the most. Casey owned a number of car dealerships, blocks of apartment buildings and untold thousands of acres of farm land in Napa Valley. This man was the one who had taken Sam's Eternia Engine to the patent office and tried to steal it. Twenty-five grand of the fifty thousand dollars in the briefcase he held close to him once belonged to Al Casey. Al was really pissed off about that.

There's no one easier to con than a greedy man.

Unfortunately, Al wasn't simply rich, greedy and pissed, he also possessed the disposition of a provoked rattlesnake. Furthermore he had the connections to get whatever he wanted done, be it legal or illegal.

The phone call that had caused Sam's hasty exit to Shakespeare came at three a.m. the day before. One thing he had learned in prison was to have a few well-paid people to watch his backside. The informer had told Sam, in no uncertain terms, that Al Casey had put a contract out on him. Even more frightening was the fact Casey didn't want Sam simply killed. A portion of his anatomy he was very fond of was to be slowly removed with a rusty knife then stuffed down his throat. Every time Sam Ransom thought back on that phone call, he drove a little faster.

Sam had been very careful to tell anyone who would listen about his ranch and oil interests in Kentucky, his beloved native home. He hoped they might at least believe *that* story and go looking for him there. Actually, Sam had been born and raised in northern California. He had been very careful never to even mention New Mexico to anyone, let alone the town of Shakespeare. The two trips he had made to put his silver mine into play there were done under the guise of seeing a professor in Los Angeles about improving the efficiency of his Eternia Engine.

Since southwest New Mexico was his goal, Sam drove south, passing through Barstow from Bakersfield, finally taking Highway 66 eastbound. He was always dismayed and repulsed by the steady stream of battered and overloaded old cars heading west. The ones that were not broken down alongside the highway chugged slowly along burdened by piles of furniture, crates of chickens, yapping dogs and an abundance of dirty-faced, unsmiling kids.

Sam knew all too well the disappointment that awaited them when they reached their goal of California. Briefly he had toyed with the idea of setting up a "job service," guaranteeing jobs to anyone who was able to pay a fee. A little research had shown that by the time these hoards of Okies reached California, other vultures had picked them clean long ago. Most didn't even have money for food, let alone the ability to pay for a nonexistent job.

Only big fish are worth frying.

Lack of sleep, slowness of the traffic and the incessant desert heat had taken its toll on Sam. He knew he should not have pulled over for a nap, but the lights of the oncoming cars had become hypnotic and more than once he had dozed off, nearly running off the road. Finally, just outside Needles he found a place where he could safely pull well away from Highway 66 and take a nap. He placed a .38 Smith and Wesson hammerless revolver under his belt, rolled up the windows to where only a small amount of air could circulate to stave off the oppressive heat, then locked the doors and quickly drifted off to sleep.

A heavy rapping on the driver's window shook him awake. "Hey buddy, you okay in there?"

Sam's grip instinctively tightened on his .38. A gaunt-looking face with a week's worth of beard pressed against the window stared blandly at him. Forcing himself to smile, Sam rolled down the window with his left hand while carefully sizing up the situation. He was doubly surprised to find a bright orange sunrise illuminating the barren landscape. He had slept for over eight hours.

Aside from the man with the beard, another much larger man sat in the driver's seat of the black Model A Roadster studying him intently. Neither looked to be packing a gun. Sam wasn't a man to take chances however, especially with a big stack of Al Casey's money offered on his private parts.

"I just got tired and decided to rest. What's it to you?" he growled.

The bearded man stepped back. "We didn't mean nothing. My uncle an' me are goin' back to Oklahoma. There ain't no work in Californy like we heard. We saw you parked off out here with a flat tire and thought maybe you were sick or somethin'. Some folks can't take this heat, ya know."

Sam kept both his smile on his face and his hand on the revolver. He knew very well how a professional hit man will try to get their victim to relax.

Carefully he stuck his head out the open window and saw that he did, indeed, have a flat. Last night in his haggard condition, he had driven over a barrel cactus.

The busted Okies generously offered to change the tire for him. Elated to be alive after stupidly letting his guard down, Sam tipped the men a dollar apiece.

"Lord Almighty. Mister you didn't need to do that," the little guy with the beard stuttered. "We'd helped you fer nothing."

"Take some good advice," Sam said, putting the Cadillac into gear. "Never do *anything* for nothing. Even a preacher gets paid."

It took until nearly noon, and a ham sandwich washed down by a few cold beers at a roadside diner in Phoenix, for Sam to settle down. He knew he had been extremely lucky. The solid-white Cadillac he was driving stood out like a billboard.

A quick stop at the local Packard dealer solved that problem. His Cadillac and twenty-five hundred dollars bought a shiny-new, red, 1932 Packard twin-six Roadster. The portly salesman nearly had a stroke when he saw the huge wad of hundred-dollar bills Sam pulled out to pay for the car. While Sam doubted any of Casey's henchmen would follow him this far, he decided to play it safe. He had taken title under the name of Ruth Simpson, saying the car was to be a present for his girlfriend. Since the transaction was in cash, the dealer gladly obliged. When he got to New Mexico he would forge the name of Ruth Simpson on the title and register the Packard in his own name.

The setting sun was washing the desert landscape with its red and orange rays when Sam Ransom pulled his new Packard to a stop in front of the Roxy Jay Hotel in Shakespeare. He simply loved this car; with the top down it had fairly soared, the V-12 motor never pulled down on hills. Powerful, sleek automobiles, slender young women and expensive whiskey were Sam's consuming passions. All of these required money, something Sam Ransom was extremely good at both accumulating and spending.

He stroked his pencil-thin mustache with manicured fingernails while he studied the remote Last Chance Mine. It was nearly a mile distant, but the ochre pile of waste rock spilling down the steep slope of the barren mountain side glittered like gold in the twilight. Sam took a thin black cigar from his pocket and lit it. After taking a deep puff and one more thoughtful look at his mine, he turned and strode through the swinging doors of the saloon.

"Well, for crying out loud, looky who's showed up!" Jason McTavish bellowed, running around the end of the long bar to shake Sam's hand.

The fat bartender's grip was sweaty, or greasy. Sam wasn't sure which. If he ever decided to become a Hollywood actor there was no doubt in his mind the name Sam Ransom would be in lights, right up there with John Barrymore and Gary Cooper. When it came to acting, neither of those two rubes could hold a candle to him.

"Good to see you too, Jason," Sam replied happily. One rule he had learned was to use a person's first name quickly and often. Another was to speak just loudly enough to be overheard at the appropriate time; make the suckers think what you wanted them to without being obvious about it. "My geologists have confirmed immense silver reserves in the Last Chance Mine. You'll be seeing a lot of me from here on."

"We all would sure enough like that, Mister Ransom,"

McTavish said fawningly, still pumping Sam's arm.

"Call me Sam, all my friends do." Sam Ransom's dark eyes scanned the room. He announced loudly, "All you men, please just call me Sam. I'm a plain and simple man. I worked hard on an apple orchard in Wenatchee, Washington, until I was twenty. Then through luck and lots of hard work, I became successful in the mining business. Believe me, I know what it's like to put in a long day for little pay."

Sam really liked that part about his having worked in the apple orchard. It sounded so good because there was a ring of truth to it, he decided. Where he actually grew up in Redding, California, his family *did* have an apple tree in the backyard.

"Give the house a round of drinks on me," Sam told McTavish loudly, while grinning happily at the few men in attendance. All but one he had seen before. This unfamiliar man was dressed in clean, ironed khakis, stood nearly a foot taller than he was and was heavier by at least sixty pounds—all of it appeared to be muscle. Sam had always been a wiry sort, having weighed no more than a hundred and fifty since he'd been kicked out of high school. What bothered him about the big fellow was the easy way he leaned back against the bar coldly sizing him up. This man wasn't simply hanging around hoping for a free beer. Sam had to know who he was. The most important task he had right now was to become everyone's friend. He stuck out his right hand, put on his "trust me" smile and strode over to the stranger.

"Reckon you know who I am. Glad to meet you Mister—?"

"Halsy, Lett Halsy," the big man answered pleasantly, returning the handshake. "I own this place since my brother, Howard, passed away."

"My deepest sympathies," Sam said. "I was *so* looking forward to knowing Howard better. I had no idea he'd succumbed."

"He didn't soocomed, he up and died," Jake Clanton

interjected. "Choked to death trying to digest one of McTavish's antelope steaks."

Sam ignored Clanton's statement and kept his attentions focused on Lett. "I hope you're prepared for the upturn in business that's headed your way. What, may I ask, did you do before coming here?"

"I've been a miner all of my life. The last fifteen years I've worked as a foreman at the Cresson Mine in Cripple Creek, Colorado," Lett answered.

"Why *excellent!*" Sam's smile broadened. "I'm in need of a local superintendent to oversee the opening of the Last Chance shaft. I trust you have the experience to organize that venture."

"Sure, cleaning out and re-timbering a mine shaft's not a big problem."

"Then you, Mister Halsy, are able to order the appropriate machinery and oversee the operation?"

Lett was awestruck but he didn't hesitate. "Yeah, it's just a matter of bringing in a hoist of, say, forty horsepower—if that's okay, building a head frame, and of course we'll need an air compressor—"

Sam stopped him. "I see you know your stuff." If Lett had asked any pointed questions, Sam would have been at an embarrassing disadvantage. He barely knew a pick from a shovel. "You are now the new mine superintendent for the Shakespeare Mining and Development Corporation," Sam told him proudly.

He pulled a roll of what looked to be all hundred-dollar bills from his pant pocket, peeled off a C-note and stuck it into Lett's hand. "This is part of your first month's salary. I'll pay you three hundred a month, every month. I dislike paperwork—it's so time consuming—right now I'm only paying every month. Lett, hire as many men as you'll need, but no one else gets their pay for four weeks. It takes a long while to get a corporation set up and things organized. After that is done and I have a secretary, everyone will be paid weekly, and at top wages, I may add. The Last Chance is going to be a bigger silver mine than the Comstock ever was!"

CHAPTER SEVEN

Every eye in the Roxy Jay watched when Lett pulled out his worn leather billfold and stuffed the valuable bill into its depths.

Jake Clanton's mouth hung open. He had never even *seen* a hundred-dollar bill before. "My God," he finally mumbled to no one in particular. "How much is he gonna pay for miners?"

Sam Ransom answered with a smile, "That's Mister Halsy's decision. His only instructions from me are to pay top money for top people."

Lett Halsy felt weak in the knees. Getting hired as a high-paid mine boss was the last thing he had expected to happen.

It wasn't as if he didn't need the money. He had spent most of the morning with Otis Tate. He and the lawyer had gone to the bank in Lordsburg and transferred all of his late brother's funds, a total of five hundred forty-two dollars, into an account of his own. Lett was nervous about having money in the bank. All over the country banks were failing by the thousands and depositors losing their money. Otis had assured him the Lordsburg Bank was safe and stable, so with great consternation he had left the bank with a checkbook instead of cash.

When they returned to the lawyer's office, Otis had carefully gone over the books of the Roxy Jay with him.

"I'd venture McTavish was nervous as a pregnant nun when he gave you these," Otis said, running a bony finger down columns of numbers.

"Didn't seem to bother his appetite none. He never said a

word, just handed them to me and went back to gnawing his way through a mountain of flapjacks that would kill a smaller man."

"The man does like his chow and, according to these figures, you're paying for it. I'd say the bottom line is when the supplies on hand are sold out, you'll either have to go into your money to buy more or close down. McTavish is carrying everyone on credit and that includes booze. Even the sheriff's five-dollar-a-month bribe is past due."

Lett had felt his Adam's apple drop to the pit of his stomach. "*Credit!* He's selling on credit! Just how much are we talking about here?"

"Oh, Jason kept a good record. All of these men ran tabs when the mines were running and they always paid up. He just kept on doing what Howard did. I really don't think you can blame him. The man's not taking any salary. He sleeps in what used to be a closet behind the bar. But to answer your question, it looks like the tabs total just over four hundred dollars."

"But if that mine does open and folks get to working I should be paid."

"Oh, they'll pay you then for sure, Lett. However, in law school I learned the biggest word in the English language is *if.*"

Lett spent the afternoon going through the supplies on hand with McTavish. He didn't confront the fat man and tried hard not to show his displeasure about his giving out credit. There were several kegs of beer and cases of whiskey and wine still in the storehouse. Foodstuffs were at a minimum, but a quick guess told him they could get by for a couple of weeks, maybe more if someone was lucky enough to shoot a deer.

He really had made no plans. This desert and running a bar were so strange to him he might as well be in a foreign country.

Then Sam Ransom had showed up and not only given him a

big-paying job that required no heavy lifting, but as a bonus said he was opening the mine. That meant men would go to work and pay their bills.

The only difficulty was Sam telling everyone it would be a month until they got paid. That could be a problem. Lett hadn't particularly cared for Ransom first off. The little man had weasel eyes and wore his short black hair parted in the middle and heavily pasted down with Brilliantine. Ransom reminded Lett of some of the rich mine owners who occasionally visited Cripple Creek to check on their investments. Lett and others like him did the hard, dangerous work of wrestling the gold from the depths of the earth while well-dressed, smooth-talking, effeminate dandies reaped the profits.

Men like Sam Ransom *did* control the money. That was for certain. All a working man could do was try to get by on what crumbs fell from their table.

Lett was more than a little taken aback by Ransom's generosity. Most of the money men he had ever run across before were tighter than the paint on a Ford.

From his earlier visit with the lawyer, Lett found his brother had made several thousand dollars a year from running the Roxy Jay before things went sour.

In 1931 alone, Howard collected over twelve hundred dollars in rent from the whores. The alcohol sales were staggering. Lett had been around mining camps long enough to know the girls out back were why booze sold so well. Most men had to work up their courage to do the act, then they would hang around and brag about it afterward.

At least he had a job, which was something few men could say in these tough times. Lett was trying to decide how to find enough time to keep the saloon going and open the Last Chance Mine for Sam Ransom.

Then it seemed like everyone in the world jumped on him all

at once wanting something. Men he did not know were telling him what good workers they were and about all of the mines they had worked in. Others were asking for credit and some for loans. His head began to spin.

"By golly boys, let's have a party," Sam Ransom said loudly, taking some of the pressure away from Lett. He tossed another hundred-dollar bill on the bar in front of McTavish's startled eyes. "Give everyone what they're drinking until this is gone!"

The roar inside was deafening. Lett had no idea where everyone had come from. He guessed there might be thirty men in the bar now. They were laughing and bragging about how nice a fellow Sam Ransom was and talking of all the good times to come.

Lett went to work helping McTavish fill beer and whiskey glasses. There was not time to wash any of them, but no one seemed to notice or care.

"Most of these guys will be outside pukin' their guts up soon," McTavish whispered in his ear.

"Why, is something wrong with what we're selling them?" Lett asked with alarm.

"Hell, no. It's just that most of these guys ain't had a decent meal for a long time. Some ain't had nothing to eat for days. When booze hits an empty stomach, a body can't help but puke."

Lett was kept so busy he had little time to think, but he did notice some of the men, when they got drunk enough, dig into hidden stashes of money in their boots or behind belt buckles and buy as many drinks as they could. Especially for Sam Ransom. Anyone who was able to come up with fifty cents bought Sam a shot of that expensive whiskey he liked.

After a couple of hours Sam motioned Lett to one side, stuck a sawbuck in his hand and whispered, "Give me a bottle of that *good* champagne. Howard kept it locked up in that drawer under the cash register." He smiled evilly. "I'll take it out back and have a little cooze from that blond whore. Personally I like 'em a lot younger than her, but like they say, 'any port in a storm.' "

Lett got the key from McTavish and gave Sam his bottle. The man had given him the best job he had ever had, and was pulling the Roxy Jay and the entire town of Shakespeare out of the Depression.

But when Lett Halsy thought of Sam Ransom and Delight together, for some strange reason he wanted to kill the greasy-haired little son of a bitch.

CHAPTER EIGHT

"I see," the lawyer said, folding his thin fingers into a ball and propping them under his chin. "You want me to form a New Mexico corporation for you."

Sam Ransom omitted his usual warm smile; this was business. "Yes, I do. I'm sure you're aware that I could have had a member of the law firm I retain in Denver prepare the documents. Then, I could simply register as a foreign corporation doing business in the state. However, not only do I prefer hiring local talent, a project of this magnitude will require the full-time services of a local attorney, and I've been told you are well-versed in mining law."

For a few moments, Otis Tate pored through the pile of papers Sam had shoved across the wide oak desk. "A very ambitious project, I must say. The Shakespeare Mining and Development Corporation is to be capitalized for ten million shares at one dollar a share per value. I'm sure you have checked with the secretary of state to make certain that name was available before going to the tremendous expense of printing up these certificates and brochures?"

The muscles in Sam's stomach tightened, but he was careful never to show anxiety. Of course he had not checked. Nor had he ever been to Denver or consulted an attorney for any purpose except how to stay out of jail. All Sam had planned was how much money he could make selling stock.

"My attorney in Denver assured me all was in order," Sam

said firmly. "And he is usually competent. However, I'm certain you'll double check. The last thing we want are any complications on this wonderful project. With the Depression as bad as it is, the jobs created by this corporation will help the area a lot."

"*Any* jobs these days are like gifts from God. I understand you've already hired Mister Lett Halsy for your superintendent."

"News does travel quickly. He seems like a good man. As I told you, I hire local people whenever possible."

"I usually take my breakfast in the hotel," Otis said. "All the talk there this morning was about the big party you threw in Shakespeare last night. A lot of folks have high hopes for your success."

Sam beamed. "This is my biggest project ever." He lowered his voice enigmatically. "Have you seen the geologist's reports in the brochure? That mountain is lousy with silver and more gold than we'd dreamed. Also there are huge amounts of platinum. The most conservative estimates of the values contained in the Last Chance Mine are over one billion dollars!"

Otis grabbed up the brochure and began perusing the beautifully colored document.

Sam took his cup of coffee, stood up and walked to the window to allow the lawyer plenty of time. He knew a mining attorney would be his worst critic. If he could get Otis Tate's approval, no one else could possibly fault the reports. He sipped the strong brew and suppressed a frown. Sam preferred fresh ground Arbuckle's coffee with a sprinkle of cinnamon.

Only the very best for Sam Ransom, he thought.

The whore, Delight, wasn't at all bad, a pleasant diversion, but in morning light a myriad of wrinkles showed through her heavy makeup. This displeased him immensely. He had tarried just long enough to get some more of his money's worth, then tipped her ten dollars. One thing Sam needed was for anyone who visited Shakespeare to hear nothing but good things about him. He had spent nearly three hundred dollars last night, but he considered it a good investment. If he was to make this venture a success he would have to spend a lot more.

It takes money to make money.

"Very impressive," the lawyer finally said, taking Sam back to the business at hand. "I dare say I've never seen such glowing reports from *any* professional geologist before. This Albert Cromwell must have spent a great deal of time on the property. Strange, I don't remember even hearing of his being in the area."

"Secrecy is a necessity on occasion, Mister Tate, especially until one gains control of the entire area of interest."

"I notice you have over a thousand acres of property, either owned or under lease. However, most of it is on the desert floor where I fail to see how your geologist could have made any determination of values without drilling."

Sam swallowed hard and tried to remember what the crooked geology teacher he had hired to help write the brochure had said. "*Professor* Cromwell is from England, where he received his PhD in both geology and physics from Cambridge University. He has invented an electromagnetic machine that is so sensitive and accurate it makes drilling for minerals as archaic as the horse and buggy is for transportation, or the use of leeches by doctors of medicine. This device"—Sam lowered his voice to a whisper—"can outline with great accuracy buried deposits of precious metals, giving not only their dimensions, but also the richness of the veins."

Otis Tate focused on Sam with a knowing stare, then a broad grin crossed his face and wrinkled his bald head. "I understand *precisely* why you would want to keep the existence of such a device secret," the lawyer chuckled. "Dowsing, consulting spirits of the dead, reading tea leaves or poking through the entrails of a chicken with a stick, are on the same level as this so-called electromagnetic device. However, I *do* give you credit for stacking bullshit higher than I've ever seen it done before!"

Sam shot the lawyer an indignant glare. "Well, I see you have no understanding of modern technology, sir. I shall take my legal business elsewhere."

Otis Tate gave out a laugh. "Oh, I really doubt you want to do that. There is a matter of attorney-client privilege here. If you retain my services I cannot divulge any part of our conversation—or your business ventures."

Shit, Sam thought. Briefly he knew how Al Casey and some of the other people he'd scammed must have felt. "I see your point, and time is valuable to me. I really hate having to travel to Denver. The going rate to form a corporation, I believe, is two hundred dollars."

Sam was fishing a roll of bills from his jacket pocket when the lawyer held up his hand.

"Mister Ransom," Otis Tate said firmly, "you have not yet retained my services. No lawyer-client privilege exists between us. I must inform you that I will only represent you on a full-time basis, for two thousand dollars a month, payable in advance—of course."

Sam Ransom's face flushed crimson and his hands shook with anger as he began peeling off hundred-dollar bills and stacking them on the grinning lawyer's massive oak desk.

Damn it all, I should have stayed away from mining. It looks like there are already too many crooks in the business, Sam thought.

"I'll have your company incorporated very shortly, Mister Ransom," Otis announced happily. "I took the liberty of phoning the secretary's office in Santa Fe earlier this morning. Everyone in town knew the name of your company. My curiosity simply got the better of me and I found, of course, there was no record of any Shakespeare Mining and Development Corporation. The name *is* open. I'd say that was a stroke of luck, wouldn't you?"

Sam gritted his teeth and spun to leave. Otis called after him, "Oh, by the way, I would make certain all of the men you hire at the Last Chance are paid promptly, every week. As your attorney, I advise that all labor be paid promptly to avoid any complaints to the state labor board. One must always comply with the law, you know."

When he stepped out into the warm, dry air of a brilliant New Mexico afternoon and began walking, Sam felt better. There was no harm done that he couldn't recover from. That snake of a lawyer had lightened his money supply, but he knew now to be very careful who he showed his investment brochures to. They couldn't be versed in mining, that was for certain.

After stopping for a few shots of passable whiskey in the backroom of a café optimistically named "The Vanderbilt" Sam felt he once again had the world by the tail. Shortly, he would take to the road, Albuquerque, El Paso, possibly even Denver and begin selling stock. If things went as planned, he could pocket maybe a hundred grand before moving on.

Back on the dirt streets of Lordsburg, Sam lit a cigar and began making plans as he walked alongside the railroad tracks. He would go to the bank and establish a company checking account with a thousand dollars and give Lett Halsy signing privileges. It would not be prudent to anger Otis Tate by not paying the men, as he had planned to do. Then perhaps he should rent a suite in the hotel and open an office there. Shakespeare depressed him. Sam hated the barren bleakness of the place. Lordsburg offered little better, but at least it could be found on a map.

Sam's planning was interrupted when, just across the tracks, he noticed a shapely young Mexican girl leaning seductively against a pock-marked adobe building. The closer he got, the younger and prettier the girl appeared. She could not have been over fifteen. Her big brown doe-eyes batted as she spoke the only English words she knew. "Feefty cents, Meester."

A smile wiped over Sam's face when he placed an arm around the girl's slim waist then felt the firmness of her breasts.

"This isn't going to be such a bad day after all," he said, as he walked through the worn doorway with the young maiden who didn't understand a single word he said.

CHAPTER NINE

Two days later, as the sun's red rays were barely peeking up from the plains to the east, Lett Halsy and his crew stood surveying the ruined shaft of the Last Chance Mine.

It seemed to Lett every man in New Mexico had hit him up for work. Bulldog, Arnold Epp and Jake Clanton were the only men he had hired. Sam Ransom had given him a measly thousand dollars working capital. Lett had decided it prudent to hire men who owed a tab at the Roxy Jay.

Bulldog stood as close to the crumbling edge of the shaft as he dared and dropped a small rock. Everyone listened intently while the stone rattled into the depths, finally fading into the dark void.

"Deep son of a bitch," Jake commented. "And ragged as holy hell on a Sunday."

"Yep," Bulldog agreed. "I'd reckon nobody's been down that hole since Moby Dick was a minnow."

"You got any maps of this mean mother?" Arnold inquired, looking at Lett. "Be nice to know where the bottom is and how many levels they drove off it."

"Nope," Lett said. "Will Green, the guy in Lordsburg who owns the claim, might have some."

"Wonder how Ransom knows what's down there?" Bulldog asked idly.

"Showed me a fancy geologist report," Lett said. "Some professor from England did it. Supposed to be all kinds of silver and gold once we get it opened up."

"Reckon geologists from over there's got better eyesight than we have," Bulldog grumbled. "Looks just like a mean hole in the ground to me. And I'd wonder if they was in rich ore, why they gave up on it?"

Lett Halsy shook his head. "No one here's getting paid to think. If Ransom had wanted thinking done he'd have hired another professor. I've got a truck coming soon with a load of mine timbers on it. You guys get to shoveling so we can frame the collar of this son of a bitch then start dropping ladders and another timber set down it."

"We're going to need a fan right soon," Bulldog said grabbing a long-handled shovel. "A pocket of bad air would cause a man to pass out and fall. That could ruin his whole day."

"We're going to need lots of stuff," Lett agreed. "Sam said he was only going to be away for a few days on business. He told me when he gets back, we could get everything we need. Until then, we'll do what we can without taking too many chances."

An ominous buzzing, like dry leaves rattling in the wind, caused Epp to quickly jump away from a crumpled pile of rusty tin. "Damn, that snake nearly got me!" he swore breathlessly.

From out of nowhere the mutt, Wesley, streaked from behind Lett toward the coiled, buzzing rattler and began circling it like a hungry buzzard.

The men watched, fascinated, as the dog's circles began narrowing, bringing it closer to the snake. Occasionally the diamondback would strike, but Wesley always remained just out of range. With a lunge so quick no eye could follow, the dog snapped onto the snake just behind its triangular head and shook it viciously several times. Then with tail wagging, Wesley carried the still writhing reptile to Lett and dropped it at his feet.

"I never seen nothing like that in all my born days," Jake

Clanton said, astonished. "And it looks like Wesley's taken a liking to you Lett. He's brought you dinner."

Lett Halsy took a step back. Snakes, be they dead or alive, gave him the willies.

"That dog has plain taken a fondness to you Lett," Bulldog said with a grin. "Delight's the only other person I know that Wesley doesn't prefer to just bite. And now he's up and given you a real nice near-dead rattlesnake."

"I never seen nothing like it," Jake Clanton repeated. "That snake shudda killed him."

Bulldog looked at Jake. "Hell, Wesley's been bit lots of times. The mutt just crawls under the porch in front of the Roxy Jay and lays around for a couple of days until he feels up to biting customers again. That dog's mean as my first mother-in-law. You couldn't kill either one of them with cyanide."

The distant groaning of a heavily loaded truck slowly climbing its way up the narrow road leading to the mine got the men's attention.

"Well, boys we've got work to do," Lett said. "That damn shaft collar ain't gonna frame itself."

As if he understood, Wesley picked up the snake, wagged his tail and trotted off down the side of the mountain toward Shakespeare.

Jake Clanton watched the dog leave, shaking his head in awe. "I still never saw nothin' like that before."

Lett's back felt like someone had stuck a knife in it and left it there when he and his tired crew walked into the saloon that evening. He wasn't the kind of man who could watch others strain themselves without pitching in to help. Being a superintendent was something that would take some getting used to.

"Give me a tall cold one," Lett said to McTavish, as he sat down at the bar. The three men he had hired stayed some distance back gazing longingly at the mug of beer the bartender was drawing. "Give these guys one too, but add it to their tabs. There's no reason not to. Ransom said I can pay them every week."

After a few beers the pain in his back eased. Lett took a notebook and began figuring what materials they would need at the mine. Long, heavy twelve-by-twelve timbers had been framed across the top of the shaft and lined up with a plumb line to square up with the old rotten timbers they would have to remove on the way down. Tomorrow, they would begin dropping in new timbers with a windlass, then hanging them six feet down with steel J bolts fastened to the new collar. When that set was in place they would lag it solid with thick planks then drop another six feet. This was slow going, but necessary to keep any loose, dangerous rocks from falling on them. Lett figured they could complete a six-foot section, with ladders installed, every other day. At eighteen feet a week, the little money Sam had placed in the bank would run out long before they reached the bottom of that deep shaft.

A hint of delicate perfume drifted by Lett, instantly taking his mind from the business of mining.

Delight took the stool next to him. When he looked at her she gave him that luscious smile that seemed to be permanently etched on her face, like those he had seen on pretty calendar girls.

"Hi, Lett," she said simply. "I was hoping you might drop by my place. Howard never really liked my coming in here. You know things have gotten a little better, so I'd like to pay you ten dollars rent. I know I owe you more, but with Sam opening the mine it shouldn't take me long to get caught up."

Delight discreetly laid an envelope on the bar in front of him. Lett swallowed hard. Even being close to the blonde made him uncomfortable in a strange way he had never felt before. And this beautiful woman was offering to pay *him* money. His guts tightened into a knot as his morals and urges played tug-of-war with each other.

"I—I don't feel right about taking money from you," he stuttered, sliding the envelope back to Delight. "With this Depression getting worse by the day you should hang on to what you got."

For once Delight was taken aback. "But I owe you. Perhaps there are *other* ways you'd rather be paid."

Lett felt his face flush and he just knew everyone in the bar could overhear the blonde's hushed words to him. "Uh—would you like something to drink? A cold mug of beer maybe?"

Then he chided himself, *You idiot, a beautiful lady like Delight doesn't drink beer. Wine or champagne is what you should have offered.*

It was Lett's turn to be surprised.

"Why thank you, actually I love the taste of beer, but seldom does anyone offer me one."

While McTavish was filling Delight's glass, Lett realized with sudden trepidation that he was still dirty and sweaty from his work at the mine. "Sorry I haven't had a chance to get cleaned up yet," he mumbled.

"You're a hard-working man, that's nothing to apologize for."

Lett's brain slid into overtime trying to come up with a polite answer to Delight's innuendo. He sorely wanted to place his arm around this alluring woman and accompany her back to his cabin and make passionate love. There was no denying Delight was a whore, plain and simple.

All I have to do is ask, he thought, *she won't say no. But she's sweet as strawberry wine and I do love her company. If I take her for money she owes me, I'll be no better than a pimp.*

He spun his mug on the wood bar then smiled and said, "There *is* something you can do for me."

McTavish decided the whiskey bottles on the bar behind Lett and Delight needed dusting. He didn't want to miss a word of this.

Delight took a sip of beer and gave him a knowing look. "And what might that be?"

"I'm a busy man lately, I spend all day at the mine, when I get back here I've got this place to worry about. McTavish is a good bartender, but his cooking is so bad it did my brother in. The last time he tried boiling eggs they hatched later on. If I had a good home-cooked meal to look forward to every evening, that would sure be worth ten bucks to me."

Delight choked on her beer and McTavish dropped his feather duster.

"That's it?" she sputtered. "You want to have dinner is *all?*"

"I think that would be wonderful," Lett said.

"I've had a lot of men ask me to do strange things, but this is the first time all they wanted from me was a decent meal."

"Then it's a deal?"

Delight shook her head in wonderment, finally forcing a slight smile. "You know, Lett, I have to eat, too. Having your company would be nice. Sure, why not. You'll find I'm a much better cook than your bartender."

A good feeling washed over Lett Halsy. He now had the company of a pretty woman to look forward to every night. It had been a long time since that had been the case.

McTavish picked the feather duster from the floor with a grunt and stomped away. Not only did he have no good gossip to spread, that quip about the eggs had really razzed him.

CHAPTER TEN

Will Green shut off the hissing assay furnace with more than a little irritation. At least, whoever was ringing the bell for service in the other room had come when they did. A little later and the crucible of high-grade gold precipitate he was preparing to smelt into doré would have been at a critical stage where he could not have stopped.

He shot a cautious glance through a peephole he had drilled in the wall. He relaxed. The big man standing easily at the counter wore khakis and no badge, just a miner wanting an assay, most likely on credit, he thought. If it was not for his buying small amounts of gold stolen from mines he would have been forced to close his assay office long ago.

Will had a reputation for being honest with the miners who brought him their meager, hard-won canvas bags of high grade. He knew how hard it was for them to "liberate" it from under the eyes of watchful bosses. A false bottom in a lunch box was a favorite trick. If the foreman made random checks of those, other more drastic measures were called for. Should a man have long hair, he could secretly hide an ounce or more there by plastering it in heavily with grease. As a last resort, the same grease could lubricate a few nuggets where they could be inserted into their rectum. No mine boss ever seemed to check *there*.

Will Green paid the highgraders for half the value of the gold in cash as soon as he had crushed the ore down and run an assay. The other half of the gold was his. He kept absolute silence and no records as to who he dealt with.

While the gold he processed made his living, it was no longer of real interest to him. For the past year, Will Green had been consumed by a single-minded quest, one which this stranger was keeping him from. He wanted—needed—to get this dab of gold smelted and get on with it. But he did run an assay office and had to put up a decent front or risk attracting the unwanted attention of the law. He could not turn away business, not yet anyway.

"Howdy," the big man said pleasantly when Will came through the doorway. "Hope I didn't catch you at a bad time?"

"Not really, I was just starting to heat the furnace and run some assays; now that it's off, there's no hurry. What can I do for you, Mister—?"

"Halsy, Lett Halsy, I'm the manager Sam Ransom hired to open the Last Chance Mine you own."

Will grinned broadly and shook Lett's hand. Leasing out that old shaft he had picked up for a few dollars at a tax sale had been a welcome stroke of luck. "I heard there was some work going on up there, but I've been too busy to visit."

"There's not much to see, we're only down a few feet. That's one ragged hole. It's going to be slow going for a while, I'm afraid."

"Do you want some assays ran?" Will inquired.

"Nothing to assay yet. What I came to see you about was Sam mentioned you might have some underground maps. It would be a mighty big help if you do."

Will handed Lett some business cards giving the cost of his services. "I don't have a thing on that mine, Lett. I bought it not too long ago. A few of the old-timers that come in here told me the last time anybody done any work there was over fifty years ago. To the best of their recollection, the shaft's supposed to be around four hundred feet deep, but that's all hearsay."

"Well, I guess we're headed for the bottom anyway, even if we do come out in China. I just hoped you might have something."

"Sorry, but for what it's worth, I hope you open a bonanza."

"Thanks for your cards. When we get to the point of needing an assayer, I'll keep you in mind."

Will breathed a sigh of relief when the man left. He had been around the mining business too long to get excited about what was going on at the Last Chance. Most likely all they would find is the ore had played out long ago. To the best of his knowledge, no one had ever found rich ore left in an old mine, just waiting to be blasted out. Those old-timers were not as stupid as most people thought they were.

He re-lit the furnace, checked his watch and grinned. He would have plenty of time once this smelting job was over. His Model A was always loaded with everything he needed.

There would be plenty of daylight left by the time he parked his car on the backside of Lookout Hill and climbed to the top with his binoculars. From there he could see the town of Shakespeare and the entire valley that contained it. Most particular, he had a good view of old Elmore Wyman's dilapidated cabin.

That white-haired son of a bitch simply had to make another trip shortly to wherever it was he got his rich gold. For a year now the old man had been selling him small lots of the highest grade ore he'd ever seen. And he saw a lot of gold ore. What intrigued him most was that the gold was contained in a beautiful deep-hued rose quartz. The Lost Dutchman Mine, as far as he knew, was the only free gold that had ever been found in rose quartz.

The babbling old fool was always telling people he had spent his whole life looking for that long-lost famous mine. Everyone had laughed, saying the Lost Dutchman was in Arizona. Will had yet to discover where it was Elmore got his gold, but he *was* going to find out. He would either follow him to it, or the old man would tell him.

One way or the other. Damn soon.

CHAPTER ELEVEN

Things had not gone well for Sam Ransom the past few days. In Albuquerque, he had physically been booted out the door of a brokerage office. He was forced to sit on a feather pillow when he drove away in his sleek red Packard. The man who had removed Sam from his presence was a giant, at least the size of his foreman, Lett Halsy.

Briefly, Sam had toyed with the idea of hiring a couple of thugs from the local Hooverville, a depressing collection of shacks near the railroad. There were always a generous supply of unwashed oafs hanging around those places looking for work. For a few dollars he could have shown that uppity stockbroker what kicking ass was all about.

Even out-of-work ruffians cost money, though. Also, there was always the off chance he might be robbed. He always kept his money with him. Sam Ransom distrusted banks. After all, it was that blood-sucking internal-revenue law that had gotten Al Capone put into prison. Sam tucked the slim, brown-leather briefcase with bright brass claps that held his future under the front seat of his convertible and decided to let bygones be bygones.

It was that damn brochure. The broker had laughed his fool head off until he read the part about platinum being in the Last Chance Mine. That was when he had gotten angry.

"You're not even smart enough to be entertaining," the broker had grumbled, just before introducing Sam to the pointy toe of his heavy, spit-polished shoe.

When he had begun researching the mining business in preparation to running the biggest scam of his life, Sam had read about an actual platinum mine. Back in 1914 the discovery of that metal in a played-out gold property in southern Nevada called the Boss Mine had created a sensational rush to the area. While very little platinum was ever shipped, huge fortunes had been made from stock sales in worthless mining companies miles away from the Boss discovery.

Hell, a mine is a mine. Why did everyone have to be so damn picky about what was in it? I didn't know platinum was rare as an honest politician.

Sam stopped in Pueblo, Colorado, and rested in a fine hotel while a printer worked overtime making up new brochures. It was basically the same imaginary report, carefully modified to eliminate any mention of platinum.

Two days and three hundred dollars later, Sam pulled to a stop in front of the pretentious Brown Palace Hotel in Denver and tossed the attendant a silver dollar to see that his car was safely parked.

"Y'all have a really good day, sir," the fawning black man wearing an immaculate red topcoat told him.

Once his money case was safely ensconced in the hotel safe, and his luggage laid out in his sumptuous lofty suite overlooking the still snow-capped Rocky Mountains, Sam grabbed up his working briefcase and retired to the gentlemen's smoking lounge. A private club for guests only. In spite of prohibition, excellent liquors flowed there more freely than in any Chicago speakeasy.

Denver's Brown Palace was well known as the favorite watering hole of the rich and famous in mining circles. The wealthiest man in Colorado at one time, Winfield Scott Stratton of

Cripple Creek Gold fame, had purchased the hotel back in the late 1890s.

He had shown up at the hotel drunk and in the company of beautiful, auburn-haired madam Pearl DeVere and asked to rent a room. The snobbish desk clerk not only refused his request, but made disparaging remarks about the lady not being his wife. After a few hasty phone calls, Stratton became the new owner of the Brown Palace and the clerk with more morals than good sense was out of a job.

My kind of man, Sam thought with a grin when he remembered this story of Stratton.

Sam Ransom was a voracious reader, a habit he had picked up while in prison. He loved to present himself as an educated, refined gentleman, even though he had been expelled from high school for cheating.

Books were a treasure house of useful information for his schemes. When he had decided to branch out into mining, Sam began poring through dozens of publications on the subject. That was how he had come to know the story of Stratton buying the hotel.

To his chagrin, the idea of him discovering platinum in New Mexico had surfaced when he had read how valuable the metal was. While Sam knew the words, he did not always get the context right. Details bored him, even though he realized now he should have read a little more on the subject of platinum— the effort would have saved him considerable money and a badly bruised posterior.

Things went more to his liking that evening. He generously bought drinks for strangers and engaged in casual conversations. As the night progressed and alcohol loosened lips, Sam made the acquaintance of Warner T. Higgenbottom, a partner in the brokerage firm of Higgenbottom and Lane.

Warner gave the impression of being cut from the same cloth

as Sam Ransom. Making large sums of money was all that counted in this world. Morals and ethics be damned.

Both agreed the reason so many were out of work was simply because they were lazy.

"Laboring men think the world owes them a living," Higgenbottom grumbled, dipping a cracker into a crystal bowl of caviar. "They want the government to take care of them, give them everything they ask for. Why, to do that taxes would go through the roof. And who pays taxes? Men like you and me, that's who, men who actually *work* for what we get."

Sam was so happy he beamed. Higgenbottom was round as a bowling ball and the suit he wore cost more than most men earned in a month. Best of all, the fat man specialized in mining stocks. Even with the depressed state of the economy, the man was an optimist.

After several more drinks the conversation drifted in the path Sam had so delicately paved. He had been ever so carefully dropping hints that he was looking for a broker to sell stock in a wonderful mining venture he'd put together. When Higgenbottom read the new brochure and kept smiling, Sam knew he had the fat man right where he wanted.

"The Dow's down below fifty points," the now drunk Warner T. Higgenbottom said with a slur. "Hell, there's no place for stocks to go but up. Buy on the ground floor and make a killing when they shoot up again, that's what I tell folks. Listen Sam, it sounds like you have a good project. Why don't you drop by my office on Market Street tomorrow morning, say around ten. As long as *both* of us can make money, I'm your man."

After Higgenbottom staggered home for the night, Sam celebrated with a glass of fine French cognac and a dozen delicious oysters Rockefeller. Then he retired to his suite where he enjoyed the most restful night's sleep he had had for a very long while.

The offices of Higgenbottom and Lane, Investment Brokers, occupied the entire top floor of a large brownstone in Denver's financial district.

Sam Ransom was impressed. He checked his diamond-studded gold pocket watch to make certain it was exactly ten o'clock when he entered the building. It was always a good idea to be punctual.

A well-built, red-headed secretary who would have been pretty, if only she had not worn her hair pulled back tightly into a bun—something he detested—politely ushered him into Warner Higgenbottom's massive walnut-paneled office.

Their affairs were swiftly concluded. Neither the portly Higgenbottom or his equally chubby partner, Bryant Lane, seemed inclined to talk of anything but the business at hand. Sam was a chameleon and immediately assumed the same no-nonsense attitude.

When the trio adjourned for a friendly luncheon celebration, papers had been signed, stock powers properly witnessed and on their way to be filed. While he had yet to receive a dollar, Sam felt he was walking on air. He magnanimously picked up the check and left the startled waiter a five-dollar bill for a tip.

The deal they had laid out was for Sam to deposit a quarter-million shares of Shakespeare Mining and Development Company's development stock with the brokerage firm. He would retain six hundred fifty thousand shares as treasury stock. These could be sold later, if necessary, to finance a mill. Additionally, Higgenbottom and Lane personally received fifty thousand shares each for their own benefit.

"Don't worry about us selling our own stock," Higgenbottom assured him. "When we establish a favorable market for the shares, we'll drop a small amount once in a while—just to sweeten the pot—but we'll never drive down the price. You can trust us, we're professionals."

It's only paper you idiots. I'll take the eighty percent your firm sends me for what stock you sell on the street, keep ninety percent of that and be long gone before you shysters can drop a dollar's worth, Sam thought.

"Gentlemen, here's to the art of the deal," Sam said, raising his glass in a toast. The glasses clinked, pleasantries were exchanged, then everyone happily went their own ways.

Sam returned to his suite and drifted off to sleep reading a novel. He was famished when he awoke. Pheasant under glass and a wonderful bottle of expensive French white wine sounded sumptuous. He was so proud of the way he had manipulated those chumps. Soon money would be flowing his way, lots and lots of it. Now it was time for celebration.

After dinner he planned to seek out some feminine companionship. In a large city like Denver he knew he would be able to find a young, tight-skinned beauty to spend the night with. For a man of means like Sam Ransom, that task was usually a simple and pleasant one.

Sam sprung from his ornate brass bed with a sudden urgency. His bladder seemed unusually full. When he reached the bathroom and finally was able to make water, he screamed. His urine was like liquid fire.

"Damn it!" Sam swore viciously. "I hate Lordsburg and Mexican whores."

CHAPTER TWELVE

"I got a telegram from Sam Ransom," Lett announced to his crew when they arrived at the mine to begin the day's work. "He's in Denver. He says he's ailing and too sick to travel. He mentioned he wired some money to the bank and for us to keep timbering."

"Hope it ain't nothing serious," Jake Clanton said worriedly. "If Ransom goes tits up, we're all out of a job."

The very thought of something happening to Sam Ransom was chilling. After a long, dismal silence, Lett spoke up. "Boys, I'd reckon it's not too serious. He probably just picked up a bug somewhere. I'd venture Sam'll be shipshape in a few days."

"Yeah, I'm sure you're right," Bulldog said, "which is more than I can say for us if we don't get a fan blowing some fresh air down that shaft. You can't even light a cigarette down there, the air's so bad."

"And we're only timbered to twenty-four feet," Epp added. "I think that hole's makin' poison gas. My head hurts like hell when I get down there."

"If you'd drink less in the evening," Bulldog grumbled, "your head wouldn't hurt near as much. But Epp's right about us not being able to go any deeper. A job don't do a body any good if he's dead."

Lett sighed. He knew there could be no more work in the shaft until he secured a blower. It *was* getting too dangerous. "Okay boys, we'll spend the day putting up a dry shack so we can have a place to eat lunch out of weather and store our tools. This afternoon, I'll go to Lordsburg. If Sam's money's hit the bank, I'll shop around until I rustle up a fan and some vent line. I think I saw one that would work out back of the assayer's office. If he don't want to sell it, he might at least rent the thing. After all, it is his mine we're fixing up."

"I don't know if he'll be there or not," Jake mentioned casually. "I got up with the chickens this morning. Went traipsing around Lookout Hill trying to stir up some kinda critter to eat, like a quail or maybe even a Hoover hog. I never saw nothing to shoot, but I did see Will Green's Model A, then I spied him sitting clean on top of the peak."

"He was most likely hunting, just like you were," Bulldog said.

Jake's brow wrinkled with puzzlement. "Sure a funny way to hunt if that's what he was doing. He kept staring down at the town through a telescope. Whatever he was peeping at sure must have been interesting because he never saw me, that's for sure."

"Probably keeping an eye on Lett's whore," Epp said.

For such a big man Lett Halsy could move very quickly. Scant seconds later Arnold Epp was dangling in midair, a ham-sized fist firmly grasped around his shirt collar. Lett's face contorted with anger. "You say one more word about Delight and you're not only fired, but I'll punch you so hard you won't stop rolling until you hit Texas!"

"Don't go and kill him," Bulldog said, calmly placing his hand on Lett's shoulder. "I know he was hiding behind the door when the brains was passed out, but he is my pard. Arnold didn't mean nothin'."

Epp tried to agree, but with Lett's hand wrapped around his neck all he could muster was a gurgle.

As quickly as he had been scooped up, Arnold Epp crashed

back to the rocky earth into a crumpled heap. "God, I—I'm sorry," he managed to croak, looking up at Lett.

After a long silence Arnold got to his feet, stuck his hands into his pockets, slouched over to a large rock and sat down. "Please don't fire me boss. I promise never to say anything about the lady again, I didn't mean nothin', really I didn't."

Lett kicked at the ground with his boot. "It's all right, no one's fired. I just got mad. All I ever do is have dinner with her. She's one hell of a lot better cook than anyone in Shakespeare. Delight's damn sure a lady, though. And don't any of you dandies forget it!"

Epp looked beaten. "Thanks boss, I'll make it up to you, you'll see."

"Okay boys, you get to building that shack. I'm going to Lordsburg now. If that assayer ain't around, I may have to spend a little time looking to find us a fan."

The three men watched in silence as Lett Halsy strode off down the mountainside toward Shakespeare. When he was just a speck among the distant cactus, Arnold Epp garnered enough courage to speak.

"If I'd known he was smitten with that whore I'd kept my trap shut."

Bulldog shook his head sadly. "When I said you was hiding when God passed out the brains, I wasn't funnin'. Anyone with enough sense to pour sand out of his boots could tell Lett's taken with Delight. We all know she's a whore, but I'd reckon not one of us had better ever use that word to describe her again."

Arnold Epp rubbed his neck. "From now on *all* whores are ladies in my book."

Otis Tate was standing in the open doorway of his office puffing on a huge black cigar when Lett walked by.

"Well, Mister Halsy, how good to see you," the lawyer said. "I trust things are going well at the mine and the men are being paid."

Lett smiled. "Things are fine. I just left the bank and there's been another thousand dollars put in the account. Sam's in Denver and mighty sick. I got a telegram from him saying it'll be a while before he gets back. Right now I'm off to find a mine fan. The air's real bad in that shaft."

Otis suppressed an evil grin. From his office window he could easily see all of Main Street and the row of weathered adobes across the railroad tracks. He knew *exactly* what Sam Ransom's medical problem was. "I'm sure Sam will be fine."

"We all hope so. The Last Chance is aptly named. Nowadays it's the only mine running in Shakespeare. The Roxy Jay's looking like it might make a go of it too. If that ore's down there like Sam says it is, Shakespeare will boom for sure." Lett wondered why the lawyer suddenly looked worried. "Is something wrong?"

"Oh, no, I've just been around mining for a lot of years, too many to go counting chickens before they're hatched. If you're looking for some machinery though, come in and I'll call Dave Jennings. He's selling off everything from when the big mines closed. They're nearly giving the stuff away to keep from trucking it out."

"Thanks, we can use all the cheap material I can rustle up. I really hope Sam gets his financing put together soon. We can only go so deep before it'll take heavy machinery to get the job done."

The lawyer swallowed hard to keep from disclosing his true feelings. "You know I represent Sam Ransom. The Shakespeare Mining and Development Corporation is properly filed. It's up to him to sell the stock. This Depression is growing worse every day. I really hope he opens a bonanza on that mountain, but things are very tough."

"Yes, I'm concerned myself," Lett said gravely. "If you don't mind I would like to see if they have a fan, then I need to get back to the mine."

The ancient Reo truck crawled slowly up the steep mountain road leaving a heavy cloud of blue oil smoke hanging in its wake.

Arnold Epp took a second to look who was coming and smashed his thumb with a hammer. *Some days it just doesn't pay to get out of bed,* he thought, sucking on his wounded digit.

Lett Halsy bounded out of the passenger door when the truck coughed and jerked to a stop.

Arnold Epp was gratified to see a smile on his boss's face. He wrapped a dirty handkerchief around his throbbing thumb, then walked over to join Bulldog, Jake and Lett as they stood surveying the cargo in the back of the truck.

"Damn, I wish I could have gotten this piece of worn-out junk turned around and pointed downhill before it quit." A skeleton-thin man wearing dirty overalls swore. He had a black slouch hat pulled down to where his big ears stuck out like flags. The man hesitated long enough to angrily kick the tires. "I don't know how many starts this old thing has left in it. Prob'ly burned a gallon of expensive oil just climbin' that hill."

"This here's Dave Jennings," Lett Halsy said nodding toward the surly driver. "He's brought us a fan and some ventube."

Jake Clanton jumped on the running board and looked the rusty machine over with a jaundiced eye. "I hope this thing's in better shape than the truck that hauled it here."

"All it needs is a coat of paint. Then I could've sold it fer new," Jennings spat.

"It *was* cheap," Lett said almost apologetically.

Arnold Epp decided it prudent to keep his mouth shut, but couldn't keep from shaking his head worriedly.

Bulldog sighed, "Well, let's grab up some timbers and skid the blame thing off. Who knows, if God's in a good mood we might get it to run someday."

After a short while the heavy machine had been maneuvered into place near the shaft and Jennings' battered truck pushed to where it pointed downhill.

Lett filled the water hopper on the Cushman two-horsepower engine and topped off the crankcase with oil. Bulldog filled the brass grease cups on the Sturtevant blower, gave them a few spins then turned the belts by hand. "At least it ain't locked up."

Dave Jennings gave him a glare that would clabber milk. "Put some damn gas in it, then stand back."

Lett carefully strained gasoline from a galvanized can through a cheesecloth until the tank was filled.

The scrawny Jennings grabbed the flywheel and rotated it a few times. The little engine let out a cough, then began chugging happily. For the first time since he'd been at the mine, he grinned as he shouted over the roar. "See I told you. It's just like new."

After the fan had run for a few minutes, Lett flipped the magneto switch, stopping the machine. "Well, boys, now we can head for China."

Jennings' usual scowl returned. "Now that you girls are all happy, give that truck of mine a push an' I'll get the hell outta here."

The Reo picked up speed quickly and the men grimaced when the driver ground the truck into gear. A huge cloud of blue smoke obscured it momentarily while a series of loud backfires echoed off the cactus-studded hills. When the speeding truck emerged from the haze, the cab was enveloped by billowing orange flames. Dave Jennings bailed out and barely missed being run over by the rear wheels. The skinny man rolled until he finally came to a stop in a thick patch of cholla cactus. The blazing truck continued speeding toward the valley floor until a front wheel went over the edge of the steep road. The Reo flipped end over end, finally crashing upside down onto a pile of granite boulders in the canyon.

"Well, *that* was exciting," Bulldog said blandly.

From their vantage point high on the mountain, the men could hear Jennings cursing loudly from pain and anger.

"He's real lucky to find a nice soft patch of cactus to land in," Jake Clanton chuckled. "Otherwise the crusty old son of a bitch mighta' gotten hurt."

"I'm havin' one of those days myself," Epp mumbled, as he grabbed up a pair of pliers to join the men as they ran down the road. He knew the machinery peddler was going to need a lot of cactus thorns pulled out of his skinny body. Arnold Epp was going to enjoy this.

CHAPTER THIRTEEN

Delight wore a worried brow when she opened the firebox door of her kitchen range and poked in a few sticks of mesquite wood. It wasn't usual for Lett to be late for dinner. After working hard at the mine all day the big man was usually ravenous.

Satisfied there was sufficient fuel in the stove to keep the huge cast-iron pot of beans and ham hocks simmering for a while, she snapped the door shut then turned the damper closed. The wonderful aroma of fresh-baked bread filled her small cabin. To keep flies away, she draped a cheesecloth over the two loaves and tray of sweet cream butter setting on the wooden kitchen table. Flies were always a big problem this time of year.

For the third time in the past ten minutes, Delight went outside to stand under the tin roof of her porch. The hot desert breeze that whipped her long blond hair felt refreshing. Cooking on a wood stove in the June heat was a stifling task.

The fiery orb of summer was just beginning to hide itself behind the jutting spire of Lookout Hill. A stinging lizard that had been poking around for crickets and cockroaches scampered away in panic, kicking up tiny dust clouds with its feet when Delight walked to where she could see the distant Last Chance shaft.

A feeling of relief washed over her when she saw the crew of the Last Chance threading their way to town, skirting patches of cactus. The road to the mine branched off some distance from Shakespeare. It was closer for the men to walk cross country than to follow a graded road.

Returning to the closeness of her shack, Delight wished for some gunny sacks hung in her windows, cooled by dripping water, as were in Lett's cabin. It seemed strange to her the big man had yet to use them. He seemed to bask in the dry heat happily as that lizard she had just frightened.

Many things about Lett Halsy perplexed her. At first she assumed fixing dinner for him would simply be a prelude for sex. She had been mistaken. The first night Lett had been nervous, reminding her of a young man visiting a bordello, preparing to lose his virginity.

One thing Delight Jones had learned a long time ago was how to calm a nervous man. She'd acted prim and proper as a school teacher, making small talk and asking about his work at the mine. There was little doubt in her mind he had a wife and family somewhere. That would have explained his undue agitation. Most men were nervous when they cheated on their wives, for the first few times anyway.

When Lett told her, unasked, that his wife and son had died of pneumonia and were buried in the mountains of Colorado, his tortured look revealed he spoke the truth.

For over a week now they had shared dinner together. Delight found herself looking forward to their time together. Lett was a charming man, surprisingly well read, with a refreshing sense of humor.

She could only think of two reasons why he had not taken her to bed. The first being that he had suffered some accident and was unable to perform.

The second and most disturbing possibility was that she simply wasn't appealing to him. Perhaps without realizing it, she had passed into that stage where she was too old for a man to desire her in bed.

There was no denying the wrinkles she covered over with makeup everyday were growing more abundant. She tried keeping her figure trim. In the mornings she would take long walks in the low hills back of town, Wesley always trotting happily in front to keep her safe from snakes.

I'm forty years old. My good God, where did all the time go? The handwriting had been on the wall for a long while, she simply tried to postpone reading it.

Delight remembered when the young whore called Brooke had come to Shakespeare and set up shop in the crib next to hers. Brooke charged five dollars, yet every night a line of eager miners waited for her red porch light to flash on telling them she was ready for more business.

Delight only charged two dollars. Still her red light was seldom extinguished. It hurt like an ice pick had been driven into her heart when she remembered some customers mentioning they had come to visit her only "because the pretty one was busy."

Soon, the whore Delight Jones would cease to exist. A middle-aged woman by the name of Sara Jane Parker would be forced to carry on as best she could in a cold, Depression-ravaged world. She fervently hoped that day was yet to come.

"Whatever you fixed for dinner sure smells great," Lett said through the open door, politely standing on the porch.

His welcome presence caused Delight to adjourn her bitter reverie.

"It's just ham hocks and beans with fresh-baked whole-wheat bread. I was getting worried something had happened at the mine."

Lett entered her cabin wearing a grim expression. "We did have an accident this afternoon. I bought a fan from a guy named Dave Jennings. He's selling off the stuff left behind when they shut the mines down. The old truck he hauled it up on caught fire on the way downhill."

"How awful. I hope he wasn't hurt bad or killed," Delight said with sudden concern.

A slight grin flicked at the corners of his mouth. "Nope, but I reckon he might feel better if he had been. When he jumped from the truck, his fall was broken by a nice soft patch of cactus."

Delight laughed from relief.

Lett continued. "It took Epp a long while to yank all the stickers out of his hide. This Jennings fellow seemed to be mad at the world anyway. Now he's got a real good excuse to have his dander up. I offered to take him to Lordsburg in my car, but he kept cussing me and everyone else out so bad, we decided to let him walk."

"At least no one was seriously hurt. I know mining is plenty dangerous."

"That old truck was the only thing that didn't make it through the day. It had one foot in the grave and the other on a banana peel anyway."

Without thinking, Delight stepped close to Lett, wrapped her arms around him and kissed his cheek. "Thank God *you* weren't hurt."

When he recoiled from her embrace, Delight's fear of being unattractive was rekindled anew. "I'm sorry, I shouldn't have done that."

Lett smiled and gently grasped her hand. "You're a sweet lady. Don't you fret about me getting hurt. I've been around mines all of my life and know how to stay out of trouble." Releasing her hand, he quickly added, "Now, why don't we get to that wonderful dinner you've fixed."

After the dishes had been washed and stowed away in the cupboard, Delight turned on her radio. It was an Atwater Kent housed in a brown baked-enamel metal case. By carefully adjusting the tuner, she could pick up a single, static-filled transmission from a station in El Paso, Texas.

Amos 'n' Andy were just starting. The popular, funny show quickly melted their earlier tensions. Listening and laughing at the fifteen-minute program was becoming part of their evening routine.

A loud knock on the open door took their attention.

"Mister Halsy, could I see you for a minute?" Arnold Epp's anxious voice intoned.

Reluctantly, Lett went to see what the man wanted. When Arnold saw Delight following close behind, he swallowed hard and couldn't keep his wide-eyes from her. "Ma'am, I really hate to bother you and Lett, but there's a phone call from Sam Ransom."

"I'd better go take care of business," Lett said through pursed lips. "Dinner sure was good."

"Miss Delight, I really am sorry," Epp apologized again.

"See you tomorrow," Delight said, as Amos shouted his famous line, "Holy Mackerel, Andy," on the radio.

Lett followed Epp from the small porch into the gathering dark for the short walk to the Roxy Jay. He heard Delight's door shut and from the corner of his eye caught the glow from her red light begin shining.

"I hope it ain't bad news," Epp said anxiously.

Lett Halsy didn't answer. A burning lump in his throat kept him silent.

CHAPTER FOURTEEN

Every eye in the Roxy Jay was focused on Lett when he hung up the phone. Only a cough from Elmore Wyman broke the heavy silence that pervaded the huge room like a fog.

"Sam Ransom just called to say the doc's told him he'll be up to traveling soon. He should be here in four or five days," Lett announced loudly.

Jake Clanton punched a nickel into the coin slot on the player piano. There was only one tune the thing could play, but the tinkling melody was a happy one. Glasses clinked, men began laughing and talking hopefully of the big silver mine. What good times could be had returned to the Roxy Jay.

Aside from the crew working at the mine and Len Miller, no one had any income. Len had taken Jake's old job at the gas station in Lordsburg. He found that paid a lot better than the occasional haircut or attempt at doctoring.

Jason McTavish was miffed at Lett over the fact he hadn't been paying him wages for his bartending and cooking efforts. He had decided the best way to get even without ruffling any feathers was to stuff himself with every morsel of food he could hold. His success was becoming obvious.

"One of these days that bartender of yours is gonna trip and fall," Bulldog commented to Lett with a grin. "He's getting so round, my guess is when that happens, he'll roll plumb to Lordsburg and do considerable damage to whatever he crashes into down there."

Assuring himself McTavish was listening, Lett said seriously, "It's a true fact that man eats more than he's worth. The problem is, he's such a *likeable* cuss. If I paid him money he'd just spend it buying pies, cakes and ice cream. Before you know it he'd be so big he wouldn't fit through the kitchen door. Then he'd starve to death, and it'd be my fault for being so blasted kind to him."

McTavish gritted his teeth on the stub of an unlit cigar, but said nothing. At least he had a place to live and his meals furnished. The way things were in this Depression, that was more than a lot of men had.

Lett no longer felt like visiting with any of his crew that night. The incident with Epp had firmly established him to be the boss. It was as if an invisible curtain had been dropped, separating him from them forever.

The sensation was a strange one. Until a few days ago he had simply been a working miner, just like they were. In a brief span of time, Lett Halsy had become not only a mine superintendent but the focus of attention for everyone in the town of Shakespeare desperately hoping for a job.

Numerous men, possibly a hundred or more, had either pitched tents on flat areas around town or moved into one of the many abandoned houses. Most had families to feed and care for. He had no idea how most of them were getting by, but he knew all too well what they were waiting around for: work at Sam Ransom's mine. And *he* was Sam's superintendent, the one they all looked to.

It broke his heart when he saw the cheerless, dirty-faced kids come to fill water cans and buckets from the spigot in front of the bar. Strangers often approached, offering to buy him a drink, a few coins in their hand held close, like a beloved family heirloom. Always, he told them, "No thank you," with a forced smile. Then, all too often they would spend their money anyway, buying Bulldog, Epp or Jake Clanton drinks, hoping they might put in a good word for them with the boss.

Lett noticed Elmore Wyman sitting alone at the far end of the bar, nursing a mug of beer. The gaunt, white-haired man was there every night, so he must have had some form of income; his name hadn't appeared on McTavish's credit tabs.

Grabbing up his mug, Lett took a seat by the ancient-looking man he had never really gotten to know and struck up a conversation. His first impression was how frail Wyman appeared. What used to be the whites of his sunken eyes were a sickly shade of yellow. Lett was no doctor, but he knew how to recognize when a man had burned out his liver with booze. He had seen it happen to a lot of men when they got too old to do anything except sit in a bar all day.

"Hey, McTavish, give us both a beer," Elmore wheezed after a few minutes of small talk.

Lett was surprised when a silver dollar rang on the big mahogany bar. He smiled and said, "You don't need to buy me a drink, I own the place."

"Hell, I know that. And I also know you ain't making any money either. Most figure me fer nothing but an old rummy, and maybe I am, but I got sense enough to know what's going on. You picked up a lot of wooden nickels when you inherited this place."

The truth of the old man's words stung like angry hornets. Lett had not only spent the hundred-dollar bill Ransom had given him for supplies, but also over fifty from his checking account.

After the bartender had set the fresh, foamy mugs in front of them and was out of earshot, Lett held his glass up to the old man and smiled. "Thanks, I appreciate this. You are right, I'm barely hanging on. If I wasn't working for Ransom, I'd have closed the place."

Elmore took a long drink and kept his gaze on the mirror behind the bar. "I'd watch that feller, just like I'd keep an eye on a hawk circlin' my chickens. There's nothing jake about Sam Ransom to my way of thinking. Be real careful or you'll wind up holding the bag."

Lett swallowed hard and changed the subject. The old man's observations were depressing him even further. "I heard you've been around here for a long time."

"Yep, I was here in the big rush over fifty years ago. Of course I was just a sprout in those days, but I remember when they hung Sandy King and Russian Bill from that beam right over our heads."

Lett looked up at the big peeled log pole that ran the length of the building.

Elmore continued. "It was back in eighty-one it was. Most folks still called the place Ralston after William Ralston, the guy who founded the Bank of California. He got skinned out of a fortune by some shysters that planted diamonds in tha' hills around here. When he found out it was a scam, he took a swim in San Francisco Bay and washed up the next day, but that's another story.

"When they found real pay dirt hereabouts, they started calling the place Shakespeare, to keep it from being associated with that fiasco. I worked in the Atwood Mine. Sandy King was on my shift. Not a bad sort really, but when he got to drinking he sort of went crazy. He shot a finger off some shopkeeper and wound up in jail with Russian Bill who had stole a horse. Folks didn't cotton much to those goin's on, so they just hauled 'em in here and strung 'em up. There weren't any trees tall enough to do the job.

"This joint was a stage stop back then. The folks who done the lynching just left 'em hang. When the stage pulled in the next morning, it had a bunch of women on board. They raised holy hell until we cut them down and carried the bodies outside so's they could eat breakfast without them dangling up there."

Elmore Wyman took a faraway expression. "I left right after that. Hell, I looked fer gold all over the West, but always came back here. That Lost Dutchman Mine gave me a fever I couldn't get over."

"I always thought the Lost Dutchman was in Arizona," Lett said matter-of-factly.

The old man finished his beer and ordered another round. "That's what tha' Dutchman wanted folks to believe. Jacob Walz was a wily cuss, he hauled that purty gold in rose quartz clear back to Arizona to sell it. Told everyone it came from the Superstition Mountains."

"But you think it's hereabouts?" Lett asked.

"Sonny," Elmore Wyman said seriously after chugging his beer, "you and me, we're drinking on money outta that mine."

The old man then clammed up on the subject and would only talk about the old days. Lett didn't mind. Elmore's story had at least taken him away from his worries. He never for a moment believed the Lost Dutchman Mine, if it existed at all, was anywhere near here.

No matter how many times he offered, Elmore refused Lett's offers to buy him a drink. Lett's head began to spin and he knew he would feel rotten tomorrow if he didn't head for his cabin and get some sleep.

"I thank you greatly for the beer and conversation," Lett said graciously, climbing from the barstool to stand on unsteady legs.

"Welcome," was all the old man got out before his yellowed eyes rolled up into his skull. Then with a soft sigh he fell backwards, to crumble into a heap on the floor.

"I'll say one thing for that old geezer," McTavish quipped, waddling around the end of the bar. "He knows when he's had enough to drink."

Lett watched wonderingly, as Jake Clanton and McTavish dragged the unconscious Wyman to the far wall and propped him up. The bartender placed an apple on top of Elmore's head. Jake walked back to where a line had been drawn in white chalk across the plank floor.

To Lett's dismay, Jake Clanton pulled out a large pistol. Then he noticed the profusion of bullet holes in the wall above the apple.

"What the hell's going on?" Lett shouted.

"Oh, they're just playing William Tell," McTavish answered. "Jake pays a dollar a shot. Wyman gets half whenever he misses. That's where he gets the money to drink on, not the Lost Dutchman Mine."

"Listen up," Lett growled loudly. "No one is going to take a shot at that old man in *this* bar. My God, I'm surprised he hasn't been killed already!"

"But boss, I ain't hit him, ever," Jake Clanton whined.

Lett's icy glare answered all questions. Jake stuck his gun back into its holster and McTavish grabbed up the apple and ate it.

No one said another word to Lett as he made his way, somewhat unsteadily, through the back door of the Roxy Jay.

The fresh night air of the desert felt good to him. It was still warm out. He breathed deeply to clear his head. A multitude of stars twinkled brightly against the black canvas of sky.

Then, bitterly, he noticed Delight's red porch light was turned off. In the dead quiet he heard moans of passion and the squeaking of bedsprings coming from her open window.

Lett Halsy entered his cabin and slammed the door closed behind him. After a long while he drifted off into a fitful sleep.

CHAPTER FIFTEEN

Sam Ransom came roaring back into Shakespeare driving his red Packard convertible on the twelfth day of June, exactly four weeks to the day after Charles Lindbergh Jr., the kidnapped only son of the famous aviator, had been found dead alongside a New Jersey road.

This heinous crime, bank failures and the growing Depression were the main topics of conversation everywhere except in Shakespeare, New Mexico. There, all talk focused on Sam Ransom and his huge, soon-to-boom silver mine.

The first thing Sam did was visit the Last Chance Mine. What he saw pleased him greatly. New and heavy wood timbers extended into the dark maw of the once-caving shaft. A chugging engine spinning a roaring fan was the best part of all. Any rube could see and hear American industry at work should they wish to visit the mine site prior to plunking down their money for stock.

At Sam's request, Lett called Bulldog and Jake up from the depths of the mine. Retiring out of the hot sun to the crude shack near the shaft, Sam praised his crew for their hard work.

"All of you will get substantial pay raises and stock bonuses in the future," he said magnanimously. Holding his arms wide like a preacher offering to save souls, Sam continued, "We are all one big happy family, working together toward a common goal. To achieve these ends, there are some things we must do here at the heart of our operations.

"Lett, I would like your crew to build a nice office building where we can offer refreshments and comforts to potential partners in our venture.

"Keep that engine running all the time, find a generator and run it too. Then we can string lights down the shaft so people can see the ore for themselves."

Bulldog looked dumbstruck, but had the good sense to keep his mouth shut.

Sam Ransom motioned for everyone to follow him outside. He nodded his head down the narrow road. "I want a substantial locked gate put up to keep out highgraders. We'll build a guard house there shortly. Then cut all the brush from alongside the road, so it won't scratch any cars. While you're at it, fill in the potholes and throw any loose rocks out of the road. We want everyone's visit here to be a pleasant one."

Sam climbed into his shiny Packard to leave, then, as an afterthought looked at Lett. "And get rid of that burned-out old truck in the canyon. It looks like hell!"

While the dust from Sam's departing automobile settled, Bulldog rolled a cigarette, lit it then shook his head. "There goes one interestin' feller. I'd have to wonder why he's so blame worried about highgraders and folks looking at ore bodies when we ain't seen any ourselves."

Epp stared at the shaft. "I ain't seen nothing down that hole that would assay more than two thousand pounds to the ton. That teeny vein we're following is narrow as a Baptist's thinking."

Lett gave a worried sigh. "One thing's for sure boys, that man pays our wages. We'll do what Sam wants done. You guys grab some shovels and axes, then get to working on the road. I'll head to town and pick up some lumber."

Jake Clanton looked questioningly at Lett. "You want that fan left running even when we're not working in the shaft?"

"You heard the man," Lett answered with a shrug. "Keep it running!"

Sam encountered little difficulty renting a wonderful office building on the main street of Lordsburg. The gray-haired old woman who owned it seemed very grateful to get thirty dollars a month for the place.

The icing on the cake was the structure had serviced a mining engineer for many years, before he had the misfortune to fall down a mine shaft. His widow, bless her heart, left the furnishings intact. The walnut wainscot-paneled walls were lined with glass cases displaying ore specimens.

A massive oak desk, even larger than the one that skunk of a lawyer, Otis Tate had, stood in the middle of the room. Looking through the huge front window, Sam could see the train depot.

This is perfect, he thought.

All he needed now was to get a phone hooked up and hire a sign painter to letter the name "Shakespeare Mining and Development Company" on the front window in ornate gold script.

He decided to go ahead and have some signs made for the mine also. Guppies simply *loved* signs. All big, successful companies had lots of them; they gave a feeling of pride and permanency. Just what he needed to sell stock.

Sam leaned back in the swivel rocker, stuck a cigarette into an ivory holder, fired it with his gold lighter and took a satisfied puff. Carefully, he went over things in his mind.

There was little doubt the Denver firm of Higgenbottom and Lane would soon be selling a lot of stock. He was *so* lucky to have met up with them.

That was why most people failed, he mused. It was because they had no guts. They were content to while away their lives in some miserable, boring existence. He, on the other hand, understood what it took to get ahead in this world. Those poverty rat sycophants who continually fawned around him simply had no imagination.

Sam Ransom did.

Shortly, when the elegant stationary he had ordered arrived, he would begin issuing glowing press statements to the mining newspapers, telling of the rich ore bodies they had uncovered in Shakespeare, New Mexico.

Possibly even the prestigious *Engineering and Mining Journal* would accept his copy. Sam knew exactly how to turn a worthless hole in the ground into a bonanza. All it took was guts and some well-placed lies printed up to look more appealing than any truth could ever be.

Sam Ransom snubbed out his smoke in a crystal ashtray and walked out into the scorching, always windy main street. He was heading for the hotel to find out what their best accommodations had to offer. Then he saw a familiar Mexican girl leaning against an adobe wall across the tracks.

He shot her a scowl and continued on his way. While he was not quite back to being interested in women yet, finding a beautiful lady would be a real problem in this hick town.

Then he remembered the blond whore out back of the saloon in Shakespeare. He couldn't remember her name, but she would have to do. She wasn't that bad looking and would provide an interesting diversion for the short time he was planning on being here.

As the old saying he was so fond of went, "Any port in a storm."

CHAPTER SIXTEEN

A diamondback rattlesnake, invisibly blended in with a jumble of rocks, strikes out, biting Sam Ransom repeatedly.

Nah, the poor snake would just die a lingering death, Lett thought.

Sam bends over to stare down into the darkness of the Last Chance shaft, a quick push and he screams like a mashed cat while plunging into the depths of the earth.

The son of a bitch never goes anywhere near that shaft.

The brakes fail on that fancy big-assed car he drives. It swerves off the road, rolls over and catches fire, just like Dave Jennings' Reo did, only Sam Ransom fries right along with the Packard.

"Yeah," Lett Halsy mumbled happily to himself, taking care not to be overheard. "That's a really good one!"

For the past several days Lett had been enjoying his flights of fantasy about Sam Ransom's demise. It was great entertainment to imagine new and novel ways the greasy-haired little pipsqueak could meet with a spectacular, hopefully very fatal, accident.

Today was the first day in the past two weeks that Sam had allowed the men to work on re-timbering the mine shaft.

To a man, they were sun- and windburned, with beet-red faces from working on the road to the Last Chance. Laboring under a blazing June sun, they had filled potholes, beaten rocks down with a sledgehammer and used rakes to make the mine road smoother than any in New Mexico.

It wasn't the grueling road work, or building the massive gate and big office building that had irritated Lett. For three hundred dollars a month he would gladly repair every road in the desert.

Lett was riled at Sam over two things. The first was those damnable signs that seemed to be everywhere. Even the turnoff for the road to Shakespeare had one. They were large as billboards and each proclaimed the same thing:

SHAKESPEARE MINING AND
    DEVELOPMENT COMPANY
LAST CHANCE MINE
PRODUCERS OF GOLD AND SILVER
LETT HALSY, GENERAL MANAGER

It quickly became painfully obvious to him why Sam's name was not up there in big gold letters. Lett couldn't even go to the outhouse without being followed by men clamoring for work. They woke him in the morning, pounding on the door of his cabin. There was simply no place of refuge from the masses of desperate men hoping for a job. And Lett Halsy was the man to see. It said so in great big beautiful lettering everywhere they looked.

"I'd reckon there's nigh onto three hundred souls camped around Shakespeare these days and they're all looking to you," Bulldog had told him last night at the Roxy Jay.

Lett thought Bulldog to be low on his count. He knew how terribly desperate these men needed work, but there was nothing he could do about it. The shaft at the mine was only timbered to thirty feet deep. Even if money was available to hire more men, there simply wasn't room for them to work down there.

While the signs were huge, the Last Chance Mine was nothing but a small hole in the ground.

The second thing that really galled Lett was Ransom's atten-

95

tions toward Delight. The slick-haired little wart had taken her into Lordsburg with him the past two nights. Lett not only missed her sweet company, along with listening to *Amos 'n' Andy*, he had also been forced to eat McTavish's cooking.

Lett had no difficulty understanding how his brother had met his demise. Last night's mystery-meat stew still weighed like an anvil on his stomach. Every time he belched he could taste its questionable flavor again.

Lett noticed Jake Clanton staring at a timber laying on sawhorses. "Jake," he snarled, "get to sawing on that timber. I'll swear the second coming will happen before we get this shaft timbered if you don't get the lead out!"

"Are we havin' a bad day, boss?" Jake said sarcastically while grabbing up the saw. "I knew you should have just ate the corn-bread last night. McTavish's stew would make a buzzard sick. Now cornbread's something he can cook that won't come back and haunt you the next day."

Lett sighed and said nothing. He walked over, grabbed the upright handle on one end of the long saw and helped Jake cut the timber. The pair carried the heavy load past the roaring fan to the edge of the shaft and tied it with a rope.

"Coming down," Jake yelled loudly down the open shaft. He then took hold of one crank on the windlass, Lett the other, and together they lowered the stout timber into the darkness.

They were getting so deep now that bells would soon be needed for communication between men on the surface and those in the shaft. In an underground mine, different bell signals were as effective as Morse code. One ring meant to hoist up, two for down, three-two meant lower slowly and so on. Seven bells was the most dreaded signal of all. An accident, usually a bad one, was the only time seven bells ever sounded.

Lett said over the noisy fan, "I reckon I'll go to town early tonight. Maybe Jennings has a couple of shaft bells and some rope."

Jake didn't answer, he was staring down the road. Lett spun to see what was so interesting. "Oh, shit!" he spat out without thinking.

Sam Ransom was already out of his red Packard, nattily dressed and wearing a smile that stretched ear to ear. Lett had been so focused on his work he hadn't noticed Sam's arrival.

A second automobile, this one a sleek, coal-black Marmon, pulled to a dusty stop behind the Packard. While Lett was walking over, an elderly couple climbed slowly from the Marmon and looked around with obvious disdain.

Sam ran to meet him. "These fine people are John and Bessie Stevens. They've come all the way from Denver to look over our operation."

Lett shook the old man's hand, it felt limp. Quickly and wordlessly the visitor recoiled from the sweaty miner. The couple were dressed far too formally to be visiting a mine site. The man, John Stevens, wore a homburg hat, along with a neat suit and tie. Mrs. Stevens in her pink, ankle-length dress and high-heeled shoes had her silver hair pulled tightly back into a bun. Both looked as if their faces would crack if they ever smiled.

Sam beamed at Lett and announced, "Mister Halsy is our mining engineer. He has had vast experience in your wonderful Cripple Creek gold mines."

A lump caught in Lett's throat when he realized Jake was just behind him and had heard every word. He didn't want any of Sam's wild statements bandied about.

Ransom never slowed down for Lett to reply. "As you can see we have a crew at work preparing the shaft to produce ore. In very short order untold thousands of tons of high-grade gold and silver will issue forth from beneath our very feet."

Lett had a difficult time keeping his mouth closed, when Sam produced two pieces of quartz from his pocket and handed them to the silent visitors. Even from several feet away he could see the little rocks were laced with wire gold.

"Here are some small samples of ore taken from the shaft," Sam boomed proudly. "As I have said, we need to buy heavy machinery to open the ore body. That is the *only* reason we are offering stock for sale at such a bargain price. Please feel free to keep those specimens. Have them assayed if you wish."

The old woman's scowl deepened. She climbed back into the Marmon and slammed the door closed.

"My wife suffers from allergies," John Stevens said in a whiney voice. "This desert makes her ill." He turned his gaze to Sam. "Would it be possible for me to look down the shaft?"

Sam nodded. "Of course it is." Then he growled at Lett. "Why haven't you gotten that generator yet? I distinctly told you we needed lights strung down that shaft so folks could look at the vein. We have other visitors coming soon—get that done straightaway."

Lett bit on his lip. "Yes sir, we'll get right on it."

"I'm afraid I'm much too old to be climbing down ladders," Stevens said matter-of-factly. "Also I'm afraid of enclosed spaces, but I would like to look at your progress."

Sam Ransom put a comforting arm around John Stevens' shoulder. "Of course sir, please allow me to assist you."

Lett and Jake stood side by side and watched while the duo walked over and peered down the shaft. Lett was truly surprised that Jake hadn't said anything.

Shortly, Ransom escorted the elderly patriarch back to his car. After promising to meet them later for dinner, Sam watched closely while the big Marmon slowly turned around then headed down the hill in a cloud of dust.

Sam wore a serious expression when he approached the miners. Then, he broke into a smile that made his trimmed mustache wiggle like a caterpillar. "You men did a wonderful job. That stock bonus I promised you will be coming shortly. Keep up the good work. And don't worry about buying that generator just yet."

Once the dust from Sam's Packard had settled, Jake curled one side of his mouth in obvious amusement. "Where did you get to be a mining engineer?"

Lett shook his head. "I'd reckon from the same place Sam got those ore specimens."

"You know," Jake Clanton sighed, "I'm beginning to think our fearless leader, ol' Sam Ransom's, as full of crap as the bottom of a year-old bird nest."

"I think you might be right. But, he's paying our wages, so all we can do is hope like hell he makes a go of it."

Suddenly, Lett thought of something to be happy about. Sam was probably going to take that old couple to dinner tonight. That meant Delight and he could be together.

"Well, Jake, I'd reckon we ought to get another timber cut and lowered down that hole before Bulldog and Epp decide to take a nap," Lett said happily.

"You should've been promoted to a mining engineer sooner," Jake commented wryly. "Now that you're educated, you're in a lot better mood."

CHAPTER SEVENTEEN

"This is one high-grade lot," Will Green said, staring hungrily at the mass of rose quartz that was simply held together with glistening wires and ribbons of pure gold. He fought down the urge to grab skinny old Elmore Wyman around his bony throat and throttle him until he revealed where he had gotten the sack of ore he had just dumped on the assayer's table.

"If it's all right with you," Elmore began coughing and had to steady himself against the table. It took him a long while before he was recovered enough to continue. "I'd like to wait for my money. I'm gonna be needin' it right away."

So you can blow it on more booze at the Roxy Jay, you old fool, Will thought. "Of course you can." He brought out a bottle of bootleg rye, poured a water glass full and handed it to the shaking, hoary-eyed drunk.

"Why thankee, I appreciate this," Elmore said happily.

"You know I've been buying gold for a long while and this is the highest grade of ore I've ever seen."

Will Green carefully scooped up the gold and placed it on a scale. "Just over ten pounds. I'll crush it down then smelt it. In the meanwhile, help yourself to all the whiskey you want."

Elmore's silence while Will Green worked nipped at the assayer's patience like a mean dog. He fervently hoped the old rummy would get drunk enough to mumble some clue as to where the Lost Dutchman Mine was. Whiskey was something he had never tried before. Hopefully booze would loosen his lips. If not, he would have to pay a visit to Elmore's house in Shakespeare some night very soon. This way was preferable, but that mine *would* be his, even it turned out to be over Elmore Wyman's dead body.

The gold had been crushed, amalgamated, retorted, and the shimmering yellow metal was cooling in cast-iron doré molds. The whiskey bottle was empty and another ready to join it, yet Elmore remained alert and silent as the stones that had contained his gold.

To Will Green's building vexation, the old geezer was shaking less and his eyes were clearer now than when he'd first walked through the door struggling with that canvas bag of ore.

Then I'll have to do it the hard way. Will managed a wan smile. "All we have to do now, soon as it cools, is weigh it, do a fineness test and you'll have your money."

"Appreciate the drinks. This ain't bad stuff, better than most a body gets these days. That damn prohibition really made good whiskey hard to find."

"Yeah," Will agreed. "I have a man who brings it in from back east. The next time you come in, I'll have some more. I hope that's real soon."

Elmore emptied his glass and poured the remainder of the bottle into it. "The future's something a body can never be sure of." He took a long drink. "So's I take every day like it's my last."

If you don't talk about that mine, you old rummy, that last day will be a hell of a lot sooner than you think. Will Green ventured a question—he really had nothing to lose. "You must have a bunch of this ore stuck back?"

"When I bring it in, you'll know."

"Why don't we make a deal? I'll do all the work, mine it and then sell it. All you'll need to do is spend your half. We'll be partners."

Elmore rolled his yellowed eyes at the assayer. "Why don't you finish your work an' pay me? I want to get home before it starts to get dark."

Will Green's hands shook from anger as he placed the doré on his scale. "Fifty-eight and a third ounces. We'll call it eight hundred fine, same as the last batch. That nets out at a little better than forty-six ounces. Let's see. . . ." He penciled some figures on a pad. "At twenty dollars and sixty-seven cents an ounce that comes to nine hundred sixty-four dollars."

All that money from ten God-damned pounds of rock.

"Give me my half," Elmore said with a hint of irritation.

The assayer gritted his teeth and his knuckles were white when he opened his safe and took out the money tray. "Think about what I said, Elmore. You could have money like this every day."

"I figger four hundred eighty-two dollars you owe me," the old man completely ignored the question.

"Oh, yeah you're right." Will Green counted out the money with a steely expression. "Here it is, just like always. I'm an honest man, remember that."

Elmore Wyman recounted the money slowly, then thrust it into the pocket of his faded and filthy pants. He shuffled over to the door. Almost as an afterthought, he turned and said bluntly, "When a person's dealing with rich gold ore, there ain't no such thing as an honest man."

CHAPTER EIGHTEEN

A pair of stinging lizards scurried for cover when Wesley, followed by Delight, made his way around a cluster of greasewood bushes on the gentle lower slope of Lookout Hill.

She smiled, watching them run so fast they kicked up little clouds of dust. Delight knew they were harmless little creatures, called stinging lizards only because of the menacing way they carried their tail curled up in the air and arched over their back, like a scorpion.

Wesley froze and cocked his head at the lizards. Satisfied the commotion wasn't a rattlesnake in need of killing, or a rabbit to chase, the wiry-haired mix of terrier and who-knew-what sat on his haunches and whined impatiently for his human companion to catch up.

Delight wiped a trickle of sweat from her forehead. The fiery desert sun had barely begun its arc in a cloudless sky, yet the temperature was already over ninety degrees. She breathed deeply, then walked over to Wesley and scratched his ears.

"Good boy," she purred, causing the dog's tail to wag furiously. "Keeping me safe from snakes. Good dog."

Delight turned and gazed sorrowfully down at the town of Shakespeare nestled in the valley below. Tents could be seen pitched haphazardly all about. Cars and trucks of every description were parked beside them.

The reality of the crushing Depression was laid bare in front of her. Every tent was occupied by out-of-work men, most with families. Too many were not only out of work, they were also hungry.

"There's not a Hoover hog within ten miles of here that hasn't got somebody chasing after it with a gun in one hand and a skillet in the other," Lett had said just last night. He was referring to the popular name for a jackrabbit in these hard times. There had been pain in the big man's voice. He knew the agony these people were going through. More than once, he had told every single man in that valley below there was no job for them at the mine. Not yet anyway. He was too gentle to tell them his doubts. Those he reserved for his quiet moments with her.

Meanwhile, the hundreds camped around Shakespeare subsisted on flour, cornmeal, what they could shoot, and hope. When nothing else was left, there was always hope.

Delight swallowed hard when she realized why Wesley hadn't been able to find a rattlesnake for days. They had been caught and eaten. Even the larger desert iguana lizards had disappeared. A stringy jackrabbit was now a prize to be savored. Instead of wildlife, all she saw these days when she took her morning strolls were men with guns.

Wesley whined sadly, as if he could understand her feelings, then rolled over on his back and waved his paws in the air. Delight sat on a large rock varnished brown by the desert sun and scratched his belly. Numerous pink, long-healed scars and lumps protruded through Wesley's short brown-and-white wiry coat.

"You poor puppy," she cooed. "Life hasn't been easy for you either."

Wesley rolled over, placed his head on her shoe and looked up with big, brown, understanding eyes.

Delight gently stroked the dog's head and thought of Sam Ransom. He was an enigma. Throughout her life of dealing with men, she had made a practice never to get involved with men beyond what their money would buy. Now, not only Lett Halsy, but the fate of an entire town lay in the dubious hands of Sam Ransom.

Sam was egotistical and vain, but certainly a man with money. He paid her twenty dollars to spend the night with him. It seemed very important to him to be seen with a woman, far more so than enjoying his time. Sam's lovemaking had been brief and crude. After quickly spending himself, he made her lie beside him, nude, for hours while he kept his nose buried in a book.

She fervently hoped the greasy-haired pompous little braggart would be good to his word and the mine on the hill would boom.

The town of Shakespeare and Lett were depending on his promises.

Lett Halsy. He was the first man she had ever known as a friend.

Delight held no illusions past their simple dinners together. She was a whore. And he knew that full well. Some day, probably soon, the big man would find a decent woman to spend time with. For now, she had the pleasure of his company.

Little things, like listening to the radio or just talking with him, she found charming.

We play the cards we're dealt, she thought bitterly. *Sometimes life gives out really bad hands.*

There was not a doubt in her mind that no matter what happened in Shakespeare, she would leave. Sara Jane Parker, alone.

Wesley barked, jolting Delight from her sad reverie.

"Okay, Wesley, want to play fetch?" she squealed like a schoolgirl.

The dog spun furiously, looking for something she could throw, finally coming up with a small, dry piece of wood.

Delight threw it hard and high down the hill toward town. The happily yipping dog ran after it.

Slowly, Delight walked back to Shakespeare to sleep away the remains of the day. Another night awaited.

CHAPTER NINETEEN

Trepidation had been nagging at Sam Ransom like a shrew for the past two days. He felt certain the Stevens couple was sold on his mining venture. A week had passed since their visit and all he'd heard from Higgenbottom and Lane was stone silence.

The way that old saphead had kept fondling the little piece of high-grade gold ore was a dead giveaway he was a Guppy. The only question in Sam's mind was how much stock they had bought and why he had not heard from those damn brokers.

God only knew how badly he wanted to see some returns start flowing in from his investment. He had spent a lot of money, *his* hard-won money, to get this scam up and running. So far not one dollar had crossed his palm, headed in the right direction.

That nefarious lawyer, Otis Tate, had gotten another two grand yesterday. Then Lett Halsy came by and there went an additional thousand dollars into the mining account.

"We're timbered to forty-eight feet and need more timbers and J bolts to keep going deeper," Halsy had told him.

Sam didn't know what the hell jay bolts were and furthermore he didn't give a rat's hind end if that shaft was timbered or not, but he was too committed to have second thoughts. The image was all important. He didn't bother to add up his expenses. There was little doubt his cash had been depleted to nearly forty thousand by now.

He sighed, leaned back in his swivel rocker and stared at the phone expectantly. Sam stuck a cigarette into his ivory holder but didn't light it. Waiting was something Guppies did. Things only transpired when you *made* them work. Sam Ransom was a mover, a man of action. He grabbed up the black receiver. A lady's voice, very business like, asked, "Number please?"

Very distinctly Sam gave her the phone number for Higgenbottom and Lane, investment brokers in Denver, Colorado.

That tight-assed, red-haired secretary took ten minutes, expensive minutes, before she had Warner T. Higgenbottom answer his call.

"Why hello, Sam, I've been meaning to phone you," Higgenbottom's gravelly voice boomed. "Things are looking very good for your Shakespeare venture."

Sam felt relieved. "I take it Stevens bought some stock."

"Mister Stevens is one of our oldest and most valued clients. I must say he's enthused over the Last Chance Mine. He said you have some extremely high-grade ore down there."

"Yes sir, there's no doubt of that. I personally believe our mine here will produce more silver and gold than the Comstock Lode did, even in its palmy days. I assume then Stevens took a stock position in our company."

Sam listened while Higgenbottom took a long puff on a cigar then exhaled loudly. "Mister Ransom, Stevens is not only a valued client, but his word carries a lot of weight in the investment community. A *lot* of weight, sir. We have found it advantageous to let a few close friends in on the ground floor, so to speak; to gain valuable investors down the line."

"Then you let him buy stock at a lower price?"

"Oh don't concern yourself," the broker said soothingly. "We would never sacrifice *your* stock at a lower price than par value without your consent. Why, Lane and I took what will certainly be a big loss to help get your company up and running. For no other reason than to ensure the future of Shakespeare Mining and Development Company, we disposed of ten thousand shares of our own stock for a mere fifty cents a share."

Sam Ransom could hardly believe what he was hearing. He had never dealt with a large brokerage firm before, so he couldn't be entirely certain they weren't acting in his best interests. In his past dealings, he had sold all stock directly to the Guppies themselves.

Sadly, that was impossible these days. All his contacts were in San Francisco. Unfortunately, so was an enraged investor by the name of Al Casey, who had a lucrative contract out on Sam's beloved family jewels.

There was nothing else to do but work with this piggish broker and hope for the best.

"Then you believe," Sam said stiffly, "that this Stevens fellow will bring in other investors. As you know, we're in dire need of funds. I'm financing the entire venture out of my own pocket down here."

"Why of course he will!" Higgenbottom boomed happily. "Bryant and I are absolutely certain we'll have a hundred thousand shares sold within thirty days. We don't take losses like we did on your stock if we don't plan on making them up very soon. We're professionals and have been in business here in this same building for many years. You can trust us."

After a few brief pleasantries Sam Ransom gently placed the receiver back into its cradle. He leaned back, lit his cigarette and stared thoughtfully through his large front window as the wind rolled tumbleweeds down the railroad tracks.

The worst part of the conversation was that Higgenbottom had told him exactly what, he himself, had asserted to every Guppy who he'd done business with.

Trust me. I'll look out for you.

CHAPTER TWENTY

"That shaft's dipping sure as hell and flattening out like this," Bulldog said, demonstrating by holding his huge, work-hardened hands together at an angle. "It's following the vein right under the mountain."

"Dad-blast the luck," Lett swore.

Up to now the shaft had held vertical. This was an absolute necessity if they were to use an efficient elevator cage and skip to bring ore to the surface.

"The only thing we can use in that crummy hole now is a bucket," Jake said, frowning.

"They're dangerous darn things," Lett commented. "Easy to get the lip caught on a timber. Lots of men riding those things have been killed when that happened."

"First we need a hoist and a gallows frame," Epp ventured blandly. "Then I reckon we'll need the bucket and some rich ore to haul out with it."

Lett rolled a cigarette to keep from saying anything for a while. He wondered deeply if Sam Ransom would ever buy the machinery they required if the Last Chance Mine was to produce even a small quantity of ore.

The fan and some hand tools were the only things Sam had bought for his "big" silver mine. Lett knew far more money had been spent on road work, signs and that fancy office building Ransom sat in everyday than the shaft itself.

Lately when he asked for money, Sam had certainly appeared

worried about something. If Sam Ransom was worried, Lett felt he should be doubly so. The Roxy Jay would be worthless if the mine failed. The joint wasn't breaking even the way it was. To Lett's way of thinking, the only good part about Sam's troubles was that he was leaving Delight alone.

Five days ago, when the little twit had come to pick her up for the night, that wonderful dog, Wesley, nailed him in front of the Roxy Jay and shredded his expensive pants along with his legs. Once Sam's wounds were bandaged he was in no mood for anything except heading home. His last command to Lett before stiffly climbing into that Packard was, "Shoot that damn dog the next time you see him."

Many people in Shakespeare would love to have had the steak bones that hit Wesley's dinner platter later that evening.

"You might want to go down and look at the vein," Bulldog said, bringing Lett back to the business at hand. "Now that it's flattening out, it's getting wider."

After putting on his hard hat, Lett grabbed up a brass carbide light, filled the base with gray crystals of calcium carbide and the top with water. As soon as it was lit and the flame adjusted, he slid the light into the holder on the front of his hat and descended into the shaft.

Once he was down twelve feet to where the ladders shifted he paused for his eyes to adjust to the total darkness of an underground mine. Only miners who worked in the depths of the earth knew the absolute absence of light. In a mine, without some form of lighting, a man was totally, completely blind.

After a moment, with a flickering yellow flame piercing the blackness, Lett continued to the bottom. There, a couple of heavy planks were laid across the lowest timber set that dangled, held in space only by long, spindly, steel J bolts.

When Lett stepped on the planks, the entire set swayed. He was expecting this and casually grabbed onto a bolt for support and waited for Bulldog to join him.

Once both miners were at the bottom of their timber work, Lett took the carbide light from his hat, bent over and aimed the light downward into the continuing depths below.

"I see what you mean," Lett said, playing the light along the side of the old shaft. Whatever timbers had been placed there in the early days were long since rotted away leaving only barren rock. The little vein they had been following contained copper. In the yellow light it looked like someone had smeared blue and green paint from top to bottom along both sides of the shaft as far as they could see. Where the vein and mine opening flattened out, this painted area grew considerably wider.

Lett dropped to his knees. Holding the brass lamp outward, he bent over the edge and studied the area below them carefully for a long while.

"You know, Bulldog, I can see a level down there about twenty more feet. And you're right about that vein, it's getting wider."

Bulldog grabbed onto a J bolt and peered into the darkness. "Well, it won't take long to get there, only around a week or so. Then we'll have some idea what had those old-timers excited enough to dig this damn hole."

When he climbed out into the hot, bright New Mexico day, Lett squinted his eyes and breathed deeply a few times. While fifty-four feet didn't sound very deep, it was the same as ascending the stairs in a five-story building.

Bulldog puffed his way over. Together they took off their lights, turned the water lever shut, then they blew out the flame and stowed them in the tool house.

"Whatta you think boss?" Jake Clanton asked, joining them to get out of the fiery sun.

"I guess we'd better wait until we get there before we say anything, but that vein sure looks good," Lett said. "Maybe it will even assay out to be ore."

Arnold Epp poked his head inside the open door. "We gonna work on the Fourth of July or can we take the day off?"

"Haven't really thought much about it," Lett said. "There's not many folks who have much to celebrate."

"We've been thinking," Bulldog interjected, trying to force a smile onto his heavy face. "Those of us that are lucky enough to be working, well maybe we could all chip in and fix up some big pots of beans, soup and the like. We could cook 'em up in the Roxy Jay then invite everyone to help themselves. God only knows a lot could use it."

"Lord a' mighty," Jake howled. "Don't let McTavish have a shot at any of this or the undertaker down in Lordsburg will croak from exhaustion, planting all those poor folks he'd do in."

Epp lit his pipe with a long kitchen match. "Even if McTavish didn't do them in, there ain't enough outhouses to take care of everyone who'd be needing 'em real quick like. I'd say we fix up the vittles ourselves and let McTavish bake lots of cornbread. That's the only thing he can cook that won't cause certain grief."

Lett clearly remembered the last meal he had eaten at the Roxy Jay. "Boys, I think that's a right nice idea, especially the part about keeping McTavish out of it as much as possible. There's a solid three hundred folks to feed though, a bunch haven't had a decent meal for a long while. It'll take a mess of food to do it right. I'd rather stop it right here if we can't carry through and give everyone all they can eat."

"Beans and cornbread don't cost a fortune," Bulldog said firmly. "Once I pay half my wages on my tab at the bar, I'll drop the rest in the kitty. There's a lot of hungry kids down there that need it worse than me."

Lett swallowed hard and knew he'd been cornered. "I reckon we can let those tabs slide another week. Hell, I'll match what you guys put in. I've got to go to Lordsburg to get gas for the fan. While I'm there, I'll see what we can buy at the store. Big bags of stuff's always cheaper. You guys lag up that last set and keep your traps shut about any of this until we get together this evening. The last thing I want to spread is false hope."

Jake looked at Lett. "We only have until the day after tomorrow. This thing'll take a lot of cookin' so we'll need to lay those groceries in. Do you reckon we could get paid tomorrow?"

Lett sighed, "I've got the checkbook, so the answer's yes. We'll start to work at six in the morning and knock off at noon. That way you guys can make it to the bank and get your checks cashed."

"Whatta you reckon Sam Ransom will think about us takin' the day off?" Epp asked.

A thin smile cut across Lett's face. "He'll probably have a screaming hissy fit. But I'll handle him."

CHAPTER TWENTY-ONE

Sam Ransom looked up from his book, annoyed, when Lett came into his office. He had been engrossed in William Faulkner's novel, *As I Lay Dying,* and wasn't happy about the interruption. "I hope you didn't come by for more money, the stock sales have been slow," he growled.

"No, sir," Lett answered in a soft voice. "Actually I may have some good news. That vein's widening out and it looks like we have our first working level only about twenty more feet below our timber."

Sam poked a cigarette into his holder. "Well, *of course* the vein is getting wider. The ore is deep up there. I've known that all along. It's right there in the report. Tell me something I *don't* know."

"Well, sir," Lett said. "I just thought you might want to be told is all."

"Thank you for your concern." Sam pulled out his gold lighter, flicked a flame to life and lit his cigarette. "Now why don't you get back to work opening up my mine. That *is* what I'm paying you for."

"I needed to buy gas for the fan, sir. The crew is working very hard I assure you. We're doing as much as we can without machinery."

Sam lowered his dark eyebrows and straightened his mustache. "You'll get your machinery. New, fine and heavy machinery, once I raise the money to pay for it. Until that time comes, be thankful you have a job."

"Mister Ransom, sir, we're all mighty proud to be working there. I do need to ask you one thing?" Lett asked humbly.

"Well, spit it out man, I haven't got all day."

"It's about the Fourth of July. The men would like to have the day off."

Sam relaxed. Unless some investors were coming to visit, they could take a week off for all he cared. "That's fine with me, but they're not to be paid for it."

"No one was expecting that, Mister Ransom. We are chipping in to fix a big dinner and invite everyone in Shakespeare. There's a lot of hungry folks just waiting for your mine to open so they can have jobs. I was wondering if you might like to help out. Maybe even come up for the evening? We'd all like to see you there."

Sam blew a smoke ring, leaned back in his posh leather chair and stared hard at Lett. "Whether or not those poverty rats hanging around Shakespeare have a free dinner is no concern of mine. There's work in California if they'd get off their lazy butts and go there. Don't look for me to waste money on the likes of those filthy people."

"No, sir, we were just asking is all. Thank you for letting us have the day off."

Lett turned and slowly headed for the door. He had just placed his hand on the brass doorknob when Sam called after him, just as he had hoped.

"Did you shoot that damn dog? My leg's still hurting!"

Lett swallowed hard, put on his most serious expression and turned to face Sam Ransom. "You know sir, I haven't set eyes on that dog since that night. I've been a little worried with all those cases of rabies around. Maybe you should see a doctor. I'd expect it's not too late, but I'm just a miner and don't know much about those things."

Color drained from Ransom's face like his throat had been cut. "What do you mean *rabies*. There's a lot of it around here?"

"Oh, sir, I wouldn't be too concerned. A few die from it every year, they tell me. Mostly it's animal bites that cause it. But I'd figure on that dog showing up again. There's probably nothing to worry about."

"My God," Sam kept muttering over and over. Finally he composed himself. "Get out of here," he nearly screamed. "And get back to work, I've got things to do."

Lett stepped out onto the blistering hot sidewalk, trying hard to contain his pent-up laughter. When he passed the big window in front of Sam's office he could see the anguished little man blubbering into his phone and overheard him yelling hysterically at the operator something about needing to find a doctor. There was none in Lordsburg, poor fellow. Probably the nearest would be found in Silver City, over seventy miles away.

Lett knew Sam Ransom would enjoy the drive more than all those shots. He made a mental note to ask him later on, if they really did give them in the stomach with a very long needle like he had heard.

When he got to the general store not only did Lett get good prices on everything they would need for the big social. He also bought two pounds of meaty neck bones.

Wesley would love them.

CHAPTER TWENTY-TWO

With a long fork, Delight turned sizzling pieces of chicken fry-ing in a deep cast-iron skillet. Her little cabin was flooded with the mouth-watering aroma.

Lett Halsy sat at the small wobbly-legged wooden table and watched her work, his hands wrapped around a steaming cup of coffee. A grin was deeply etched into his face that had a stubble of gray beard showing. He loved these times. Delight moved with the grace of a dancer. Always, the pretty lady seemed happy. When he was with her the Depression and all of his problems seemed a world away.

"You look like the cat that ate the canary," Delight said, plac-ing a heavy lid on the skillet to stop the grease splatters. "Want to tell me about it?"

He took a careful sip of boiling-hot coffee and decided not to tell her what he had pulled on Sam Ransom. She would likely find out quick enough anyway. "We're taking the Fourth off. The boys at the mine and me, well, we decided to celebrate by cooking up a dinner for the whole town. We'll have it at the Roxy Jay. Beans, soup of some kind and cornbread is all it'll be."

Delight looked happily taken aback. "Why Lett, that's so nice of you guys. It's going to cost a fortune though."

"Oh, we're all pitching in. I priced stuff at the store in Lords-burg. There won't be any money left over, but I'd reckon everyone will get their belly full."

Lett watched as Delight fairly skipped to the nightstand beside her neatly made brass bed. She opened the top drawer, thumbed through it for a moment and brought out some dollar bills which she carried over and laid on the table.

"I want to help out, too. There's a lot of folks hereabouts," she said sadly, "some haven't had a decent meal for a long time."

"Thanks—I'm sure they'll appreciate it."

"The only thing is, what about the next day and the day after that? This Depression is terrible!"

"It's pure hell, that's what it is." Lett's earlier good mood was vanishing along with the scarlet setting sun. "Maybe if we get rid of Hoover, and Roosevelt gets to be president, things will be better then."

"Lett, I hope so, I surely do."

"Would you like to help us cook?" Lett ventured. "We can't have McTavish do much of the cooking or the whole dinner will be a washout."

Delight made that cute little smile of hers and flicked a strand of blond hair from her forehead. "I'd love to, but what do you think people would say? Howard always wanted me to stay back here and not be seen."

"I'm not Howard," Lett said with a familiar lumping in his throat that always appeared when Delight made references to her occupation. "You're as sweet and nice a lady as I've ever met. If anyone makes even a slight comment about your being there, I'll take care of him."

Delight ran her soft hand gently over the stubble on Lett's cheek. He noticed a slight tear forming in the corner of her eye when she said, "Then, I'll be proud to help."

Lett reached up and grasped her hand. She'd expected him to push her away as he always did when she attempted to show affection. To her surprise he took his other calloused hand and placed his palm on top of hers.

"Don't you ever, ever, believe you're not a lady," he said firmly.

Delight pulled herself away and quickly returned to the stove. It was difficult for her to check on the biscuits through the stinging wetness in her eyes, but she managed.

CHAPTER TWENTY-THREE

News of the big social spread like wildfire through Shakespeare once Lett informed his crew that they had sufficient money for the dinner and Sam Ransom had given them the day off. Even McTavish seemed not to be miffed about being relegated to just baking the cornbread.

"Delight's chipped in enough money we can add salt pork to the beans. That gives them real flavor," Lett said.

"And chili peppers," Bulldog asserted. "You need some jalapeños in beans, lots of 'em, to give 'em body."

"For Christ sakes," Epp said with a worried look. "If McTavish ain't gonna send a bunch of good folks running off to find an outhouse, you're gonna do the job for him."

"We'll need to make up several pots," Jake interjected. "Bulldog can make his two-step beans and I'll make up some for the rest of us."

"Two-step?" Lett asked idly.

"Yep," Arnold Epp said with conviction. "After eating his beans you're two steps away from taking a dump. Outhouse or no outhouse."

Lett quickly tired of listening to the good-natured arguments over who was going to do what. He grabbed his foamy mug of beer and stood up to wander outside.

"Hey, Mister Halsy," a small voice called out. It was Elmore Wyman, sitting on his usual stool at the end of the bar. Lett walked over and leaned his elbow on the mahogany counter. He was shocked how gaunt the old man appeared. It seemed he had failed considerably in just the past few days.

"I heard about the big dinner," Elmore said. "Nice of you to do that. Damn nice. Most folks are hangin' onto what they've got these days."

"It's not just me. Every man at the mine and even Delight kicked in to help."

"Bet you a plugged nickel Ransom didn't toss in a dime."

"He chose not to help," Lett answered without emotion.

McTavish had been listening in. He plopped his bulky arms onto the bar and said, "I heard tell Sam's ailing again. Folks said he tore out heading for the doc's in El Paso, like a bat outta hell."

"He *is* a sickly one," Lett said holding back a smile.

"Hope he'll be all right." McTavish looked genuinely worried. "We can't afford to lose him. This whole town will dry up and blow away like some ole tumbleweed if that happened."

As if a cue had sounded, Wesley, the mutt, walked through the open swinging doors of the Roxy Jay. He sniffed the air for a brief moment and headed back outside where the air smelled better than the aroma from whatever McTavish had in the stew pot.

"Oh, I'd venture Sam Ransom will be right as rain shortly," Lett said with assurance. "There's nothing to worry about along those lines."

"Can I see you outside?" Elmore asked Lett.

"I got cooking to do and folks to wait on," McTavish growled and stomped away, heading down the long bar.

"That man shudda been born a female," Elmore quipped. "He's a bigger gossip than you'll find at a church women's social meeting."

"Yeah, but he works for nothing," Lett said. "And he's worth every penny of it. What can I do for you?"

The old man rolled his watery yellow eyes to make sure the bartender was long gone. "I want you to do me a favor."

Lett took a sip of beer and wondered how big of a tab Elmore was going to ask for. It didn't matter, the answer would have to be no. The ledger book for the Roxy Jay wasn't lying to him. There was no denying the place was going broke.

Elmore must have read the doubt in Lett's face. He cleared his throat and said, "Rein in yer horses, sonny. I ain't askin' for credit. I found that Lost Dutchman's Mine, ya know."

Lett gave him a kindly smile. He genuinely liked the old man. His stories of early-day Shakespeare and crazy ideas about the Lost Dutchman Mine were always entertaining. "A long as it don't cost me anything, I'm all ears."

"For that big celebration you got planned. . . ." Elmore Wyman broke into a deep, ragged cough. He pulled a tobacco-stained handkerchief from out of his pant pocket and spit into it.

Lett was shocked. What he'd taken to be tobacco stains was dried blood. "You need to see a doctor," he said with concern.

"Done seen one, sonny boy," Elmore said, gaining his breath. "An' he's seen me. Damn sawbones don't know nothin'. Son of a bitch said this cancer would kill me in six months. Hell, that was near a year ago."

Lett felt his gut tighten. "Can't they do anything for you?"

"He gave me somethin' for the pain. That panther piss you peddle here works better, and it's cheaper, to boot."

"This favor you want, what might it be?"

Elmore washed his throat with a heavy swallow of beer. He shot a glance down the bar to make certain he was not being overheard. Very carefully he reached into the front pocket of his grimy khaki shirt, pulled something out and pressed it into Lett's hand. "It's been a long time since I heard any kids laugh. Reckon this social you're plannin' will be the last time I'll get the chance."

Lett opened his palm. It was filled with twenty-dollar bills. "My God," was all he could say.

"Get some fireworks. Lots of 'em. Rockets that shoot up in the sky an' explode, firecrackers an', of course, watermelons. Kids love watermelons, I know I did—a long time ago."

Lett shook his head and had a hard time speaking. "I'll do the best I can. We only have tomorrow to get ready."

"They's plenty of money there. Run someone to Deming or Silver City, if you gotta. Reckon next year won't work out for me, so's we gotta do it day after tomorrow, fer sure."

Lett sighed, "You've got it. I don't know what I can rustle up, but we'll get those kids some fireworks, even if we have to blow up dynamite!"

"Wouldn't be tha' Fourth of July if there weren't dynamite."

"I'll take care of it."

Elmore cocked his white cropped head and grinned. "I reckon you'll have lots of time tomorrow fer shoppin'. That was a good one you pulled on Sam Ransom. I hear tell those hydrophoby shots hurt worse than getting shot in the gut."

Lett's mouth dropped open.

Elmore Wyman shot him an evil smile and said, "McTavish ain't the only one around here that likes to know what folks are up to."

CHAPTER TWENTY-FOUR

Lett Halsy felt as if dark and heavy hands rested on his tired shoulders. He trudged with leaden feet through the back door of the Roxy Jay to stand beneath a black canopy of twinkling stars. The desert air felt strangely hot and oppressive. Until now, he had found it tranquil and soothing.

The big man hesitated for a while and rolled a cigarette. In the distance, somewhere near the mine, a coyote howled its mournful tune. Crickets chirped their mating song. Inside the bar someone had plunked a nickel into the coin slot of the player piano. Its off-key tinkling music clashed with the sounds of nature.

Delight's red porch light glared against the darkness like a beacon. It was intended to draw men, like a moth to a flame.

Lett fought down a nearly overpowering urge to run and knock on her pallid door. He desperately wanted—needed—her companionship. He wanted to tell her about Elmore Wyman. He wanted to tell her his deepest fears about Sam Ransom and his dark premonition there wouldn't be a big silver mine for him to open on that barren mountain back of Shakespeare. He needed. . . .

He couldn't do it. Delight had a right to her own life. She, like himself, was simply trying to get by in a world gone mad. A lady like Delight had endless opportunities to pick and choose men. She was sweet, intelligent and very pretty. He had no right to intrude on her with his problems.

Their brief dinners together were all he could ask of her. Lett knew he was no longer a young man. His days of hard work at a mine were drawing to a close. He had no other skills. It was better to have no illusions, he had nothing to offer any woman. Most likely, he would spend his last years like Elmore Wyman, living alone, hoping to hear someone else's kids laugh, just once, before going down that trail from where no man returns.

A shooting star streaked across the heavens. Lett watched until it burned out over Lookout Hill. He spat out his cigarette, ground the butt into the dry earth with the heel of his work boot, then headed for his cabin.

Footsteps. Carefully muffled for certain. But Lett had no doubt he'd heard the sounds of nervous feet grating against the rocky desert floor alongside his cabin.

He froze. Every dollar that had been donated for the holiday, including Elmore's money, was stuffed in his pant pocket.

Someone must have seen the old man hand me all that cash. He silently chided himself for taking no precaution from being robbed. In these times, with people going hungry, it should have come as no surprise to him such a thing could happen.

His hard fists were all he had to defend himself with. They would be of little use against the gun that would most certainly be shoved in his face. He was too close to spin and run. Whoever was lurking in the darkness alongside his cabin would be on him in an instant.

There was no choice but to face them head-on. The money he carried belonged to everyone in Shakespeare—he wouldn't give it up easy. "All right, I know you're there. Come on out where I can see you!" Lett roared, gruffly as he could.

Nothing. Then a rustling sound came from down low. With a slight whimper the hidden "highwaymen" stepped from the shadows into the light radiating from the bar.

Lett felt his mouth drop open in relief and astonishment.

Instead of a man with a gun, he found himself gaping at two very small and very scared little kids. The oldest, a dirty-faced little girl with stringy long blond hair looked to be maybe seven. Her big blue eyes were wide with fear. Grasping onto her waist was a boy, dressed in baggy shirt and pants, who hid his face. Lett thought he might be five at the most.

Gently now, Lett asked, "What are you two doing out this late? Does your mother know where you are?"

The little girl stepped closer, dragging the boy with her. Lett saw her lips quiver but in a brief moment she looked up at him with big doe eyes and asked, "Mister Hoolsey, would you please give our daddy a job?"

Lett felt his heart drop somewhere into the pit of his stomach. He bent to his knees where he could look into the children's faces. "Honey, it's mighty late, your mommy's going to be worried about you two."

"We don't have a mommy anymore," the girl answered in a surprisingly strong voice. "When tha' bank took our farm she took to bed and the angels took her to heaven. Daddy don't do nothin' these days but sit an' stare. He never laughs like he used to and he says there ain't no use lookin' for work. We don't got much to eat, either."

An all-too-familiar burning was in Lett's throat when he asked, "What's your names?"

The girl spoke, her voice brave now. "I'm Melissa, this is my brother, Avery. He's only a little kid, an' I have to look out for him all the time. I'm almost nine, he's only four."

A man with a gun would have been easier to handle than this, Lett thought. "Did your pa put you up to this?" he asked.

Melissa shook her head sending her long hair waving. "Uh-uh, he'd whomp me good if he knew we was out this late. Everyone knows you run the big mine. Mister Hoolsey, if my daddy had a job there, he'd be happy agin and then we'd have good stuff to eat. I hate oatmeal, but that's all we got."

"My name is Hall—sea, Lett Halsy. Melissa, why don't you bring your brother and come inside with me. I just might have something you'd like."

Lett flipped a switch and his small cabin was suddenly bathed in bright light. Avery squinted his eyes and stuck a thumb into his mouth but kept his other arm tightly wrapped around his sister's waist.

"You two go sit at the table," Lett said, trying to remember to speak gently. He hadn't been around kids since. . . .

Melissa pushed her brother away and marched him over to the table. When she had him in a chair, he plunked the thumb back into his mouth and turned to face into the plank wall.

"He's awful shy," Melissa sighed and shrugged her shoulders. "He'll just have to outgrow it like I did."

Lett unwrapped a half loaf of Delight's tasty homemade bread. He sliced it thick and smeared the pieces heavily with peanut butter and grape jelly. It was to be his lunch for tomorrow, but now he couldn't care less. These helpless little hungry kids had torn into his heart worse than any robber's bullet could have done.

The two children began devouring the open-faced sandwiches with obvious relish. Lett took the reprieve to lean in the open doorway, roll a cigarette and think. His first idea was to give the kids a dollar and send them home. Then, he remembered Delight's heartbreaking statement from earlier: "What about the next day and the day after that?"

"Mister, I'm sorry about my kids bothering you," an apologetic voice intoned from the dark. "I seen them go inside. I was just too late to stop 'em."

"Come on in," Lett said kindly. "I gave them some peanut-butter-and-jelly sandwiches. They're not being any problem at all."

When the man stepped into the light streaming from his cabin, Lett was surprised at how young the children's father appeared. He was a tall man, towering a good half-foot over Lett's six feet. The dirty overalls he wore hung loose on his lanky frame.

Your youngsters have been getting all the food haven't they? I'll bet it's been a long while since you've eaten a square meal. Lett kept his thoughts unspoken. He didn't require an answer. The sunken cheeks beneath the man's stubble of black beard were acknowledgment enough.

"Grab yourself some of that bread and fix yourself a sandwich. I was going to toss it out tomorrow, anyway. Why don't I warm us up a cup of coffee on the hot plate?"

"I'm truly sorry my kids bothered you, sir," the tall man said unmoving. "We'll leave you be, right shortly. If you wouldn't mind, I'll allow 'em to finish their snacks first."

A man needs his pride. Lett offered up his hand. "My name's Lett Halsy, not sir, and I'd appreciate if it'd take the time to come inside so we can visit."

"Kay—Joel Kay's my name, sir. I would take the coffee if it ain't too much trouble," he said, grasping Lett's hand firmly.

"Gee, Daddy, this is really good," Melissa squealed at her father.

Avery had his cheeks stuffed so full they pouched out like a chipmunk's. Purple jelly and brown peanut butter smeared across his small face.

Lett noticed the longing way Joel looked at the leftover bread and shrugged his shoulders indifferently. "I was gonna toss it out anyway. You might as well help 'em finish it off, while I warm up our coffee." He took an exceptionally long time fiddling with coffee cups and hot plate. From the corner of his eye Lett noticed Joel slice Melissa and Avery another piece of bread, then he spread the heel with peanut butter and quickly wolfed it down.

"I'm glad your kids came by," Lett said casually, pouring the steaming coffee and carrying a cup to Joel. "Not only did they save me from wasting that bread, but now I don't have to rustle up another hand at the mine. You look plenty fit and I imagine you'd put in a good day's work for six dollars a day."

"See, Daddy, I told you Mister Hoolsey would give you a job," Melissa said knowingly between bites.

Joel Kay's coffee cup shook in his hand. A look of sheer disbelief washed across his bearded face. "Sir, I'd do most anything for that kind of money."

"Well, you're hired. Just do me a couple of favors. First, keep this quiet. There's a lot of folks looking for work and I only have one opening. Second, please just call me Lett."

By the time the coffee had been drunk, Lett knew Joel was twenty-eight years old. His parents had come to this country from Scotland and bought a farm in eastern Kansas. After they passed away, the farm passed to him. Like thousands of others Joel Kay had taken a mortgage to expand his operations when prices for farm products were at an all-time high. Then, the Depression struck and the worth of his crops plummeted to unheard of lows. A bushel of wheat that sold for three dollars in 1920 was now worth less than thirty cents. The bank foreclosed and the search for work that followed was a heartbreakingly familiar story.

Lett carefully avoided asking Joel about his wife. A deep feeling inside told him she had committed suicide, not an uncommon occurrence. Some questions were best left unasked.

"Well, we'd better get some shut-eye," Lett said with a feigned yawn. Avery was leaning against the wall, blissfully sleeping. Melissa's blond head was bobbing. "We're starting work at six, and knocking off early. We have a lot of shopping to do for the

Fourth. By the way, you'll have a check for the day's work."

Joel scooped up his brood into his long arms. Melissa quickly lost her battle with sleep and dropped off into dreamland.

"See you at the mine in the morning," Lett said casually.

"Yes, sir—I mean Lett, and I want to thank you for the job and seeing to my kids."

Joel Kay spun quickly and plunged into the night carrying his sleeping children who had just eaten their first meal for what Lett knew must have been a long while.

He shut the door to his cabin and closed his eyes. "Oh, Lord, how many more out there need help too," he sobbed quietly. He wiped the table clean, then fixed a pot of coffee so that all he would have to do in the morning was perk it.

Sam Ransom wouldn't even notice he had hired another man. The little prima donna with a pencil-thin mustache had yet to even descend the shaft to check on their progress.

What concerned Lett the most was the building premonition that he had hitched his wagon to a mighty sorry horse, and a lot of good folks were waiting to climb on board.

If that ore wasn't really down there like that glowing geologist's report said it was, in mighty short order he would find himself in the same boat with the rest of the people in Shakespeare.

All Lett Halsy could do was keep timbering that shaft and hope.

Chapter Twenty-Five

Now that Joel Kay had been hired, there were two men available to operate the windlass. This allowed Lett to go into Lordsburg early. He wasn't at all surprised to find Sam Ransom was still among the missing.

Len Miller saw Lett's car and ran out to flag him down. "We've got something at the gas station you need to look at!" Len said excitedly.

What had Len so worked up turned out to be a decrepit old truck loaded with five tons of ripe watermelons. Its engine blown beyond any hope of repair.

After some hasty negotiations, using Len as an interpreter with the hapless Mexican driver—Lett didn't speak a word of Spanish—he bought the entire load for five dollars.

After a quick stop at the hardware store to purchase a case of dynamite, some blasting caps and a roll of fuse, Lett visited the general store. There he bought several sacks of pinto beans, cornmeal, butter and, just to keep Bulldog happy, ten pounds of fresh jalapeño peppers.

The fireworks that Elmore Wyman had asked for were not difficult to come by. Lordsburg had a fair supply, but only a few of the high-flying exploding rockets the old man wanted. The young couple who ran the hardware store were more than happy to run their Model A to Deming where they could fill Lett's order with no problem.

When he arrived back at the mine, just past noon, Lett pulled out Sam Ransom's checkbook and paid everyone, including himself. Joel Kay's hand shook like a leaf in the wind when he grasped his six dollars. Then began the task of transporting to Shakespeare everything Lett had bought.

The setting sun was painting the low hills to the west with a red hue when the men were finished with the task. Five tons turned out to be an awfully big bunch of watermelons.

Elmore Wyman grinned like a satisfied cat when Lett walked into the Roxy Jay. The old man called him aside and discreetly slipped him two hundred dollars more.

"Give everyone free beer tomorrow and soda pops for the kids until it's all gone," Elmore instructed quietly.

Lett tried to talk Elmore out of it, but it was useless. The white-haired old fellow simply said, "It's my money an' I want to see one hell of a party."

At a nickel a beer, Lett had absolutely no doubts that Elmore Wyman would get his wish.

"Arnold, you idiot," Bulldog fumed. "Don't go cutting them jalapeños open and scraping the seeds out. They don't have any taste when you do that to 'em. Just snap the stems off and toss them in the pot."

Jake Clanton cast a dubious eye into the big metal cook pot. "I hope you two are planning to add some beans to that mess of hot peppers. No matter, I reckon, but the first flatlander who takes a bite of that shit will scream loud enough to cause a panther way up in the hills to pee down its leg."

Bulldog grinned at Jake like he had just received a compliment. "This pot of beans is for us *men*. Delight's cooking up beans for the ladies and little kids. Lett's doing his for flatlanders and pantywaists. This pot's reserved for guys with hair on their chest."

Arnold Epp chugged his mug of beer and headed out back of

the Roxy Jay to use an outhouse.

Lett tapped Bulldog on the shoulder. "After slicing open those jalapeños, I'd venture your pardner should have washed his hands with soap and water before handling what he's getting ready to wrap his mitts around."

"I told him not to mess with 'em," Bulldog replied, with an evil twinkle in his eye. "He's about to get a lesson in the culinary arts."

The pair walked to the open back door and waited expectantly. Shortly, Epp's howling and cursing boomed from inside the outhouse he occupied.

"Maybe he'll listen to me next time," Bulldog chuckled. "It's for sure he won't do *that* again."

It was nearly noon on the Fourth of July. In the gentle cactus-studded valley and the town of Shakespeare smiling people milled about like busy ants. The center of activity was, of course, the Roxy Jay.

Now that the big social was underway, Lett could see his trepidations about the free beer in spades. McTavish was in a dither trying to bake cornbread while contending with a line of people clamoring impatiently for him to draw them a glass of beer.

Lett studied the situation and realized something had to be done. He jumped on a chair and yelled loudly for everyone to shut up and listen to him.

"Boys," he said, "I know it's been a while since you've had a party like this one. If you don't slow down on the beer though, it'll be gone before it gets dark and we have our fireworks display. We can't have that, so I'm shutting the tap off until the food's done. Then you can all drink up."

Only a few muttered complaints. It would not be wise to anger the manager of the soon-to-boom big silver mine on the mountain back of town.

McTavish appeared relieved as a man whose pardon had come just as the noose was being adjusted around his neck. "Thanks boss, now I can get back to cooking up my delicious cornbread. Bulldog gave me some jalapeños and I chopped up a big bunch to add to the batter. That'll make it mighty tasty."

Lett hopped down from his chair, walked over to the bartender and stared into his chunky face. "One pan for Bulldog is all. You add those blasted things to more than that and I'll have to kill you."

McTavish shot him a sullen look, then tromped off to tend the stove.

"Thank you," Delight said over Lett's shoulder. "Cornbread's the only thing McTavish can cook and he was on his way to botching that."

Lett smiled. Her presence here pleased him greatly. Delight had carefully dressed demurely in a high-necked, loose-fitting, ankle-length, blue chemise. It did little to hide her tempting figure, however. To his relief not one man had ventured a comment about her that had not been complimentary. Earlier he had overheard Arnold Epp and others tell several men it would be *very* wise to treat Delight like the lady she was.

"I don't know what all the fascination is around here with hot peppers," Lett said casually. "Jalapeños are fiery enough to put a kink in the Devil's tail."

Delight said happily, "New Mexico folks sure seem to like them. They grow some peppers down here that make even jalapeños seem mild."

Arnold Epp came trotting through the back door, bent over like someone in terrible pain. His eyes were watery and his face flushed. He hurriedly passed them to go and join Bulldog.

"What's wrong with him?" Delight asked with concern.

"He caught a New Mexico disease called peppers on the

pecker," Lett quipped without thinking. When he realized what he had said, his heart did a double-thump.

Delight howled with laughter, while Lett's face grew redder than Arnold Epp's.

"I'm sorry," he said sincerely. "I shouldn't have talked like that."

Delight chuckled, "Don't be. I haven't had a good laugh like that in a long time." She hesitated, looked up at Lett and said, "That poor man." Then bent over in laughter.

Lett couldn't help but join her. Not another person in the Roxy Jay had any idea what they found so funny about cooking beans.

CHAPTER TWENTY-SIX

By four o'clock, mountains of beans simmered in every large pot that could be found in Shakespeare. Stacks of yellow cornbread and heaping bowls of sweet cream butter lined the long mahogany bar inside the Roxy Jay. Watermelons had been hauled out from underneath porches, sliced and laid out in washtubs filled with ice beside the swinging front doors.

Anxious kids laughingly teased each other and feigned grabbing a hunk of melon. But not a single one touched a slice until Bulldog climbed the slight hill behind the bar and fired off a stick of dynamite to sound the opening of Shakespeare's social dinner.

A long line of men, women and children, each carrying their own plate and silverware, began threading through the Roxy Jay. What made Elmore Wyman the happiest was the kids. It had been a very long time since he had heard the laughter of children in Shakespeare, New Mexico.

Perched contentedly on his usual stool at the far end of the bar, Elmore nursed a frosty mug and beamed. True to his words, Lett had told no one that he was their main benefactor.

Bulldog and most of the others thought a lot of the money for their holiday was being secretly furnished by Sam Ransom. Elmore simply smirked when he heard that rumor. He didn't give a gnat's fanny if Ransom got the credit, as long as everyone—especially the kids—had one whale of a good time.

Elmore knew all too well that this was to be his final party.

He wanted it to be one to remember. The white-haired patriarch couldn't help but chuckle when some greenhorn made the mistake of scooping up a heaping pile of Bulldog's torrid beans. Many would choke them down. Some surreptitiously dumped their plates alongside the porch in front of the saloon. Wesley helped himself to them until he had eaten his fill. Then the wiry-haired mutt sauntered in and curled up under Elmore's feet. There he kept a stern eye on the passing multitude of legs to make certain none of them needed biting.

Watching Lett Halsy and Delight working and laughing together caused long repressed memories to flood his senses like a dam had burst. Elmore harshly remembered the distant past when he had had the opportunity for a family and the companionship of a beautiful woman.

Elmore Wyman took a sip of beer and tried futilely to shove his rueful recollections into that niche of his mind where they had been tucked away all these many years.

Gold was what had destroyed his life. Lust for the yellow metal had pushed him into the barren expanses of desert and kept him there. And gold he had found. More gold than most men could fathom. That was what had ruined his life.

It had happened many long years ago when he and his partners, Jasper Kellogg and Billy Webster, had finally found the fabled lost Dutchman Mine.

The damnable vein of glistening gold in rose quartz had been their downfall. At camp that very night, tempers had flared over how the mine would be shared. Bitterly, he remembered he was just as greedy as his partners.

Quicker than a rattlesnake can strike, pistols had been drawn and gunfire split the still night. When it was over, he alone stood.

The bleached bones of his long-dead partners still rested inside that well-hidden tunnel burrowed into a nearby mountain.

He never filed a claim. News of a rich find always brought people who asked questions. Elmore Wyman, who had murdered his two partners, could never have that.

For many years he had subsisted by making occasional trips to that mine, bringing back only a few pounds of ore. Lately, his trips had been very few. Not only was he a sick man, he had begun more and more to dread seeing those skeletons staring at him with hollow, accusing eyes.

"Hey, McTavish," Elmore yelled feebly, sending a twenty-dollar gold eagle ringing onto the bar. "Keep my mug full, and keep this fer yer troubles."

Once the chubby barkeep set eyes on that coin, Elmore became the focus of his attention. McTavish even brought him a platter of Delight's tasty beans. He ate but little. Food held no appeal. Beer kept the pain—and old memories—at bay.

He felt content on this, his final holiday. Best of all was the laughter of children. That, more than anything, made him happy.

The bright desert day waxed slowly into dusk. Elmore's vision began to fog and his movements muddled. Tonight of all nights he could not afford to drink himself into blissful oblivion where no eyeless skeletons glared at him from the shadows of his memories.

Elmore slowly sipped on a fresh beer—he'd spilled the last one into his lap—and waited until Lett Halsy and Delight came close enough so he could draw their attention. By the time this occurred, darkness had begun to blanket the gentle valley.

"Hey, Lett." He tried to speak clearly, but his words were slurred. "I've had a real good time, however, I ain't young as I used to be." He smiled warmly at Delight. "You done right well helpin' out like you did. Make sure those kids get all the watermelons they want."

Delight placed a soft hand on his shoulder. "No problem, they're having the time of their lives."

Elmore was pleased at that statement. "I'm gonna head home an' watch the fireworks from my place. Growin' old is hell, you two take care to enjoy life before it's too late." He rolled his yellow eyes at Lett. "Before you go to the mine in the mornin' come by my house. There's something I want you to have—it's important."

"Sure thing," Lett answered firmly.

Elmore took time to watch Delight grab onto Lett's hand and usher him outside. He choked back tears, then staggered home through a milling crowd of happy people.

The first skyrocket bloomed loudly, showering the little town of Shakespeare with twinkling red streamers of fire.

Elmore Wyman sat in his cane-backed rocker, staring intently through the front window. The explosion echoed from the distant hills, followed by raucous laughter.

Tonight he would face his old partners again.

Another explosion—this one he knew was dynamite—rattled the window panes. Elmore kept his eyes glued on the fireworks. His right hand rummaged on the table by his side, finally closing on the bottle of painkiller that doctor had given him.

Ain't no man can hide forever. I just hope God is in a forgivin' mood. Most likely Jasper an' Billy won't be.

The stopper came out easily. Quickly, before he could change his mind, the old man downed the contents. A feeling of warmth coursed through his frail body. Lastly he tucked the envelope addressed to Lett Halsy between his legs where it could easily be found.

Two rockets exploded outside at nearly the same time. This time he joined with the children in their joyful laughter.

CHAPTER TWENTY-SEVEN

Will Green couldn't have asked for a better night to finally corner that white-haired drunken old bastard. With all the fireworks exploding and people yelling, no one would hear Elmore Wyman's cries of pain.

He was sorry it had come to this. Not a soul knew how hard he had tried to find that old man's source of gold. Hell, he had even offered to go partners with that doddering fool.

All Wyman ever did was waste his money at the bar anyway. Tonight would end his long quest. When the sun rose over the eastern flatlands, Will Green would know where the Lost Dutchman Mine lay hidden.

Stuffed into the pockets of his overalls were short pieces of rope, a folded straight razor, a pair of pliers, and handkerchiefs to use as a gag. That skinny rummy would spill his guts before *this* night was over.

Stealthily, Will circled the town. From all the ruckus going on down there he was certain not a single soul noticed his approach.

Moving quietly as a snake gliding through wet grass, Will approached Elmore's house from the rear. Quickly he was through the open rear window.

There was that old fool, sitting in a rocker staring mindlessly out the front window. Elmore's white head never moved as he ran up behind the old dummy and draped a length of manila rope across his throat.

Something was *very* wrong.

Elmore made no resistance, no movement. Moonlight streaming through the window illuminated his smiling, gray face.

He can't be dead.

But he was.

The realization hit Will Green like a shot.

"No," he cried. "This can't be! He has to talk to me. He has to tell me where he got that gold!"

Trepidation struck. Someone may have heard him! Carefully, Will shot a glance out the window.

Nothing.

Then he noticed a white envelope tucked between the old drunk's legs.

He grabbed it up and thrust it into the yellow moonlight. Elmore Wyman's cold eyes were open wide. Staring. Watching.

Will moved the sealed envelope to where there was light enough to read a penciled inscription:

"To Lett Halsy—my funeral instructions and money to pay for it."

Will began shaking like a man with palsy. He shook so hard his teeth rattled. He knew there was money in that envelope. Money for the old man's funeral. He had come to find where Elmore Wyman got his gold, even kill the old fool if necessary.

Not to rob him.

Will Green was no petty thief.

Sobbing now like a baby, he dropped the unopened envelope.

He tripped going out the rear window and fell into cactus. The pain went unnoticed as the sobbing, shaking assayer staggered to his feet and melted into the warm desert night.

CHAPTER TWENTY-EIGHT

"That blasted sleep's mighty rough on a man," Lett grumbled. He grabbed up the clanging alarm clock from his night stand and fingered it until he found the correct lever to stop its awful noise. "I felt really good when I went to bed last night."

A faded orange glow from the beginning sunrise was barely peeking through the window by his bed. He tossed the rumpled bed sheet aside, forced his legs to the floor and sat up on the creaking double bed. A little man with a big hammer began pounding away inside his skull.

"I'd reckon I should've passed on that last beer," he said with conviction.

Four aspirin and two cups of strong coffee later, Lett felt as if he might actually live through the day. He knew he was probably in better shape than a lot of the men in Shakespeare.

More people than he would have thought turned out to be Baptists or some other breed of zealot who didn't drink. That left way too much beer for those who did. Waste not, want not sounded like a really good philosophy last night. In the painful growing light of day, Lett felt nothing but admiration for teetotalers, whatever their cause.

Briefly, he thought about fixing some breakfast. When his stomach got the news, it told him in no uncertain terms to hold off for a while. He needed to pick up a timber saw he had left at McAllister's hardware store to have sharpened. This would give him a good excuse to go to Lordsburg. There he could eat breakfast at the Vanderbilt Café and check on whether or not Sam Ransom had returned from El Paso after getting started on all those rabies shots.

Just thinking about that little rat getting stuck in the belly with a long needle put him in a better frame of mind. He finished the pot of coffee, laced up his heavy work boots and stomped out the door, headed for the mine.

Lett was at the edge of Shakespeare when Wesley came streaking from behind a long abandoned store building and began yapping.

"Wesley," he said softly, "I appreciate the fact you haven't bitten anyone except Sam Ransom for quite a spell, but do you think you could find it in that black heart of yours to shut the hell up?"

It was like someone had spun the dog's barker dial over to full blast. Not only did Wesley begin sending shock waves shooting through Lett's already tortured brain, the mutt began jumping around wildly, running up the slope toward Elmore's house and back down again.

"Okay, dog, I remember now," Lett shouted. "I would have gone to see him eventually. He didn't need to send you after me."

The moment Lett started toward Elmore Wyman's place, Wesley grew silent. The dog trotted along a few feet ahead, occasionally looking over its shoulder in irritation at the man's slow progress.

Lett stepped onto the worn plank porch and knocked softly on the door. Wesley tugged briefly at his pant cuff, let out a whimper, then ran over to the front window. The dog reared up, placed his paws on the window sill, looked at Lett and began to whine mournfully.

"What is it, fellow?" Lett asked with sudden concern. When he stepped over and peered inside, the cause for Wesley's urging was sadly made clear.

He patted the dog's head gently. "You knew, didn't you, Wesley? I don't know how, but you knew."

Lett opened the unlocked door and walked over to where Elmore Wyman's cold body sat with open eyes, staring out over the little town of Shakespeare. He didn't bother checking for signs of life, the old man's face was gray as weathered wood. When he touched Elmore's hand, it was stiff. Rigor mortis had set in.

Lett bent over and picked up the empty bottle of painkiller from where it had rolled underneath Elmore's rocker. "You had this planned all along, didn't you friend?"

Slowly, he turned to leave and call the sheriff. Then he noticed a white envelope lying in the middle of the living-room floor. Lett was puzzled as to why it was there and moved closer. *His* name was clearly written across the front.

The seal was intact. He took out his pocket knife, carefully slit one end open and extracted the contents. There was money, possibly as much as two hundred dollars—Lett didn't bother to count it. A note to him, shakily scrawled with a pencil, read:

Halsy, you seem to be a good man, so I'm trusting you.

I doubt Sam's mine will ever pay. I know of one that will.

The Lost Dutchman Mine will give jobs to a lot of good folks. Take the map and stake it yourself. Don't bring any crooks like Ransom in with you. Pardners are trouble. The bodies in that mine are my old pardners. Yes I killed them.

Make Shakespeare boom again. Then maybe the kids will laugh a lot. Send my dead carcass to Missouri. I write where on the back of this. I have kinfolks and want to be planted there with them. If there ain't enough money tell the undertaker to send me a bill. I'll be in Hell. Give my best to Delight.

Your friend,
Elmore Wyman

P.S. I hope that mine brings you better luck than it done me.

Lett pursed his lips. "You poor guy, I guess you told that story so many times you got to believing it yourself."

He unfolded a map the old man had stuck in with the note and money. It had obviously been done earlier. The lines were steady and the writing plain. Elmore had very clearly laid out the location of his imaginary mine in degrees and feet, using the top of Lookout Hill as the starting point. Anyone who could read a compass would be able to follow the directions easily.

Lett sighed, refolded the map and tucked it in the pocket of his jeans. There was a writing tablet and pencil on Elmore's table. He knew this was where the old man had written the letter he held. He copied down the address of the undertaker where Elmore wanted to be shipped, then wadded Wyman's note and thrust it in with the map. He headed for the Roxy Jay. Sheriff Mayes had to be called. There was no need to sully the memory of the man by showing his crazy rambling about the Lost Dutchman Mine to anyone.

Delight sobbed and men took off their hats when the black Cadillac hearse took Elmore Wyman's body away.

The sheriff of Hidalgo County had simply filled out routine paperwork, stating death by natural causes. Then he used Lett's phone to call the undertaker, hit Lett up for his monthly five-dollar bribe and returned to the comforts of Lordsburg.

Once the somber hearse had climbed the low hill leaving Shakespeare and was out of sight, Lett realized Delight's arm rested around his waist. It felt comforting to him.

She rolled her sad blue eyes. "He was such a nice man. I

146

think he enjoyed his last night, though."

Lett thought briefly of telling her the truth, that Elmore had paid for most of the big holiday celebration, then taken his own life. The old man had made him promise secrecy about the money. That empty bottle from underneath the chair lay buried in a trash can behind the bar. It would be better to simply have everyone believe what was written in the sheriff's report.

"Elmore knew he didn't have much longer. His heart just quit beating. It's an easy way to pass on."

Delight's arm squeezed him tightly. "These times are always hard. I don't know if it's because we lost someone or it reminds us that one day it will be our turn."

Lett chewed worriedly on his lower lip. It was time to change the subject. "Reckon I should head for town. There's a saw I have to pick up that they need at the mine."

"You take care," she said. "I'll fix you a good dinner."

He forced a grin. "And I'll bet we have watermelon for dessert."

Delight slid her arm away, dabbed her cheek and said, "All you can eat and then some."

Lett walked over, climbed into his Chevrolet and started the engine. As he drove toward Lordsburg, he noticed gray dust from the hearse hanging in the still desert air.

Chapter Twenty-Nine

Sam Ransom was too sore to sit upright at his magnificent office desk. He felt weak and scared. For the past two days he had been unable to keep food on his stomach. His visit to the doctor in El Paso kept playing over and over in his mind like a stuck phonograph record.

It's impossible to tell if we caught it in time or not. All we can do is inoculate you and watch for any symptoms to appear, the doctor had said coldly.

What if they do? Sam asked.

I'm sorry, there is no treatment. Once the disease has begun, it's invariably fatal.

Invariably fatal. Those two words had been far worse than the shots and they were terrible. That needle looked to be a foot long. He remembered well how the nurse—who under different circumstances would have looked pretty—had grabbed up a handful of his belly, then quickly jabbed in the needle to its hilt. Sam remembered feeling as if a nest of angry hornets had attacked him there.

The bottle of serum the doctor had given him rested in his briefcase. He needed to drive to Silver City and take it to the only physician within seventy miles and receive the rest of his shots. Sam worried if he would be strong enough to make the trip.

Invariably fatal. Sam fretted over anything that could possibly be a symptom of rabies. He nearly cried every time he felt the urge for water. He knew it could be a death sentence, so he refused to even think about drinking.

Sam placed a shaky, sweaty palm to his forehead. "My God, I've got a fever," he sobbed. "I have it and there's not a thing anyone can do!"

The slamming of his front door caused him to look up. It was that stupid Lett Halsy. Sam fought down an urge to run over and bite him.

"Sir," Halsy said with concern, "you don't look well. Perhaps you should see a doctor."

"I'm a sick man, Halsy!" Sam snapped. "That damn dog, the one that bit me, was mad."

"You mean Wesley, sir?" Lett asked blandly.

"Of course, you dolt, the one that ran away. I've been to see a damn doctor and he don't know if I'll live or not. It's *your* fault for not telling me sooner!"

"I'm sorry, sir," Halsy said, with a stupid, blank look. "I didn't expect you to worry so. I said it was probably nothing—"

"*Nothing!*" Sam interrupted viciously. "You call getting bitten by a mad dog nothing. Here I am dying and you call it nothing."

"Uh, sir, I tried to get hold of you later that night, but you had already left."

"Well, spit it out man. I don't have time for this." When Sam said the word "time" a tear ran down his cheek.

"Wesley seems fine, sir, that's what I wanted to tell you. He was under the porch when I got home. He's been real friendly ever since he bit you. He certainly doesn't act like a mad dog."

Sam straightened up, grimacing from pain. "That dog doesn't have rabies?"

"I'd reckon not. Like I told you, he's fine and seems to be in a good mood."

"And you let me go through all of this. Why, I should fire you right now!"

"I'm sorry to see you so upset, sir. I *did* try to let you know, and it would seem an awful waste to have to repaint all of those signs."

Sam swallowed hard, his mouth was dry. "Okay, you're not fired. Now, get the hell out of here and go back to work! And by tonight, that dog better be dead."

"Uh, sir," Lett said.

"What is it now, Halsy?"

"If that dog's dead, we'll never know if he's rabid or not. I've been told it can take a long time to find out. That's why I kept him around. Safe's better than sorry."

Sam wanted to bellow out cuss words at this ignorant simpleton, but his belly was much too sore. "Just go to the mine," he ordered softly.

"Yes, sir. And I really hope you come out of this okay," Halsy said, on his way out the door.

Sam Ransom breathed a sigh of relief once he was alone. He got up and painfully walked over, filled a glass with water and drank deeply. It was wonderful. He poured the glass full once again. Then he thought back on what Halsy had said. "It can take a long time to find out."

My God, how he wanted more water. He had never felt so thirsty in his life. Sam sobbed, then began fumbling frantically through his pockets for his keys. He had to go to Silver City. The doctor there might yet be able to save him.

It can take a long time to find out. Invariably fatal.

Sam Ransom simply couldn't get those words out of his head when he staggered outside to climb into that sleek red Packard.

CHAPTER THIRTY

"I simply can't understand why Sam Ransom would think Wesley had rabies," Delight said, daubing melted butter on the crust of a fresh-baked loaf of bread.

Lett drew up his cheek in thought. "Beats me. I think he's just one of those people who likes running to the doctor a lot."

"Those shots are supposed to be really terrible."

"Yep," Lett agreed. "That's what I've heard."

Delight gingerly scooted the bread loaf over to cool. When she turned to Lett, her face appeared sad. "Did you see to it that poor old Elmore Wyman was taken care of?"

"The mortician got him preserved and boxed up for the trip. He'll be on the train tonight, headed for Missouri."

"I'll miss him, he always treated me like a lady," Delight said with teary eyes. "A lot of people thought he was crazy, the way he carried on about that Lost Dutchman Mine."

Lett had completely forgotten about Elmore's map and letter he had tucked away in his pocket. "It's sad, but getting old does that to folks sometimes."

Delight swished past Lett, leaving a hint of her sweet-smelling perfume hanging in the air. "I'm going outside for a while. It's really hot working over that stove. Would you like to take a walk with me?"

"Just a minute," he answered, standing up and fishing in his pocket. Without a second's hesitation, Lett brought out Elmore's papers and went to the big Majestic stove, opened the firebox door and dashed them into the flames.

Delight had been watching him from the doorway. "What was that?" she asked.

"Oh, nothing," Lett said. "Just some private papers Elmore left me. I didn't want anyone to see them. They were ramblings about that Dutchman's gold. I'd like folks to forget the fact he'd lost his mind and just remember how nice a guy he was."

"That's sweet of you. Are you ready for our walk now?"

Lett clicked the stove door closed and turned to her with a smile. "Sure, I'd love some fresh air."

CHAPTER THIRTY-ONE

"Guess what we've got for free at the Roxy Jay tonight?" Lett asked with a smirk.

Bulldog marked a line on a heavy timber lying on sawhorses and looked up. "Well, let me think on that for a spell. Would it by any chance be watermelon?"

"You're a hard man to stump," Lett replied.

Bulldog snorted, "Yep, I'm a regular college perfesser type. Just how many of those darn things are left, anyway?"

"We're down to the last hundred or so," Lett answered cheerfully.

"Wonderful, simply wonderful," Bulldog grumbled, stomping off toward the tool shed.

"It's been a week since the Fourth," Joel Kay said. "Even my kids are mighty tired of 'em. They just eat the hearts out of 'em nowadays and leave the rest for the coyotes."

"I can't understand coyotes eating watermelons like they do," Lett commented.

Jake Clanton spoke up. "Coyotes'll eat anything that don't eat them first—kinda like McTavish—I suppose watermelons are a real treat after munching on dead gophers and the like."

"Speaking of McTavish," Epp interjected. "He done a first-rate job patching over all those bullet holes Jake made in the wall playing William Tell with ole Wyman."

Lett's face grew serious. "I told him to do it. Elmore was a good man, don't forget that."

"No, siree," Arnold Epp said quickly. "I was just commenting on McTavish's carpenter work."

Briefly, Lett wondered as to how Wyman had come up with all of the money he had spent. There didn't appear to have been that many holes in the wall. No matter, lunch break was over and it was time to get back to work.

Bulldog and Joel had hung a timber set within reach of the first level. This afternoon, once some heavy planks and a ladder were lowered, the miners would have an opportunity to inspect the tunnels driven off the shaft by the old-timers, probably well over fifty years ago.

Hopefully, Lett thought, they might find signs of ore. The vein had widened and appeared mineralized. When he had mentioned to Sam Ransom it might be a good idea to run some assays, Sam had angrily told him no, which made him wonder anew about the promoter's intentions.

The little twerp had returned to his usual arrogant self after the doctor in Silver City allowed him to stop taking those shots as long as the dog appeared healthy.

Lett remembered having to painfully pinch himself to keep from grinning when Sam had ordered him to "Take good care of that dog and keep a close eye on it."

Bulldog came stomping out of the tool house followed by Joel Kay. Both had hard hats and carbide lights tucked under their arm.

"Friggin' watermelons," Bulldog grumbled as he passed Lett.

Joel climbed onto the mortised wood ladder and descended into the earth, followed by the still mumbling Bulldog.

Lett was glad that he had hired Joel Kay. The kids' dad was stronger than he appeared and a willing hand. It hadn't taken him long to get used to working in absolute darkness with only a flickering yellow flame to see by. The man did everything asked of him without complaint and seemed genuinely interested in becoming a miner.

Arnold Epp brought out a timber saw and Lett pitched in to help cut the planks where Bulldog had marked them.

Jake Clanton pulled in driving Lett's Chevrolet just as the last planks and ladder were being lowered into the depths. The moment the windlass cable grew slack, signifying Bulldog and Joel had the load under control, Lett walked over to see if Jake had gotten the ventube "T" they would need to ventilate the tunnels.

"Dave Jennings has something new to bitch about," Jake said, taking the ventube from the backseat.

"That man would complain if he was hung with a brand-new rope and woke up in heaven," Lett remarked. "What's his problem now?"

"The price to mail a letter just went clear up to three cents," Jake answered.

"At least he found a legitimate gripe," Lett fumed, shaking his head. "The government must have gone crazy. Here we are in the worst depression of all time and they go do something stupid like raising postage rates a whole penny!"

Jake grinned. "I'll swear Lett, you sound more and more like Jennings ever day."

The bell cord dangling down the shaft twitched and two bells sounded. It was Bulldog signaling that the old tunnels were now accessible.

Arnold Epp joined them. "What do you think, boss? The air's been pretty good down there lately. We might be able to check things out before we hang more vent line. We could use a candle. Those things'll go out if we run into any bad air, then we can skedaddle and ventilate the place."

Jake commented, "The way Sam has us run that fan all of the time, I'd bet the air down there's better than the air in the Roxy Jay."

Lett thought for a moment, then said, "Okay boys, grab up your hat and lights. It's time for us to see what's down that hole."

The shaft had flattened out and the last timber set lay jammed against hard rock. This time there was no swaying when Lett stepped onto the plank floor. The sound of clomping boots echoed eerily from the dark cavernous opening only a few feet below where Joel and Bulldog stood. Air hissed from the end of the ventube like the sibilance of some great dying beast.

All five miners crowded onto the wooden platform. Lett Halsy took the carbide light from his hat, bent to his knees and sent the yellow flame stabbing into the blackness. After a long, careful look he said, "Well, I can't see anything ready to cave in. Bulldog, you come with me. The rest of you guys stay here until we find out what we're faced with."

"You be careful, boss," Joel Kay said worriedly.

Lett stuck the lamp back into its holder on his hard hat. "Anytime a man goes into old mine workings, he has to be." Then he swung around to face the ladder and climbed down into the stygian darkness.

The tunnel level was only six feet below their timber. Lett tested the floor with his boot, found it solid, stepped inside the ancient opening and waited for Bulldog.

Both men focused their flickering lights into the chasm.

"Air seems fine," Lett commented, taking a candle from his pocket and lighting it from the flame of his carbide light.

"Yep," Bulldog agreed, "but bad air looks just like the good stuff. I'd say we go mighty slow."

Lett held the candle at arm's length and began inching his way ahead. The miners' heavy boots grated on the rock floor where no man had set foot for over a half century.

Both men flicked their carbide lights continuously to the roof, sides and floor. They knew all too well the myriad of dangers that awaited the unwary. Aside from bad air and loose rocks, there was a possibility openings from a deeper level could reach to just below their feet, with only a few rotting debris-covered timbers keeping them from plunging to their deaths.

"Seems solid enough," Lett said, halting for Bulldog to join him.

"Yep, and the workings are bigger than I'd have expected. My guess is they drove this big enough to haul ore out of."

Lett ran his fingers across the copper-stained vein on the tunnel roof. "By golly, it looks like it might be ore. Only an assay would tell for sure."

Carefully, the men proceeded. A few more feet and Lett froze. "Take a gander at that mess, Bulldog."

Flickering yellow lights played along the tunnel roof which, for as far as they could see, was lined with timbers. To their left a wooden chute for loading mine cars dropped from above. Just beyond it, loose rock spilled into the tunnel from some long ago cave-in.

"That vein did make ore," Lett commented. "Those old-timers mined the hell out of it, taking the high grade and leaving the rest behind."

"Yep," Bulldog said seriously, "and what they left behind is held up by those old timbers we're looking at. I'll bet my hole card there's thousands of tons of loose rock above our heads just itching to follow the law of gravity."

Wordlessly, Lett moved ahead and carefully thunked the first timber. "This dry desert preserves wood really well. It not only sounds solid but looks like it was put here yesterday."

"Old mine timbers are like dominoes, one of 'em goes and the rest follow. We're so damn close to the shaft all of that loose rock over our heads would not only bury us, but if the guys back at the shaft didn't run like hell, they'd get buried too."

Lett sighed, "We've got to check it out. That's why we get

paid the big bucks."

"Hard to spend money when you're squashed flat," Bulldog said, pushing ahead of Lett.

"Look at the bright side, if those timbers give way, you won't have to eat anymore watermelons," Lett quipped.

Bulldog ducked under the old chute and climbed onto where muck from the cave-in half filled the tunnel. He dragged some rock out of the hole with his hands, grabbed a chunk up and held it close to the flame of his light. "I'll be a monkey's uncle."

"What do you see?" Lett asked, coming closer.

Bulldog grabbed more rocks from the pile. "I think college perfesser stock just went way up in my book," he nearly shouted.

"What the hell?" Lett blurted, when he joined Bulldog and hefted a chunk handed him. "Why, this is like lead."

"Take a closer look, boss. That ain't lead or zinc. Those wire-looking masses are mainly pure silver with a sprinkling or two of gold thrown in for good measure."

Lett broke a big chunk with his rock hammer. When he flashed his light onto the glistening pile his hand was shaking. "My God, Bulldog. This is as high grade of ore as I've ever seen!"

Bulldog pushed a heavy chunk with his hand. "Dang few folks have seen anything like this before. Now I know why Ransom had that guardhouse built. A ton of this is worth a small fortune."

Lett played a flickering light along the far-reaching line of aged timbers. "That might be, but if you'll notice the vein of high grade runs right alongside of and just below where those old-timers left thousands of tons of loose muck hanging over our heads on fifty-year-old timbers. It'll be dangerous as hell to mine any ore without bringing the whole damn mountain down around our ears. Like you said earlier, it's hard to spend money when you're squashed."

Bulldog took a moment to look things over. "Blast it all if you ain't right. Here we are looking at a fortune and one stick of dynamite or one swing from a pick in the wrong place will bury it forever."

"Yeah," Lett said seriously, "right along with everyone who's in the mine."

"Shit," Bulldog grumbled. "I should've listened to my granpappy and took a government job. All I'd have to do then is sit on my butt in some office and do nothing. A guy could get killed down here before God gets the news."

"It's a little late to get educated, now," Lett said. "We've opened Pandora's box and Sam Ransom's going to make us mine this no matter how dangerous it is. He's talking like he's desperate for money."

Bulldog shook his head so hard his cheeks rolled like ocean waves. "I should have listened to my granpappy."

CHAPTER THIRTY-TWO

Sam stared in bewilderment at the dirty lump of rock Lett Halsy had just dumped onto his immaculate desk.

"Mister Ransom, I reckon that geology professor you hired really knew his stuff. There's a footwall vein of this laying right alongside where the old-timers mined. It's only a couple of feet away. The wall air slacked and caved, laying it open."

The natty promoter was even more puzzled. He had absolutely no idea what Halsy was talking about or why this disheveled simpleton seemed so proud of that grimy hunk of rock.

"That mine's full of ore," Ransom snapped. "I've known that all along. Now clean off my desk and go back to work."

"Yes, sir," Halsy said, "only I was sure you'd want to get it assayed. This vein should run at least five thousand dollars a ton."

"What!" Sam blurted out, giving the rock much closer scrutiny. He was suddenly *very* interested in what his foreman had to say. "Are you telling me this really is high-grade ore?"

Halsy's brow narrowed. "Few men ever set eyes on ore this rich. Now we all understand why you had that guardhouse built. What we *don't* understand is how that geologist knew it was down there. The only problem is—"

Ransom interrupted by reaching over and dragging the heavy chunk to him, furrowing a deep scratch into the top of his beautiful wood desk. "Are you sure this is really rich ore?" he asked again with obvious disbelief.

"Just as rich as you've been telling folks it would be."

Sam hefted the rock and pored over it like a doctor examining a sick baby. "My God. That *is* gold and silver. Five thousand dollars a ton you say!" His eyes widened. "How many tons of this stuff is down there anyway?"

A look of perplexity washed across Lett's face. "Well, sir, since you've had extensive experience with mines, I'm certain you know it's far too early to tell. The strike appears to be a large one. There's just one problem—"

Sam stuck an open palm toward Lett's face. "I don't give a damn about your petty problems. I hired you to mine this ore and that's just what you'll do. Right now, I want to see this vein of high grade with my own eyes!"

Half an hour later, after Lett had showed Sam Ransom how to adjust the band of a hard hat and fire the carbide light, the wide-eyed promoter stepped off the ladder and onto the dusty floor of the Last Chance Mine.

Sam had never been underground before. He was so excited about actually striking ore that he no longer cared what the men thought of his ineptitude. They worked for him. If someone made so much as a wrong comment, he would fire them on the spot.

"It's this way, about seventy feet," Halsy said, taking off his brass lamp and flashing the light into the dark maw of the tunnel.

Sam shuffled along behind his foreman and the miner with a wrinkled face everyone called "Bulldog." The closeness of the opening and shadowy flickering yellow lights that seemed woefully inadequate gave him the willies. Only the lure of awaiting riches drove him on.

"Watch your head, sir," Halsy said, pointing out some wooden timbers jutting down.

"Where is it?" Sam demanded, ducking under the chute and joining the miners.

Halsy and Bulldog looked at him strangely. "Right here," the foreman said, pointing to where a heap of rocks spilled out from the side of the tunnel, half filling it.

"I knew that," Ransom snarled. He dropped to his knees and pawed at the grimy mass. Even in the pitiful light he could see shimmering silver and gold scattered throughout the heavy rocks. In his wildest dreams he had never imagined wealth like what was laying at his feet, simply begging to be taken to the surface and sold.

"The vein's up here," Halsy said blandly, shining his light into a hole from where the unbelievable high-grade ore had fallen.

Sam Ransom gritted his teeth. "Of course it is."

Sam poked his head into the cavity and for the first time in his life was speechless. Everywhere he looked his gaze was rewarded by glittering thick wires of silver and gold. The carbide light shook in his trembling grasp. Here was the wealth of Solomon laid bare. His Shakespeare Mining and Development Company Stock would go to ten, maybe even twenty dollars a share. He would be rich beyond measure, a legitimate mining magnate like Winfield Scott Stratton. There was no time to waste, he had to rush back to his office and phone Higgenbottom. The brokers *had* to know what was actually in his mine.

Sam's hard hat crashed to the rocky floor when he forced himself away from his rich vein. "Men, I've got to hurry and get back to my office," he said breathlessly and started running toward the shaft.

"Watch that chute," a voice yelled.

Then something very hard struck the top of Sam Ransom's head and blackness enveloped him like a shroud.

Chapter Thirty-Three

"When Ransom saw that vein of high-grade ore he got so excited he took off like a striped-assed ape," Lett told Delight with a satisfied grin. "The little squirrel ran right into a chute and knocked himself out colder than a wedge."

"I hope he wasn't hurt too badly," she said with concern.

"Nah," Lett answered, "he just hit his head. I don't reckon there's a lot of damage that could be done there. I'll swear Sam Ransom had never been in a mine before. He acted as spooked as some little kid visiting a dentist."

Delight asked, "Then he'll be all right?"

"Oh, sure. He'd most likely have had a heart attack if he'd come to while we were winching him out of the shaft with nothing but a rope wrapped under his arms. But he didn't. It only took Len Miller a dozen stitches to patch him up."

"You didn't take him to a *real* doctor?"

"Nah. Sam was a tad upset over that fact himself until I explained the situation." Lett leaned back in his chair and took a sip of coffee. "With him being knocked out and bleeding like a stuck pig, I decided closer was better and wheeled into Dugan's station. Len swabbed his cut out with iodine and used a clean needle to do the stitching. I don't imagine the doc would have done it much different. He came to when I got him back to his room. Once he drank a few shots of whiskey he was fit as a fiddle."

A little too fit, Lett thought. His coffee tasted bitter as Sam's last order rose in his throat like bile. "Tell that blond whore to come down and spend the night. Now that we're into rich ore, I've got some celebrating to do." Just being reminded of Delight's occupation tortured him. Lett felt caught between a rock and a hard place. He couldn't afford to anger Ransom to the point where he might get fired. Sending Delight to spend the night with that weasel would tear his heart out—

"Hey, cheer up," Delight said happily. "You look like your dog died. With the mine full of high grade this place will boom!"

Lett forced a slight smile. "There's rich ore in the mine all right, but whoever came up with the saying about a fly in the ointment had the Last Chance in mind when they coined it."

In simple terms, Lett described to her how the two veins lay side by side only three feet or so apart. How one vein had been mined out by the old-timers who left the opening filled with thousands of tons of loose waste rock.

Then he said seriously, "To mine the newly discovered ore and keep from breaking into the old workings will take a forest of timber and even more luck."

"You make it sound very dangerous." She reached over, grasped his hand and rolled her worried azure eyes. "I don't want anything to happen to you."

Her soft touch caused Ransom's order to crash back into his head. Lett set down his cup and placed his hand on top of Delight's. "If Sam would give us the money to do it right, we could mine that high grade safely. He's money hungry. I don't think he understands if that vein caves in he'll not only lose the shaft along with the ore, but anyone in the mine will likely get buried alive."

She chewed on her lower lip. "Now I see why you are so worried. And I have the feeling you still aren't telling me everything."

Lett swallowed and tightened his grasp on her hand. Suddenly a loud knock on the open door stopped him from speaking.

"Sorry to bother you and the lady," Arnold Epp said nervously, "but Sam's here and buying drinks for everyone. He told me to fetch you and her to come over and join him. 'Cept for having a bandage on his head, he seems fine as a frog hair."

Delight slid her hand away with a sigh. "I don't suppose we should say no. He's the only reason this town or any of us are still here."

A sharp pain shot down Lett Halsy's back when he forced himself to stand. Wordlessly, he walked over to the sink and dumped out his coffee. He gazed through the open window at the low, cactus-studded hills bathed in pale yellow light of a full moon. He tarried long enough to watch as an owl swooped down from the dark sky and carried off a small mouse in its sharp talons.

"Are you all right?" Delight asked.

Lett chocked down his emotions and painted a smile on his face. "Sure. It's just been a long day and I'm a little tired is all."

Lett was silent for a long while once they joined the raucous crowd at the bar. Whenever he saw Delight and Sam Ransom together, all he could think about was that hapless little mouse.

CHAPTER THIRTY-FOUR

Warner T. Higgenbottom snipped the end off a long Havana cigar with a silver cutter. He slid his ornate brass desktop lighter close, flicked a flame to life and held one end of the cigar in the fire, rotating it slowly to bake the tobacco, so when lit it would burn evenly. Enjoying a good cigar was like many things in life; they couldn't be rushed. At the moment, aside from contemplating his fine Havana, Warner was savoring the telegram from Sam Ransom that his partner, Bryant Lane, seemed to find equally entertaining.

"I was wondering how long it would take that little turd to strike 'pay dirt' down there," Bryant said with a sneer. "He must think we're real rubes to believe that phony report of his or anything else he says."

Warner chuckled. "My only problem is, he's too easy for it to be *fun*. If Ransom's brains were dynamite he couldn't blow his nose."

"We can use his telegram to unload our last few thousand shares of Shakespeare stock. That'll give us fifty grand, not bad for the way the economy is."

Warner lit his cigar, leaned back in his posh leather chair and blew a smoke ring. "The arrogant little nit must be used to being a big fish in a little pond. If any legitimate brokerage house took to selling stock based on a fraudulent report, everyone connected with the scheme would go to prison."

"You were right about that geologist not even existing. These things are *so* easy to check out. I did think the part about that electromagnetic ore finder was a nice touch though."

"Yes, it was," Warner agreed. "It certainly helped sell our personal stock. Thank God we can still do that without getting into legal problems." He smiled contentedly and continued, "Securities laws are wonderful when you understand how they work. As long as we only sell our own stock we might have some angry investors, but there are no laws broken. If we had put Ransom's stock on the exchange and used fake reports to promote it to the public, the outcome would be a lot different."

Bryant held the telegram close and read it again. "Richest ore strike since the Comstock. Huge masses of wire gold and silver everywhere."

Warner T. Higgenbottom took a long satisfying puff on his Havana and cast a glance through the office window at the distant snow-capped Rockies. "Well, I suppose we should get on the phone and tell that cock-and-bull story of Ransom's to some numskull who might believe it."

CHAPTER THIRTY-FIVE

Sam Ransom glared down his nose at Lett from across his massive desk. "Why in hell do you want to build a gallows at my mine?" he growled. A few years past Sam had lost a good friend to one of those ominous devices and couldn't fathom any possible good use for one now.

Halsy looked perplexed. "Well, sir, it's a tower over the mine shaft. A gallows frame is made from wood. We'll need one thirty feet high or so. Perhaps you call them a head frame."

"A head frame is the *proper* term," Sam snapped. "I want you to remember that I have always been in management and am not familiar with many of the slang terms used by uneducated miners."

"Sorry, sir," Lett said through gritted teeth and forced smile. He felt as if he was talking to a spoiled brat who needed a good spanking. There was no longer any doubt in Lett's mind, Sam Ransom knew nothing of mining. On the other hand, there was also no doubt that Sam was his boss, no matter how arrogant or incompetent he might be. Three hundred dollars a month was big money for these hard times. He couldn't afford to anger Sam to the point of getting fired.

If he would just stay away from Delight he'd be a lot easier to be around. Lett swallowed hard and continued. "We're going to need several pieces of machinery to mine that high grade; a gasoline-engine-powered hoist, an air compressor and drill, mine rail and dolly for the ore bucket—"

"Yes, yes," Sam interrupted. "I don't want to be burdened with all of your petty details. Just tell me where we can buy this stuff at the best price and how much money you will need."

"Dave Jennings has everything, including a good supply of timbers and some dynamite that's not too old to use. He'll deliver the whole package to the mine for three thousand dollars cash."

"You're talking about a lot of money Halsy. Are you certain this machinery you claim to need can't be purchased cheaper elsewhere?"

"I don't believe so, sir. Jennings' prices are as good as we're likely to find and it's all right here in Lordsburg. With any luck, we can be set up to begin pulling out high grade in a couple of weeks."

Sam mulled that over in his mind. If he could sell a few tons of ore, the price of Shakespeare stock would skyrocket. "Okay Halsy, I'll put four thousand dollars into the account. This will cover wages and expenses. I warn you, there had better be some ore shipped before you ask me for more money."

"Yes sir, we'll do our best."

"I don't care about your best. See to it those men you have hired work like they're paid to do and get that ore out."

Sam Ransom waited several minutes after Halsy had left. Then he went to the door, locked it, and dropped the blinds. The combination to the safe was a simple one. Moments later the contents of his slim money case were spread out on the desk before him.

Methodically as a banker, Sam counted and recounted his funds. Four thousand dollars to the operating account and two for that bloodsucking lawyer, left him thirty-six thousand. He sighed, extracted a grand for personal expenses, stuck it into his pocket, then ran his hands lovingly over the remaining stacks of green bills. Not even the silken skin of the loveliest woman could compare to the exquisite feel of money.

"God, I love this stuff," he said with a soft passion men usually reserved for sweethearts. Sam picked up a stack of hundred-dollar bills and ran the edges slowly up and down his cheeks. "When that stock takes off I'm going to cover the bed with these things and roll around on them naked with an eighteen-year-old girl."

The thought of stock shook him from his delightful reverie. Carefully Sam placed his remaining thirty-five thousand dollars back into their place in his leather case and returned it to the safe. He spun the dial and tried the bolt. Satisfied that his money was secure, he reopened his office and picked up the receiver on his telephone.

Strangely, Higgenbottom and Lane hadn't answered either his telegram or any of his calls.

They are a large brokerage firm, he thought. Now that he had struck high-grade ore, they were most probably busy working on press releases and sales calls for Shakespeare stock. He told the operator their number and waited expectantly.

"I'm sorry, Mister Ransom," the haughty secretary said tersely. "Both Mister Higgenbottom and Mister Lane are out of the office at this time."

"Well, when will they return?" he growled into the black mouthpiece.

"They are on vacation, I really don't know when they will be back."

"What! We have business to take care of. My stock—"

"I will leave a message that you called, sir."

Sam Ransom found himself talking into a dead phone. He grew livid from fury and frustration.

"Vacation!" he screamed, slamming the receiver back onto its hook. "Those idiots are costing me a fortune."

Sam's hand shook when he grabbed a fountain pen and began

scribbling a telegram to Higgenbottom and Lane demanding either the immediate return of his stock or their diligent efforts to promote it.

After folding the scathing telegram and sticking it into his pocket, Sam grabbed a silver flask from his desk drawer and took a healthy belt. The burning whiskey felt soothing. Another drink and his red rage begun to subside.

Once he went to the bank and his message was sent, he knew just what he needed to recover his spirits. The Roxy Jay was a pitiful excuse for a tavern and the only whore there had seen better days, but at least he would be able to get his mind off business for a while.

CHAPTER THIRTY-SIX

"Not all yo-yos come on a string, do they Mister Halsy?"

Lett spun and saw Otis Tate standing in the doorway to his office. The lawyer's stubble-bearded face displayed a jovial grin.

Stepping from the fiery desert sun into the welcome shade of the two-story brick building Lett said, "You wouldn't be referring to a certain weasel of a promoter would you?"

Tate's grin widened. "Heavens no, Sam Ransom is a client of mine so I can't talk about him personally. I was simply referring to stock boomers in general. Say, I've got a pot of coffee that shouldn't damage a healthy man. Why don't you take time for a cup? The high-grade ore in the Last Chance Mine has been there a few million years, it will wait for a while."

"I've survived both McTavish's cooking and that awful stuff he passes off as coffee. I reckon I'm game," Lett said, as he followed the lawyer inside.

"Not everyone enjoys coffee with some body to it," Otis said, plunking two steaming mugs down on his desk.

Lett eyed the tar-like contents of his cup with suspicion. He grabbed it up, blew a cloud of steam, took a sip and grinned. "Compared to McTavish's brew, this stuff is a might weak, but I guess it will do." His face grew serious. "What have you heard about the strike at the mine?"

Otis plopped down in his swivel chair and leaned his elbows on the desk. "Only that it makes the Comstock and Cripple Creek look pale by comparison. What's the truth of it?"

Lett couldn't restrain a chuckle. "From what we can see the vein's about a foot wide. There is only a small hole into it from where a cave-in laid it open. The ore lays alongside an old stope gobbed full of waste rock. It will be dangerous as hell to mine, even if it turns out to be a big deposit. As to the value, well you can see the silver and some gold with the naked eye so it's high grade for sure. I'm going to take some samples in for assay tomorrow."

The lawyer made a moue. "You're aware the nearest assayer is in Silver City?"

"Did Will Green go out of business?"

"No, unfortunately he lost his mind. The sheriff took him to the insane asylum in Santa Fe. I'm helping his wife obtain guardianship so she can sell off the assay equipment."

"That's too bad," Lett said with concern. "Does anyone know what caused him to snap? He seemed fine when I met him."

"With this Depression on, who knows. From the mess this country is in, I'm only surprised more people don't lose their way. He just curled up into a ball and started crying, won't say a word to anyone."

Both men were drawn to Sam Ransom's sleek Packard as he sped past the office.

Otis watched through his huge front window until the red convertible turned south. "It looks like Sam's taking off early and heading up the hill to the Roxy Jay."

The lawyer noticed the subdued rage that flared in Lett Halsy's gray eyes and knew the rumor he had heard about him being smitten with Delight was true. Otis took a sip of coffee and sat in silence a few moments before saying, "All she's doing is trying to get by in this crazy world."

Lett's hand gripped his cup with white knuckles. "Who do you mean?"

"Delight," Otis said soothingly. "She's no different from you

173

or me. She's simply making a living the only way she knows."

Lett pursed his lips. "I didn't realize I was so obvious about liking her."

The lawyer gave a sly smile. "There may be a dozen or so people in Hidalgo County who *don't* know about it." Then he grew solemn. "Lett, women are judged by a different standard than men, an unfair standard to my way of thinking. Bible thumpers don't like to be reminded that Jesus himself once defended a prostitute against accusations from the Pharisees and forgave her. If more people would actually read what the Bible teaches instead of pounding on it and using the Good Book to look down their noses at someone, this would be a better world."

Lett was plainly surprised at Otis Tate's words. "I thought you were a lawyer, not a philosopher. I must admit, Delight being with the likes of Sam Ransom rankles me."

"Ransom's a different story." Otis waved his hand like he was swatting a fly. "I'm simply trying to tell you that it's all right to care for Delight. She's already been forgiven by the only one who matters. Maybe it's time you followed suit."

Lett swallowed hard, a familiar knot had formed in his throat. "She *is* a sweet lady."

"Then, for Pete's sake *tell* her that. All women like to be told they are desirable and a good person. This lesson is one I learned the hard way, myself."

The lawyer's lips trembled slightly as he continued. "Once, a long time ago, I had a wonderful wife and two precious sons. I was a hotshot lawyer who thought money was the only thing that mattered; make lots of it and you'll have a happy life. I worked seven days a week and the money poured in. Someday, I told myself, when I was sufficiently wealthy, there would be time for my family.

"Lett, money is like opium. The more you get, the more you

want. There never is enough of the stuff. One night I came home to an empty house. Vivana, that's my wife's name, had taken my sons and left me. I spent the next three years trying to track them down. I wasn't successful. Finally I drifted into Lordsburg and have been here ever since."

"I'm sorry," Lett said.

"Yes, I am too," Otis answered. "Being a Catholic, I have no choice but to remain alone. Take care not to wind up like me."

"Well, I need to go over to Dave Jennings and buy some machinery." It felt good to change the subject. "Thanks for the coffee."

"You're welcome, the next time you drop in I'll attempt to have some brewed up with more body to it."

Lett Halsy stepped from the lawyer's office into the blazing afternoon sun. He tilted his hat forward to keep the glare from his eyes and headed for the bank while the ever-present wind blew ragged tumbleweeds down the dusty streets of Lordsburg.

CHAPTER THIRTY-SEVEN

Warner T. Higgenbottom waddled from his office struggling with a large cardboard box. He dropped it heavily onto his secretary's desk. "Penelope, my dear," he puffed. "Please see to it that this gets sent to Sam Ransom by registered post. I trust the letters to the secretaries of state were mailed as I instructed."

"Of course, sir," the prim secretary replied. "I'm certain this Ransom fellow will soon be having a *very* bad day."

Higgenbottom took the smoldering black cigar from his mouth and grinned. "He's nothing but a petty crook, my dear. You must not concern yourself with the likes of him. By the way, my wife's visiting her mother in Chicago. Why don't we go to the cabin in Eldora for the weekend? It will be nice and cool in the mountains."

The redhead rolled her green eyes at him and smiled seductively. "You know how much I love spending time with you. Of course I'll go."

Higgenbottom stroked the nape of her neck with his pudgy hand. "You're such a sweetheart." He stuck the half-smoked cigar between his lips and turned to leave.

"Oh, sir?" the secretary asked.

"Yes, my dear, what is it?" Warner said, returning to his devoted Penelope.

"We received a letter asking about Shakespeare Mining stock and more particularly about Sam Ransom. It is from a man in

San Francisco by the name of Al Casey. Do you want to reply to him?"

Higgenbottom admired the redhead's beautifully manicured nails and slender fingers when he plucked the proffered letter from her hand. He read it and quickly said, "Unfortunately we no longer deal in Shakespeare stock. In the spirit of cooperation, however, send him a brochure on Shakespeare Mining and also enclose some information on our firm. He very well may become a client someday."

Penelope caressed the back of his hand when she retrieved the communication. "I'm counting the hours," she purred.

Warner smiled warmly. "We always do have such wonderful times together."

The broker was hesitant to leave his secretary's charming company, but he pried himself away and trudged back to his plush office. No matter how trying, business must always come before pleasure.

Chapter Thirty-Eight

"The Last Chance should be producing ore in a few days," Lett said to Delight, as she poked garlic cloves into a steak.

This was his favorite meal. A thick, marbled steak slit open and filled with garlic, then slowly fried in pure butter, was food for the gods. Watching the beautiful Delight gliding busily around the little shack completed his enjoyment of the moment.

"Then you'll be hiring some more men soon?" she asked. "There are a lot of folks just barely hanging on, waiting for that to happen."

"I'm afraid it may be a while," he answered with a hint of sadness. "There's simply no way I can put anyone else on. Ransom has made it plain we'll get no more money from him until he sells some stock or we get paid for selling some ore. If we ship the high grade to the smelter in El Paso, it will be several weeks before they issue a settlement check. Ore buyers move with the speed of a crippled turtle when it comes to paying out money."

Delight flicked a wild strand of blond hair from her rouged cheek. "Sam's plenty upset with the brokers. He told me he was going to find another firm if they don't start moving some stock shortly. With this terrible Depression on, I really worry about him selling any stock at all."

Lett winced, then quickly masked his displeasure with a smile. Hearing Delight refer to the cocky little promoter as "Sam" was a much too familiar term.

"Ransom's a hard case to figure out," he said coarsely. "I know for a fact he's never been around a mine before, no matter what he says. He's a mighty big talker and an arrogant person to boot."

"I know he is all of those things," Delight said worriedly. "But, Lett, if he fails what is to become of us and this entire town? Everyone here is depending on him opening a big mine. There are over two hundred people still hanging around here living on nothing but hope."

"There *is* ore in the Last Chance," he answered firmly. "I do worry about how much we'll be able to take out and not cave in half the mountain."

Delight bent over and refilled his coffee cup. Lett forced himself not to stare at her tempting cleavage and the wonderful way her jutting breasts accented the plain print dress she wore. He always felt like a jittery virgin schoolboy when she came close.

Otis Tate's advice of several days ago roared into his head like a Colorado mountain avalanche. *Tell her how pretty she is. Say you'll take care of her. Forget the fact she's a whore. Tell her the way you really feel toward her.*

Lett tried desperately to force his mouth to move, but it felt as if it was chiseled from granite. He wanted more than anything to wrap his arms around her slender waist and draw her to him. Delight's cherry-red lips glistened with promise.

If I do, he thought, *she won't refuse me. I know that, but then I'll be no different from any of the countless number of men who have paid for her pleasures. Delight is special to me, I want to be special to her also. I just don't know how to go about it—*

"Hey, cheer up," Delight giggled, mussing Lett's hair with her free hand. "You look like your dog died. On the bright side, we've got steaks for dinner and *Amos 'n' Andy* are on the radio later. Things could be a lot worse."

"Speaking of dogs," Lett replied seriously, "I'm plumb concerned about ole Wesley. He hasn't so much as taken a nip out of anyone since he bit Ransom. I hope the poor pooch hasn't come down with a sickness from it."

Delight laughed aloud, then her happiness faded like a black cloud had descended on her soul. "Wesley's just depressed because he can't find a rattlesnake anymore. Lett, those poor people camped out there waiting for a job at the mine are actually hunting snakes and eating them. Folks are so desperate they boil sagebrush to make tea. It might be a good idea to put out the word there simply won't be any jobs. Then maybe those folks could move on."

"Move on to *where?*" Lett joined in her despair. "Delight, darling, from what I hear, things aren't any better in California, possibly even worse. There is no running away from this damn Depression. Besides that, if Ransom got wind of my saying his mine won't boom, I'd be out on my ear."

Delight sighed, knowing he spoke the truth. "I understand," she said and turned her attention to the stove. "It just hurts to think about it."

"Yeah." Lett watched her tap some fresh butter from a knife into a skillet. "I know."

As usual, Delight had prepared a sumptuous dinner. Both left a large portion of their steak for Wesley, which the dog wolfed down bone and all without making any attempt to chew first.

"That dog just isn't normal," Lett said, carrying his empty dinner plate to the sink and sliding it into soapy dishwater. "He'll eat anything that don't eat him first."

Delight's usual good humor was back. She flashed a foxy smile. "I have the feeling when Wesley bit Sam, he was just taking a taste. If, for some reason the mine doesn't make a go of it,

Wesley will probably eat him out of desperation."

"Maybe Wesley's more normal than I thought," Lett said. "I'd prefer rattlesnake over weasel myself."

"*Amos 'n' Andy* will be starting in a few minutes," Delight said with a chuckle. She spun a black dial on the radio. As the tubes warmed, the round speaker begun spitting static.

It took her a while to tune into the distant station. While Delight fiddled with the cantankerous radio, Lett slid two chairs more closely together than ever before and sat two steaming cups of coffee down on the small table in front of them.

Satisfied the crackling reception was as good as they were going to get in this remote location, Delight came and eased into place alongside Lett. The show they intended to listen to had yet to start. A popular song, "Brother Can You Spare A Dime?" was playing.

Delight brushed an unruly strand of hair from her face, then blew gently on the cup of coffee. She rolled her blue eyes toward him and said softly, "Earlier tonight you called me darling. Better be careful or I may take to thinking you mean it."

Every muscle in Lett's body tensed as if an electric shock had passed through. He swallowed hard and felt what he knew was a crimson blush wash across his tanned face. Summoning all of his willpower he managed to say softly, "I *do* mean you are a darling. Why wouldn't I? You're a pleasure to be around and pretty as a flower."

Delight set the cup down, reached over and caressed Lett's calloused hand. "Why thank you," she purred. "A girl always loves compliments, you know."

"And you are a lady who deserves them."

"I never thought you to be such a romantic, but I like it."

Gaining courage, Lett gently ran his fingers through her long hair. Bathed in the yellow moonlight gleaming through an open window, Delight's blond locks shimmered like the finest gold.

She turned toward him and flowed closer, her sensuous ruby lips slightly parted, inviting.

He cupped his hand behind her head and gazed deeply into her azure eyes. "There is something I've wanted to tell you for the longest time," Lett said, his voice soft and gentle as the night breeze.

"Oh, Lett," she cooed, squeezing his hand tightly.

Their lips had nearly touched when heavy footsteps thudded onto the plank porch. The door flew open. In unison they drew back to stare at Jason McTavish. The fat man's wrought face spoke of trouble.

"Boss, you've got to get up to the mine real quick," McTavish wheezed excitedly, poking his thumbs underneath his apron straps. "Jake Clanton and Bulldog's got guns. There's gonna be killings for sure if you don't stop 'em!"

CHAPTER THIRTY-NINE

Lett Halsy bolted from Delight's shack into the moonlit night and ran south up the dirt main street of Shakespeare. He had not taken time to question McTavish about details. The portly bartender wasn't a man to get as rattled as he appeared about a petty problem.

This had better be serious, Lett thought. He was madder than a wet hen over being taken from Delight's sweet company, especially when he had been so rudely interrupted. *If someone is in need of killing, I might do it myself.*

The waning light only faintly illuminated the well-trodden path that turned up the gentle slope of the hill and wound a sinuous course around clumps of cactus on its way to the Last Chance.

Before he reached the mine, Lett saw glaring lights from two vehicles near the shaft house. A sharp pain stabbed at his side forcing him to stop and catch his breath. He was close enough to hear cursing and loud shouting over the ever-chugging little engine that spun the fan. Thankfully, he had not heard any shooting. He regretted not grabbing a gun before plunging into unknown trouble. McTavish kept an old double-barreled twelve gauge behind the bar. Right now that shotgun would be a comfort.

Lett shrugged his muscular shoulders and grumbled, "Reckon I'll have to do like a politician and talk them to death."

The pain eased. He took a deep breath and ran ahead. He

hesitated before popping over the hill into plain sight of whoever was doing all of the yelling. Not only did he want to size up the situation, he had to get his wind before he could even shout at anyone.

From the cover of a large greasewood bush, Lett cautiously poked his head up to where he could inspect the mine area. To his relief, one of the cars parked near the shaft belonged to the sheriff, Victor Mayes. Bulldog, Epp and Jake Clanton, rifles or shotguns cradled in their arms, stood facing the lawman.

Realizing the situation, whatever it was, appeared under control, Lett sauntered onto the flat area by the mine. Bulldog spun and pointed a mean-looking shotgun at him. Instantly Bulldog recognized who was approaching and lowered his aim with an apology. "Sorry boss, I didn't know but maybe those ore thieves might have had company."

"What do you mean," Lett gasped with a winded voice, "about ore thieves?"

The sheriff stepped forward and answered. "Highgraders have been hauling ore out of here at night. I got word some toughs from Silver City were stealing ore from these parts. Since this is the only mine operating and everybody and his dog knows about the strike here, I decided to pull a stakeout. I nearly caught 'em red-handed, too. They'd blasted and were sitting in their truck down by the main road waiting for the smoke to clear, when these yokels came charging in like G-men and scared 'em off. By the way, nice of you fellows to leave the fan running for them."

"Hey, I said we was sorry," Jake Clanton whined. He gave Lett a hangdog look. "Bulldog, Epp, and me was just leaving the Roxy Jay when Arnold caught a flicker of light from the mine. We was studying on that when we heard a distant 'whoof' and the ground shook a little. That was when we knew they'd touched off a blast and were stealing ore. We grabbed our guns and hopped into Bulldog's car to stop 'em. There weren't no way we could have known the sheriff had the place staked out."

Lett squinted into the car lights at Sheriff Mayes. "Couldn't you still chase them down and arrest them for Pete's sake?"

"For what?" Mayes answered sharply. "I saw them drive up the mine road then come back a few minutes later and park by the main road. I knew they hadn't had time to load up any ore so I was biding my time, planning to nail 'em after they had stolen something." He sneered at Clanton and continued his tirade. "I'd have sent those three yeggs to prison for a long spell. Now, thanks to your men here, I doubt the judge would fine 'em for trespassing."

Lett stepped close to Mayes. Keeping his gaze on the sheriff he tilted his head toward Bulldog and Clanton. "Sheriff," he said firmly, "it sounds like you're mad at the wrong folks. My men had no way of knowing you were anywhere near. They were simply protecting the mine."

Victor Mayes kicked angrily at a rock. He kept his head down when he spoke. "You're right, Halsy. I shouldn't have went off half cocked and yelled at 'em like I did. It's just such a bitch to have been so close and not nail those thieves."

Bulldog stepped over to the office and stowed his shotgun inside. He came out scowling at the mouth of the mine shaft. Smoke from the highgraders' dynamite blast was billowing from it into the night. "I wonder just how much damage those bastards did down there? We needed to do a good week's worth of timbering before setting off any dynamite."

The sheriff shook his head. "There's nothing more I can do here. I got the license number of their truck. If I run across them, we'll have ourselves a little talk." He patted the black handle of his revolver. "I think they'll get my drift."

Mayes traipsed stiffly to his patrol car. Before climbing in, the sheriff pointed toward a small building alongside the road that was only vaguely discernable in the dark. "Nice guard-house," he commented dryly.

Dust from the departing cruiser had yet to settle when Jake Clanton remarked, "That man has one evil temper."

"He's just doing his job," Lett said. "So were you guys. Thanks for trying to help. Jake, you and Epp crank up the hoist. Those fumes should be aired out below. Bulldog and I will get suited up and ride the bucket down. Then we'll see what shape the mine is in."

Carefully Lett and Bulldog stepped onto the wobbly rim of the steel ore bucket that dangled over the open maw of the shaft. Both men held a firm hand on the spindly cable. Lett grabbed the bell cord and yanked a three-two signal. Slowly they were lowered into the still smoky depths of the Last Chance Mine.

Acrid fumes from exploded nitroglycerine chafed at their eyes and irritated their lungs. In less than a minute the bucket eased to a stop at the working level.

"Man, we're going to have a headache from this," Lett said with a cough. "Too bad we don't have any grapes, they're the only thing that will stop a powder headache."

"Can't be any worse than a man feels the next morning after drinking that Mexican panther piss you sell as beer at the Roxy Jay," Bulldog said wryly. "Besides that, I'm curious as you are about what damage those highgraders caused and just how much ore they managed to steal."

"At least the air is fresher down here," Lett said. "The fan cleared out the tunnel like we thought."

The duo wasted no time reaching the open end of the ven-tube. They took off their carbide lights so the flame wouldn't blow out and bathed in the cool, sweet air blowing into the mine.

"That's better," Bulldog remarked. "At least my eyes ain't

burning anymore."

"The headaches won't start for a spell. Before they do, let's see what those highgraders did to us."

Flickering yellow flames stabbed into the darkness. Before reaching the area where the rich ore was exposed, their progress was stopped by a pile of freshly blasted rock spilling from the side of the tunnel.

"Those bastards!" Bulldog growled. "They shot a round into the wall trying to find more high grade."

Lett poked his head into the newly blasted hole. "Look at this," he said flatly.

Bulldog pushed alongside him with a grunt and surveyed the situation. "Hell's bells," he said unbelievably. "There's the vein all right, but it sure don't carry any ore. This is the first place we were gonna blast into it ourselves. I've got the sinkin' feeling maybe the strike ain't as big as we hoped."

Lett ran his fingers along the narrow black streak. "Well, it's for sure the high grade don't run this way. It could still run up and ahead," he hesitated before saying the obvious. "Right alongside that old mined-out area and a few thousand tons of rotten rock."

"Yep," Bulldog agreed. "That's the way I see it too. We can crawl over this and see what's left of our original strike. Maybe things will look better."

"Horse feathers," Lett spat when the yellow light disclosed that not only had every pound of the rich ore laying in the tunnel been scooped up and hauled off, the thieves had used chisels to gouge upward several feet, extracting possibly another ton or more. "They must have been working here for several nights."

Both men's hearts skipped a beat when an old timber above their heads let out a deep groan and dirt sifted down through cracks in the planking.

Bulldog jumped back and spoke in a hushed tone as if even

the sound of his voice could cause a cave-in. "We'd best make like a shepherd and get the flock out of here. That blast shook the bejesus out of this mountain!"

Lett agreed by following hard on Bulldog's heels as they made a dash back to the shaft.

"We're gonna have to stuff a bunch of new timbers down here," Bulldog grumbled. "All of that rock's just itchin' to fall now that it got rattled around a bunch."

A grimace crossed Lett's face. "I should have put a guard on. This is as much my fault as those highgraders," he spat. "Tomorrow start timbering back from the rotten rocks and keep lots of new timbers over your heads. The last thing I want is to get someone hurt or killed."

"You got it boss," Bulldog said, climbing on the bucket rim. "I reckon Ransom will be a tad upset when he finds out about this."

"Oh, I wouldn't say a tad," Lett said joining him. "I'll be lucky if he just shoots me."

Chapter Forty

The last whore in the town of Shakespeare stood leaning against a wooden post on the porch of her crib. She stared forlornly through the star-covered desert night toward the distant Last Chance Mine. She wore a worried brow and fretted over the safety of Lett Halsy.

A sudden gust of wind mussed her long blond hair. She was too busy struggling with unfamiliar emotions to pay it any mind.

Delight had never believed a time such as this would ever arrive. Since that terrible night of long ago when her stepfather raped her, countless men had spilled their seed inside her. Every single one of them had paid for the privilege.

A short while ago she came very close to sharing her bed with a man without being paid.

Decent women call it love, Delight thought. *Giving of yourself without demanding something in return first.*

It came as a shock when she realized she *had* been paid. Lett's company was all she looked forward to these days.

Little things like sharing dinner or listening to a popular radio show together were precious memories. Memories were something she could take with her when she left Shakespeare.

And leave she must. Soon.

Lett Halsy was a good and decent man. He deserved better than a forty-year-old whore.

From somewhere near Lookout Hill a coyote began singing its mournful tune. Suddenly a cold, wet nose poked against her bare leg, shaking Delight from her sad reverie.

"Why hello, Wesley," she said. The dog whined and rolled over on his back, happily flailing his legs in the air. "You know something's wrong don't you, boy?"

She dropped to her knees and scratched the mutt's scar-ridged belly. "I wish people could be more like dogs. Dogs don't care if you have done things to be ashamed of."

Wesley wiggled closer and licked at her foot.

"People aren't like that at all. I'm a whore and nothing will ever change the fact." She hesitated for a moment. "And they never allow you to forget."

The dog jumped to his feet, tail wagging furiously. Delight wrapped her arms around him tightly and began crying softly.

The distant coyote wailed like a lost soul.

Chapter Forty-One

"Goddamn it!" Sam Ransom fumed. "Is there anyone in the mining business who's *not* a crook?"

He slammed the registered letter from Higgenbottom and Lane onto his desk and shot it a glare that would blister paint. Those piggish peckerheads had returned his stock, less the hundred thousand shares he had given them personally, along with most of his promotional brochures.

Sam's thin black mustache twitched like a nervous caterpillar when he read the scathing letter again. "Shakespeare Mining and Development Corporation is an obvious swindle being promoted by false reports," he spat and continued. "Our brokerage firm does not wish to associate itself with a scheme to defraud the investing public." The worst part was what followed, "Since we feel it is our patriotic duty to restore trust in the stock market, copies of this letter have been mailed to the secretary of state and the Attorney General in New Mexico, Colorado, Arizona and California."

Sam was so furious he nearly bit his tongue. He tapped the last cigarette from a crumpled pack and lit it with his gold lighter. He inhaled deeply then slowly blew the smoke from his nostrils. Better.

Calm down. An angry man makes mistakes, he thought glumly. *Only losers get steamed up. Winners get even.*

He fought down the urge to take a jolt from his hip flask. It was nine-thirty in the morning. A little too early to begin drinking.

Ideas clicked into his head like the easy movements of a well-oiled machine. Sam Ransom was not a man easily defeated. He had the dazzling ability to turn adversity into victory—and money. All he needed to do was clear away the anger and think on the situation.

Before Sam crushed out the butt of his cigarette a smile washed across his pinched face.

Winfield Scott Stratton, the famous mining magnate of Cripple Creek, had made a fortune by selling his Independence Mine to a bunch of foreigners for eleven million dollars. What impressed Sam was the fact that Stratton had already gutted the mine of most of its gold before the sale. The Guppies never recovered a fraction of their investment.

My kind of man, Sam thought, his good humor returning. *If that old sot could do it, so can I.*

The more he pondered, the more he drew a remarkable parallel between himself and Stratton. His Last Chance Mine contained rich ore; five thousand dollars a ton, the manager said. All he needed to do was have those lunkheads working for him ship a thousand tons or so of high grade. Then, when he felt the ore might be running out, he would sell his lease on the mine for a million dollars and move on.

"Hell, that wouldn't even be illegal," Sam blurted out, totally amazed.

Winfield Scott Stratton was remembered as going from rags to riches in a style that would have done a Horatio Alger story proud. No one lamented the hapless Guppies who bought his mine. Thanks to the hatchet job Higgenbottom and Lane had given him, he now had an opportunity to make a vast—and legal—fortune.

The thought of making money and not having to go on the

dodge was nearly incomprehensible, yet oddly appealing. He began feeling very pleased with himself. He had gotten those prosaic, greedy stockbrokers out of his opulent mining venture without lifting a finger. He was *so* lucky to have been blessed with a keen business sense along with no irritating scruples to impede his progress.

Someone might even write a book about me like they did Stratton. A poor boy makes it big in spite of all odds.

A rude knocking on the door destroyed his delightful planning.

"Yes, what is it?" he growled loudly.

The office door swung slowly open. Lett Halsy, his half-witted mine boss, entered holding a battered fedora close to his chest like it was a sick baby. Something was obviously troubling him.

The fool has spent all that money I gave him. He will either learn to live with what I dole out or I'll hire a manager who can.

Sam glared at him and said sharply, "I told you, no more money until some ore is shipped!"

"I'm not here about money, Mister Ransom," Halsy replied. "There's been trouble at the mine."

"Well, speak up! I'm a busy man."

Lett Halsy did as he was instructed. In a few short moments Ransom was angry enough to bite nails. "Goddam thieves," he pounded on his desk and screamed. "I had that guardhouse built to keep this from happening. You idiot! I trusted you to keep my ore safe and you failed me."

"Yes, sir," Halsy agreed humbly. "I couldn't blame you for firing me on the spot. Only sir, there never was any money allotted to hire a guard. It's hard for me to believe the gall these men had. They even used your hoist to haul ore out of the shaft."

"You should have been more alert."

"I'm very sorry. As we speak, I have the men timbering up

the damage the ore thieves caused. With any luck we'll be pulling out high grade in a few days."

"Thieves can remove tons of ore in the dark of night, but it takes a crew of my men a whole week to start taking out ore. What are you pulling, Halsy? I'll bet you and your men are stealing ore, too."

Lett's teeth clinched and his eyes narrowed. "If you truly believe that, Ransom, perhaps you had better hire a new crew of men and another manager."

Sam sported a gold tooth, courtesy of a man who wore an expression like the one that had just washed across Lett Halsy's face. "That won't be necessary," he said in a more conciliatory tone, hoping to stifle the big man's anger. "However, I *will* be keeping a very close eye on operations from here on."

Halsy swallowed hard and took a moment to answer. "We could use another hand up there. If those old workings aren't timbered solid, the whole mine might cave. The highgraders only took what was easy to get. We have to plan on being there a long time. I don't want to get anyone hurt needlessly."

Sam Ransom leaned back in his swivel chair and locked his fingers behind his head. "I don't intend to do menial labor, if that's what you're alluding to. We have to start selling ore however, or the whole venture will fold. If that was to happen, your pathetic little saloon and the entire town of Shakespeare will dry up and blow away."

"I'll do my best."

"Losers always whine they did their best. It's *your* job to drive those pantywaist miners and ship some goddamn ore. Timbers be damned. Get out of here and go do what I pay you for. Remember, everyone is depending on you. If the Last Chance fails, people will know who to blame because they're out of work. And it sure as hell won't be me."

Sam breathed a sigh of relief when the muscular mine boss

left his presence. It was too bad he'd lost a ton or two of ore. He had to admire the bravery of the men who had seen an opportunity and seized it. If he could hire good help like that, he would. Halsy was far too concerned about safety to get the job done. Once the mine was operating, he would fire him and hire a new manager more attuned to his way of thinking.

Nothing has changed. I'm still going to be a very rich man.

Sam rummaged in his desk for another pack of cigarettes. Not finding any he decided he needed to take a drive. Shakespeare was not very far. He could pick up some cigarettes and go there. Soon he could have better to pick from than Delight. For now, just like Lett Halsy, he would make do with what was available.

Bulldog came to greet Lett when he piled out of his car, a wry smile on his wrinkled face. "Well, boss, I don't see where you're leakin' from any bullet holes. I guess Ransom must have been in a good mood."

Lett widened his eyes innocently. "He's a regular pussycat." Turning serious he asked, "How's the timber work going?"

Tipping his hat to keep away the sun, Bulldog looked toward the shaft. "I've got Clanton and Joel Kay down there now. We're mucking out all the loose rock those highgraders blasted out so we can start timbering. I wish like hell that ground would quit moving around above us. It's spooky as hell down there."

"And dangerous as shaving a wildcat's butt with a dull razor. I'm going to suit up and go help them. Clanton's an experienced hand, but Joel's green when it comes to bad ground. I'll take over for him. Joel can start cutting timbers to length and helping get them in the bucket."

"You got it, boss," Bulldog replied.

Lett spun to go toward the mine office. He froze in his tracks. From somewhere in the depths beneath his feet a low rumble began building like the approach of a distant thunderstorm. *"Oh my God!"* Bulldog yelled in near panic.

CHAPTER FORTY-TWO

The earth shuddered beneath their feet like the flesh of some giant, mortally wounded beast. The ominous deep rumbling sound grew steadily louder.

Bulldog had been through a tornado once long ago when he was just a kid growing up in Texas. Briefly, he thought it strange that a collapsing mountain growled the same deadly tune as a prairie twister.

"Holy shit!" Lett cried out, his face contorted with helplessness. "We have to get those men out of there."

Bulldog spun and joined Lett in a headlong dash to the shaft. Boulders, dislodged by the undulating tremors began rolling down the cactus-studded hill behind the mine site. When they were only a few feet from the opening, the bell cord that snaked into the depths whipped with a desperate jerk from below. A single bell rang clear against the building thunder. Arnold Epp, who was operating the hoist knew the signal well; raise the bucket quickly. He threw the throttle on the hoist engine wide open.

"I think they might have made it," Bulldog gasped hopefully.

The old Model-T motor that powered the hoist belched a cloud of blue oil smoke skyward from its exhaust pipe, then sputtered and died.

From inside the hoist house Arnold Epp cursed loudly and wildly spun the crank, trying in vain to restart the worn engine.

"My God, the head frame's going to fall!" Lett yelled.

Bulldog jumped back and focused on the newly built thirty-foot-high wooden tower. It swayed drunkenly against a cloudless blue sky. "Goddamn it, Epp," he bellowed, "get that friggin' hoist running!"

It was a futile order.

Untold thousands of tons of fractured rock shifted as the wounded mountain continued to heal the scars man had inflicted upon it.

Puny timbers snapped like matchsticks against nature's relentless onslaught.

A sharp crack split the air like a rifle shot when the bucket holding the two miners was driven deeper down the shaft, severing the spindly cable that held it.

The earth rolled like an ocean wave. Arnold Epp sprang from the hoist house joining Lett and Bulldog to watch in horror as the gallows frame sank downward into the spreading maw of the shaft with a deadly gasp.

Only a few feet of the long, heavy tower was left in sight when the rumbling and shaking stopped. A sudden quiet lay heavy on the devastated hillside.

It was over. One final rock rolled with a thud into the collapsed pit where the Last Chance Mine shaft had been, putting a harsh period to the moment.

The three miners stood together silently staring at the caved shaft. They had spent too many years doing the dangerous work of underground mining to hold any false hopes.

Jake Clanton and Joel Kay were dead.

No one could have lived through such a massive cave-in. Even in the slight—very slight—chance they had made it safely from the bucket before the cable broke and found refuge in some chamber it would be of no use. Lack of oxygen would suffocate them within hours. Digging a new shaft ten stories deep in badly shattered rock could take months.

Beside the hoist house the little fan motor continued chugging away, spinning the air blower like an empty promise. The metal ventube had been jerked apart and crushed when the shaft caved. Lett walked sluggishly to the machine and shut it off.

In the oppressive silence that now pervaded the hillside, a gambles quail ventured a cautious song from a nearby clump of greasewood. Another chirped an answer. The sounds of nature were returning to the rolling hills behind the town of Shakespeare.

It was left for the humans to deal with the enormity of what had transpired.

"Mother of God," Lett said when he returned to his anguished companions.

"I didn't mean to stall the hoist motor," Arnold Epp said, keeping his moist eyes focused to the ground. "But I threw the throttle open too fast and went and killed 'em."

Lett placed a comforting hand on Epp's shoulder. "You never had time to get that bucket to the surface before the shaft caved. It's not your fault. If anyone is to blame, it's me. I should have been down there timbering—"

"And those ore thieves shouldn't have set off dynamite either," Bulldog interjected. "And Sam Ransom shouldn't have told everybody and their dog about that high grade. And God shouldn't have invented gravity. Lett, what happened here was an accident. We all knew that ground was rotten as a politician's promise. It could have been any one of us that got buried."

Lett Halsy sighed and pinched his lips. A motion from the blue sky above caught his attention. It was a black turkey buzzard riding easily on warm currents of rising air. Quickly he shifted his gaze down the hillside toward the town of Shakespeare. His thoughts flashed back to a snow-covered Colorado Mountain and the last time he had felt so powerless, so utterly destroyed. *Then it was a disease that killed my wife and son. Something a man can't foresee or hold back. This time it's all my fault. I sent those men down there, knowing full well how dangerous that mine was.*

"What are we gonna do, boss?" Epp asked softly.

Bulldog spoke up. "Not much a man *can* do. Reckon we'll need to notify the sheriff and the state mine inspector." He hesitated a moment. "Then Sam Ransom's got to be told."

"That's my job," Lett said. "You men had better climb in the car and go with me. There will be lots of questions asked. Ransom won't be easy and the mine inspector will surely put the blame square on me. I can handle that. Then I've got to go do the worst part of all."

"What's that boss?" Epp asked innocently.

Bulldog's wrinkled face contorted into a mask of pain.

Lett swallowed hard and said, "I have to go to Shakespeare and tell a little blond girl and her four-year-old brother the only parent they had in this world isn't coming home—ever."

A tear trickled down Bulldog's anguished cheek when he climbed into Lett's car. During the drive to Lordsburg, the burly miners with calloused hands rode together in stone silence.

CHAPTER FORTY-THREE

Delight read the anguish in Lett's steely gray eyes before he could utter a word and knew something was terribly wrong.

"What happened?" she asked, standing wide-eyed in the doorway to her crib, pulling a pink bathrobe tight about her body.

It took Lett a moment to find his voice. "The mine caved," he finally said. "Jake Clanton and Joel Kay were buried. Delight, that whole damn mountain just fell in. The worst part was all we could do was stand there, helpless, and watch it happen."

"My God!" she gasped.

"Halsy, is that you?" the familiar harsh voice of Sam Ransom boomed from the depths of the little building. There was a squeaking of bedsprings and the sound of feet hitting the floor.

Delight's jaw slackened from shock and embarrassment.

Lett had been so distraught and intent of purpose that he failed to notice Sam's pretentious Packard parked in front of the Roxy Jay. He wanted Delight's gentle help when he broke the sad news to little Melissa and Avery. Also, he desperately needed a friend to talk to. Over the past several weeks the blond lady who prepared his dinner every night had become his best friend. Now, the reality of what she did for a living came crashing down on him with the weight of a shattered mountain.

"Oh, Lett, I'm so sorry," Delight said before Sam Ransom brusquely swept her aside.

Sam hooked his belt buckle and faced Lett with a snarling

look of seething hatred. "Just what the hell did you mean about my mine caving in?"

Lett Halsy told him.

Everything.

Sam Ransom's cheeks grew tight and turned red as a fiery desert sunset.

Delight pressed the back of her hand to her mouth and began sobbing.

"Shut up that infernal whining, whore!" Ransom barked at her. "Here I've lost a goddamn fortune and all you can do is cry like a baby for the brainless fools who let this happen to me." He glanced at Lett. "Halsy, you and your ore-stealing buddies are all fired! I'm going to have my lawyer sue you. When I'm finished with you everything you own, including the Roxy Jay, will be mine."

Ransom's fists knotted in blind rage. In his fury he had to lash out at someone. His beady eyes darted from Lett to Delight like a rattlesnake trying to decide where to strike. True to form, he chose the weakest. Quickly he grabbed Delight's trembling shoulder and spun her to face his clenched hand. Before Sam Ransom could launch his blow a heavy arm coiled tightly around his neck and lifted him from the wooden floor.

Unable to break the iron grip that constricted him so strongly he couldn't breathe, all Sam could do was kick futilely when Lett dragged him to the edge of the porch.

Ransom's face grew increasingly purple while Lett surveyed the surroundings. His gaze finally settled on a spindly cholla cactus plant a few feet away. Easily as an angry child tosses a rag doll, Lett sent a shirtless Sam Ransom flying to land square on the cactus, smashing it flat.

Screams, curses and threats gave way to sobs of pain. Sam rose slowly to his hands and knees, eyes wide like a cornered animal. With a loud howl of pain he bolted upright and ran past

Bulldog who had watched the proceedings through the open back door of the saloon.

Bulldog sauntered over to Lett, hands stuffed into his pockets, a concerned look on his furrowed face. "Wisht you hadn't done that, boss," he said nonchalantly.

"Son of a bitch had it coming," Lett boomed, his rage building. "He was gonna hit Delight."

"I didn't mean about you tossing him into a cactus. What I meant was, there's a real nice big patch out back with longer stickers on 'em that woulda' worked better."

In spite of the terrible events that had transpired, Lett couldn't keep a thin smile from crossing his lips. "Next time I see that little shrimp, I'll haul him around there and toss him in. Any man who'll hit a lady deserves the best effort I can give them."

"Hope I'm here to see it, boss," Bulldog said.

Lett sighed. "Reckon you can stop calling me boss. We're all fired."

Bulldog shrugged. "I was looking for a job when I found this one."

A delicate hand with painted, manicured nails softly touched Lett's face. Delight's heady perfume glided by on the hot desert breeze soothing his boiling anger.

"Thank you," she said. "No one has ever stepped in to protect me like that before."

Lett's knotted muscles began to relax. "There's no excuse for a man to ever hit a woman," he said. "Ransom might have more money than Rockefeller, but it's a sure bet no one ever taught him any manners."

"I'd venture he's a little more educated now than he was a few minutes ago," Bulldog quipped, before heading back inside the Roxy Jay.

They were alone now. Delight stepped around, looked up

into Lett's stolid face and asked, "Has anyone told those little kids about their dad?"

Through gritted teeth Lett replied, "No, and that's something I need to do real quick. I'd hate it if some stranger told them first. I was the man in charge. If I hadn't felt sorry for Joel and made a job for him at the mine he'd still be alive. It's my fault Avery and Melissa are orphans. You know Joel's wife died. He told me he didn't have any other relation. I simply don't know what to do about those poor kids."

"I'll take care of them, at least for a while," Delight said with a decisiveness and strength that took Lett aback. "They can stay with me."

He couldn't keep from shooting a glance at the red light over Delight's door. While the bulb was turned off, a flash of sunlight caused the globe to shimmer like a fire that could never be completely extinguished.

Delight knew what Lett was thinking. "Just a minute," she said heading inside the crib. She returned carrying the heavy cast-iron skillet in which she fried succulent chicken every Sunday. One quick swing and the red light shattered into hundreds of pieces. She placed her free hand on her hip and surveyed the damage with obvious satisfaction. "There, that should do it. Lett, if you'll sweep this mess up while I get dressed, we can do what we have to do."

Lett just stared at her, dumbstruck.

Delight hesitated for a second then said, "Don't worry, you've gotten fired and I've quit being a whore. Things can only get better from here."

Taking care to make sure all of the shards of glass were cleaned up, Lett Halsy desperately hoped Delight was right about things getting better. The hardest task he ever faced was only moments away.

CHAPTER FORTY-FOUR

Joel Kay, like many others, had scrounged the desert for building materials. From weathered planks found at abandoned mines, cardboard boxes beaten and driven by the ever-present wind and limbs of greasewood no larger than a man's thumb, he had constructed a habitable structure.

The old car that had carried Joel and his children westward formed the backdrop for their crude defense against the relentless sun. Two of the tires were flat and Lett figured the gas tank was long dry. Joel had been a frugal man, preferring to walk to Lordsburg for supplies rather than splurge on expensive gasoline. Briefly, Lett wondered how the makeshift hut would fare in a rainstorm, should such an event occur. Since he had come to Shakespeare not a single drop of moisture had fallen on the parched earth.

The aroma of simmering stew greeted Lett and Delight when they stepped inside. Melissa had a small fire burning in a tin sheepherder's stove. On its metal top an open pot bubbled gently. The little blond girl was chopping onions and carrots to add to the mix. Avery was curled up on the car's backseat, lost in sleep.

"Why hello, Mister Hoolsey," Melissa said, obviously surprised to see them. "And you too, ma'am. Our daddy's not here. He's at the mine working. When he comes home tonight I'm going to surprise him with the best dinner ever. I'm even going to make cornbread. At least I'm going to try. This stove's got no oven, but daddy makes biscuits in a cast-iron kettle and they turn out good. I don't see why cornbread won't cook in it."

Lett dropped to his knees. The diminutive girl still had to look up to meet his eyes. "Honey," Lett said softly, "do you remember when the angels came and took your mommy to heaven?"

Delight kneeled beside Lett and placed a comforting hand on his shoulder.

The little girl's face took on the emotionless countenance of stone. "My daddy's dead," she said simply, her words ripping into the adults' hearts far worse than tears ever could.

Delight reached and grasped Melissa's hand. "Sweetheart," she said, "we are all so sorry."

"Folks said they was sorry when mommy died, too." Melissa's flint eyes focused on her sleeping brother. "I cried back then, but now that I'm older I can't do that. Avery has to have someone to take care of him. Daddy told me to be strong."

A huge knot had formed in Lett's throat. He knew if he tried to speak all he would do was sob.

Delight sensed this and said, "Honey, it's all right to show how you feel. Sometimes when people have a good cry, they feel better."

"I know," Melissa said in a flat voice. "Avery will bawl his eyes out when he's told."

Delight swallowed hard. "I would like it if you and your brother came and stayed with me for a while."

Melissa pulled her hand from Delight's, walked over to the bubbling stew and began stirring. "Okay, we've stayed with lots of diff'rent folks. Can I take the stew with us? Avery really likes stew."

Looking at Melissa through stinging wetness, Delight remembered back to long ago when she had been a devastated little girl named Sara who never cried a tear when her world fell apart. *You've had to grow up way beyond your years. I just hope you haven't seen so much hurt and pain you destroy your life like I did.*

Delight put a sudden firmness to her demeanor. "Mister Halsy and I will help you bring along everything you want."

Struggling with leaden feet Lett carefully scooped Avery into his arms, carried the still-sleeping boy and laid him in the back-seat of his Chevrolet. He tilted his hat to keep the glaring desert sun at bay and watched in sadness while Delight and Melissa scoured the ramshackle hut, packing everything of value. Through a black fog of anguish, Lett wondered deeply what wonderful well of strength a woman could draw on to make it through trying times like these. And he thanked God that they could.

Chapter Forty-Five

Only two days after the disastrous cave-in, Shakespeare began to resemble the ghost town it was destined to become. With hopes of employment at Sam Ransom's mine dashed, nearly everyone loaded their meager possessions and returned to the heartbreakingly familiar search for work.

It was like chasing a will-o'-the-wisp.

California with its golden rumors drew the majority like a moth to a flame. Most were to find greater ravages of poverty and oppression there. Conditions in the larger cities were desperate. Women pawned even their wedding rings to buy food. When that money was gone, especially if they were burdened with children, they resorted to begging. Humiliation lost its meaning. Hunger and suicide were commonplace.

And the Great American Depression had yet to reach its most crushing depths.

At the site of the ruined Last Chance Mine, a sad-eyed old Mexican priest with a sun-wrinkled face that resembled time-worn parchment led a funeral service for the two miners who would remain interred there forever.

The padre spoke the ritual in Latin and contemplated the assemblage with pensive eyes that had seen far too much suffering.

"I can't understand a word he's sayin'," Arnold Epp complained quietly. "Wisht he could talk American."

Bulldog glared at him. "Reckon as long as the good Lord

understands, that's enough."

Epp thought for a moment. "Yeah," he agreed, "I'd reckon."

Melissa and Avery stood on each side of Delight. The boy close and quiet, grasping her hand. Melissa kept a discreet distance. She petted Wesley on the head and watched the proceedings without betraying any emotion. Since the children had come to live with Delight, the dog had been their constant companion.

Lett Halsy held his hat close to his chest and wondered if the burning in his throat would ever heal. Yesterday, Bulldog, Epp and he had chiseled the names and date of death of their fallen comrades into long plank boards. They had nailed them to each of the twin wooden stubs of the sunken head frame, all that remained above ground at the Last Chance shaft. With the old padre standing in the forefront, Lett pondered how much the markers resembled crosses.

Soon the service was concluded. The old priest and several Mexican men and women who had accompanied him donned their hats and started walking back to Lordsburg.

"Hope the Devil's in a forgiving mood and ain't too rough on Jake Clanton," Bulldog said. "He always tried to do what was right. Joel wasn't a miner long enough to fret over. He's likely already got a harp."

Lett started to say something when McTavish interrupted by slamming the door on his Model T. The men watched in wide-eyed awe when the chubby Scotsman hoisted a set of bagpipes over his shoulder and headed toward them.

Bulldog's mouth dropped and he mumbled. "If he actually plays that thing we won't need to worry about the Devil. One hair-raising screech and ole Scratch'll pee down his leg and move to Canada."

"Joel was a good man and one of my countrymen," McTavish commented gravely as he tramped by. The fat man went to where the priest had stood and turned to face the remaining assemblage. He took off his fedora and stuffed it inside his khaki shirt. The bartender took a long, deep breath then bent his head down to the mouthpiece and inflated the instrument with a wail.

"Son of a gun's actually gonna do it," Bulldog said. "Leastways he ain't wearing one of them funny lookin' dresses."

"They're called a kilt," Lett corrected.

"He's got one of them things," Arnold Epp said. "He just can't fit into it nowadays."

"That's no surprise," Bulldog said. "He'd have a hard time finding a tent his size."

Lett thought briefly he should mention they were at a funeral. He realized, however, that people handle grief in different ways. Bulldog and Epp were grieved as he was. The two men buried beneath the rocky earth had been friends to them all.

The cactus-covered hillside reverberated with a grating screech that reminded Bulldog of chalk squeaking across a blackboard. Every eye turned toward McTavish. He sucked in one more deep breath and continued. To everyone's amazement the bagpipes' faltering howl turned hauntingly symphonic.

"Reckon he knows how to play that thing after all," Bulldog said with obvious wonderment.

"Sounds like a lost soul," Lett murmured.

As the anguished trilling continued, the old padre and his flock returned to listen in awe and reverence to the gripping music.

The burning in Lett's throat reached a new plane. He swallowed hard but all he accomplished was to utter a sob. From the corner of his eye, he noticed Bulldog's lower lip quivered like the leaf of an aspen tree.

The sad lamentation of McTavish's bagpipes was more heartbreaking than many could endure. A few of the ladies began weeping openly.

Delight kept a stony countenance until Melissa turned to her and said flatly, "Daddy would have liked this."

Delight sobbed. "Oh darling, I'm sure he does." She reached out and drew the little girl, who remained stoic as a statue, to her. Wesley followed. The dog sat on his haunches at her feet and stuck his nose skyward. To her horror, Delight thought Wesley would begin howling. Instead the dog simply whimpered and licked Melissa's face.

By the time McTavish folded his bagpipes, the only dry eyes on the desolate mountainside above Shakespeare were Melissa's, whose hurt was too deep for mere tears to express.

CHAPTER FORTY-SIX

Things had not gone well for Sam Ransom since that ungrateful wretch, Lett Halsy, tossed him into the cactus. Even putting on a shirt was torture. Sam regretted his generosity in paying Len Miller five dollars to pluck out the stickers. The skinny gas station attendant had, on purpose no doubt, broken off several spines leaving them to painfully fester their way out of his skin.

He was furious how many people actually felt sorry for those idiots who had buried themselves at his mine. *Hell, they were too busy stealing ore to put in timbers,* he thought.

Isn't it too bad about those poor kids being left orphans? It seemed everyone he met had asked the same question. Sam was a chameleon. He looked appropriately broken-hearted, agreed with them, then left their annoying presence as quickly as possible. The fate of those little crumbsnatchers was no concern of his. If the dolt they called Father had done his job properly, the mine wouldn't have caved and most importantly, Sam would be sitting pretty today, on his way to being a respected and wealthy man.

Unfortunately, the only high-grade ore Sam ever received from his Last Chance strike was a single lump he kept on his desk. He got a good look at it every time he glanced over at the gray-haired, hatchet-faced, idiotic excuse for a mining engineer, who sat contentedly puffing on a pipe while telling him more than he cared to know about rock.

When the pain from his unexpected encounter with a cactus

lessened, Sam realized he would require the services of an expert to recover his buried fortune. Fred Johnson was a reputable engineer who maintained an office in Silver City. The very afternoon of the disaster Sam climbed stiffly into his Packard and endured the jolting drive. The engineer charged five hundred dollars to make a professional assessment of the cost of reopening the Last Chance.

Johnson and his assistant had spent the next day poking about the mine.

Now, the report was completed. The engineer seemed gratified to deliver every minute detail of his findings using some of the largest words in the dictionary.

"I'm certain with your background in mining," Fred Johnson took a long puff, blew the smoke skyward and continued, "you know that we are dealing with an ore zone along an unstable and badly fractured fault plane."

"Yes, yes," Sam growled, impatience showing, "what I *want* to know is how much it will cost to mine my ore; the high grade?"

Johnson's eyes squinted into a frown. "With the massive shearing that has occurred there is no option other than to sink a new shaft. I would think to a depth of not over one hundred and fifty feet. The zone of supergene enrichment should extend to that depth—"

Sam interrupted. "The *cost*, man. What will all of this cost me?"

The engineer slid a stack of neatly typed papers across to Sam and shot him a glare that would peel paint. "Everything you ask is in my report. Most *professionals* would wish to know how I arrived at my conclusions."

Sam reared back in his chair and looked down his nose. "You are obviously not used to dealing with busy executives who have great demands on their time."

Johnson rolled his eyes around the office. He noted a telephone that never rang, an open copy of the novel *The Maltese Falcon* by Dashiell Hammett lying to one side of Ransom's massive desk. The wastebasket contained only an empty bottle of expensive whiskey. "I can't say I have ever been retained by a man with such pressures as yours. No, sir, I really have not."

It rankled Sam when anyone patronized him. "I paid you good money for your services. When I hire someone who is a *supposed* expert, I expect results." He thumbed through the engineer's report. "Perhaps you're unable to give me the figures I require."

A sinister smile washed across Fred Johnson's face. He knew now Sam Ransom didn't know a pick from a shovel. The little man was nothing but a greedy stock promoter. Two men had been killed at the Last Chance. Not one word of regret had passed Ransom's pinched lips. He would enjoy the rest of this. "Mister Ransom, sir. On page three I describe in detail the terrible conditions that must be overcome. A new shaft and tunnel work is estimated at fifty thousand dollars."

Sam's eyes widened and a slight tremble came to his fingers. "Fifty thousand dollars!"

"At the very least. There should always be a reserve of at least twenty percent to cover unforseen expenses."

"That's sixty thousand."

"Your arithmetic is impeccable."

"You fool, I don't have that much money."

The engineer grinned with satisfaction. "I'm not your banker or a priest. You paid for a professional report and now you have one. What you do with the information is not my affair."

"But, what about my high-grade ore?" Sam whined.

Fred Johnson slid his chair back, stood up and donned his hat. "My best guess is it will stay put, right alongside those two poor men who were killed trying to mine it for you. Good day, sir."

Once the engineer departed, Sam's anger boiled. He grabbed for the empty whiskey bottle, planning to smash it against the door. He howled when sharp pains from dozens of imbedded cactus spines flashed across his back.

"Damn it all!" Sam swore. "And damn Shakespeare and damn Lordsburg and damn the mining business and damn the whole state of New Mexico."

He forced himself to calm down. There was a full bottle of whiskey in his desk drawer. Carefully he bent his whole body over and retrieved it. He drank deeply of the fiery contents. A welcome and warm feeling flooded his entire being. Another drink and he began putting things into perspective.

He had made the mistake of delving into a field that was already overpopulated with thieves and liars. It wasn't really his fault. The men he had run across were simply very good at what they did. A little *more* skilled than he was, it seemed.

Cut your losses and run. Good advice from an old cellmate. Sam didn't have to count his money to know there were thirty-four thousand dollars in his leather satchel. All in cash. A decent stake for a smart man to parlay into a fortune. The mining business be damned.

Florida real estate was the hottest thing going. It would be a simple matter to buy up a thousand or so acres of worthless swampland, chop it into acre tracts, then sell them to unsuspecting Guppies as choice waterfront properties.

At least I won't have to lie about the water part, he thought with a grin.

It was a simple matter for a sharp fellow like him to make a bundle. All it took were guts and imagination, both of which Sam Ransom was amply blessed with.

There were a few things at the mine he could sell. Perhaps

that Jennings fellow would buy them back—at a huge discount of course. Sam didn't mind. He had no further use for mining machinery. If he could get enough money from the stuff to cover his expenses to Florida he would be happy.

Sam shook loose a cigarette and lit it. He admired his heavy gold lighter with a satisfied smile. Through the front window the ever-present wind chased tumbleweeds down Main Street. Soon, very soon he could leave this forsaken place. Florida with its tropical climate and dark-skinned dolls beckoned with a siren's song. The Last Chance Mine and the town of Shakespeare were dead. A man in his profession needed to move on occasionally.

The occasion had just arisen.

CHAPTER FORTY-SEVEN

When he returned to the Roxy Jay after the deeply moving ceremony, Lett was so depressed he felt the need to make a respectable attempt at getting drunk. Only the fact that the saloon was nearly out of booze foiled his efforts.

Lett had thrown open the bar for everyone. The meager stock on hand didn't last long. The last keg of beer in Shakespeare blew empty on his second mug.

McTavish cooked up two huge pots of pinto beans mixed with a few onions that had seen better days. Then he found a case of canned sauerkraut which he opened and dumped into the beans.

"Dag blast it, McTavish," Bulldog fumed. "If you could cook as good as you play them pipes, Howard would still be walking around. No one with sense enough to pour sand outta their boots tosses kraut into beans for Christ sakes."

"You might know good music when you hear it, but you sure don't know good cooking," McTavish replied with a miffed glare. "One day I'll be a famous chef in some fancy hotel where folks appreciate imagination when it comes to preparing food."

Bulldog lowered his head, squinted at the simmering pots and shook his head. "Thanks for the warning. When I get rich and stay in some fancy joint, I'll make sure to ask who's doing the cookin' before ordering anything."

McTavish sighed and shifted his attentions to Lett. He chewed worriedly on his lower lip for a moment, working up courage to speak. "Boss, if it's all right with you I reckon I'll be leaving tomorrow."

Lett answered, "Can't say as I blame you, since you weren't getting paid anyway. Do you know where you're heading to?"

The pudgy bartender grinned. "San Francisco. Where else have they got better restaurants?" He scooped up a big bowl of beans and kraut and set it in front of Bulldog. "Folks *there* know good food when they see it."

"Crazy folks and birds of a feather flock together," Bulldog grumbled before spooning a steaming bite. A look of disbelief crossed his wrinkled face. "You know this ain't half bad," he said. McTavish's satisfied grin broadened.

Bulldog polished off the bowl. Then, to McTavish's gratification, asked for another.

Arnold Epp poked listlessly at his food, his brow furrowed with worry. Finally he looked sadly down the long bar at Lett who had just drained the last drop of foamy beer from his glass.

"Reckon we oughtta tell him now?" Epp asked Bulldog.

"I suppose we should."

Bulldog laid his spoon on a napkin and spun from his barstool. Epp joined him as he approached Lett.

"We hate to tell you this, Lett," Bulldog said. "You've been real good to us. But a man's gotta go to where he can make a living. This Depression don't give one much choice. Epp and me heard there's some good mining jobs up in Butte, Montana. Guess we'll be heading that way in the morning."

"What are *you* planning to do?" Epp asked. "There's not much reason to stay around here."

Lett's thoughts flashed to Delight and the two children. He could hold no illusions. His friends were leaving for good reason. Shakespeare was dead as the famous bard who was its namesake. He was simply attending another wake.

"I wish you guys the best and I don't blame you for leaving

here," Lett said. The back door was open and he looked long-ingly through it towards Delight's shack. "I wish I had some decent plan, but I don't. Others are depending on me."

"She's one handsome woman," Bulldog said.

"And a lady," Epp quickly added.

Lett's gray eyes twinkled. "I know," he said, then his face grew serious. "What I *don't* know is if she could abide a broken-down, out-of-work miner who has two little kids to look after."

"Only way to find out is to ask her," Bulldog said firmly.

"I will—in good time," Lett replied.

Epp ventured a hand on Lett's shoulder. "Sometimes a man don't have all the time he wants to do things in. A pretty lady like Delight might be stronger and lonelier than you suspect."

Lett stared into his empty mug. "You men have a safe trip," he said.

Long, dark shadows draped the desert. For the first time since he had inherited the saloon, Lett was alone in the Roxy Jay. In the deep, strange silence his emotions played tag with reality.

More than anything, he wanted to rush to Delight, wrap his arms around her and tell her he loved her deeply. She was with Melissa and Avery, just a hundred feet from where he stood. The little shack would smell of fresh-cooked food and sweet perfume. Like a home.

You killed those kids' dad surely as if you'd kicked those timbers loose yourself.

And Delight. She needed a man with money. Something he could not offer. When the time came for him to leave Shake-speare he would be as broke as the hundreds of poor souls who had already packed up and headed off.

Lett had absolutely no idea where to go. Perhaps there really was work in Montana, but he doubted that. Rumors of jobs were far more plentiful than fact. He simply could not drag

Delight and those poor kids along while he spent his last few dollars pursuing some distant, elusive hope.

On leaden feet, Lett walked slowly behind the bar and cranked open the huge brass cash register. He scooped up a few nickels planning to dump them into the player piano, thinking perhaps the tinkling, happy music would bolster his sagging spirits. Then he saw the keys to the cabinet where Sam Ransom's whiskey supply was kept.

The single bottle inside was nearly full. It was Canadian whiskey, smooth and silky. When the warm amber currents coursed through his being, Lett felt more alone and confused than ever.

He took one more hefty pull, tucked the bottle into his pant pocket, then walked through the swinging front doors onto the dirt main street of Shakespeare. A small dust devil snaked its way through the deserted town. In the twilight he could see Bulldog and Epp checking over their car for the long trip to Montana. He wanted no company, so he headed east, skirting the hill.

It was dark and the whiskey bottle nearly empty when he came to the cemetery. He found his brother's tombstone bathed in yellow moonlight. Lett ran his calloused fingers through the marble grooves of Howard's name.

"Big brother, when we were kids growing up you were always there to tell me what to do. God, how I wish you were still here."

A red rage roared into Lett's soul like a dam had burst. Whiskey had supplied the lubricant for his pent-up anger and frustration to slide from its resting place.

Lett sprung upright on legs of steel. He jerked the bottle from his pocket and finished the contents with one gulp. Shaking like a man with palsy he looked skyward into the canopy of twinkling stars.

"*You just don't care, do you God?*" he shouted, nearly screaming.

Lett glared into the heavens as if awaiting an answer. None came.

"People are hurting down here." His tirade continued. "We cry for help and you do nothing."

He felt the heft of the empty whiskey bottle in his hand and flung it skyward. "Wake up, will you. Are you asleep or what!"

Lett bent over with a stumble, picked up some rocks and started throwing them at God. First one rock then another sailed toward the firmament. He scooped up another armload and ran yelling at God, tossing stones as fast as he could.

"I hope this gets your attention," he shouted just before a sharp blow alongside his head drove him to his knees. Warm, red blood trickled down the side of his face. One of the falling rocks had struck him.

A firm voice said from over his shoulder, "I've seen some sights in my time, but I never saw God hit a man in the head with a rock before."

Lett bolted upright. He had thought he was alone. He spun to look into the grinning face of Otis Tate.

"I got mad," Lett said simply.

"I can see that. A lot of people get mad at God, but darn few get into a rock fight with him. You shouldn't be surprised you lost. He *is* the Almighty."

In spite of himself, Lett couldn't restrain a chuckle. "I guess I must have looked plenty stupid."

"I'd say you managed that really well."

"How did you find me?"

"I'm a lawyer. Lawyers know everything. Actually I was looking for you. McTavish said he saw you and a whiskey bottle heading east. Somehow I figured you would wind up here. Most folks when they're hurting, either go to a church or the cemetery."

"I'm gonna miss that Scotsman. He's got sharper eyes than a hawk and he's a worse gossip than a washwoman."

Otis took a handkerchief from his pocket and handed it to Lett. "You've got a nasty cut."

"Reckon I had it coming. What did you want to see me about?"

"Those two kids who lost their father."

Suddenly Lett felt more sober than he cared to be. "I don't know how, but I'll take care of them."

"What happened was not your fault. Sam Ransom is to blame. He killed those men and the town of Shakespeare. Him and no one else. You simply followed orders."

Lett looked at the lawyer with sad moist eyes and said nothing.

"It's only right that Ransom, or his money, help those poor kids," Otis said. "I've been gouging that little weasel ever since he started running his schemes here." He held out a fat, white envelope. "Take it. There is three thousand dollars inside. I'll trust you to do right by them."

"My God," Lett said. His hand shook when he accepted the money.

"Maybe God's not asleep after all."

"I—I just don't know what to say."

"Don't say anything. It's not *all* of the money I skinned from Ransom. After all, I am a lawyer."

The envelope fell from Lett's trembling grasp. When he picked it up, Otis Tate had melted into the night.

Alone once again, Lett held the money close, like a drowning man clutching a life preserver. He dropped to his knees and cried bitter tears while blood ran from his forehead and dropped, glistening in the moonlight onto parched earth.

From the shadow of a large tombstone Otis Tate watched and thought, *Why is it that only the good ones feel pain?*

The lawyer turned and picked his way carefully around patches of cactus to the road. Then he trudged from the hills through the hot desert night to his lonely house on the outskirts of Lordsburg.

CHAPTER FORTY-EIGHT

Death woke Lett the next morning, banging on his open door. At least it looked like death—a cadaverous, bony figure wearing a black suit and hat to match.

Lett didn't feel like putting up an argument. Canadian whiskey might be smooth going down, but in the harsh light of day he felt like a stick of dynamite had exploded between his ears. His head throbbed with pain so badly he would welcome a trip to the netherworld.

He staggered to his feet and went to face the specter head-on.

"You looking for a day's work?" the death figure asked. "I'll pay you ten bucks."

Lett realized death probably wouldn't be offering him a job and blinked his eyes into focus. Death molded itself into Dave Jennings, the machinery peddler. The black suit was actually a pair of overalls that were so plastered with grease and grime, Lett figured the skinny man had to climb out of them when he went to bed at night.

"Yeah," Lett answered far more vigorously than he felt. "What do you want done?"

"I bought back all of the machinery that Ransom feller bought from me. He seemed mighty anxious to sell. Most folks like to make a little game out of it. He just took my first offer." A frown crossed Jennings' face. "That son of a bitch did run the hell outta my fan. I'll bet it's plumb worn out."

Aspirin was more of a concern to Lett than a fan engine. "No, we took good care of it. The thing runs as good now as it did when you sold it to us."

Jennings spat a stream of brown chewing tobacco at a lizard. "Wish you'd overhauled it," he grumbled.

Lett rolled his eyes to the red glow in the east. He was not surprised to find even that caused pain. If there had been a rooster in Shakespeare, Jennings would have woke it up. Lett figured it was around five o'clock in the morning.

Lett said, "I'd like to get some breakfast first. Would it be all right if I met you at the mine in say an hour?" The very mention of food sent his stomach rolling like a small boat on a rough sea. What he really needed was a little time to recover.

Jennings pulled his black slouch hat lower on his bony head. "I reckon it'll have to be. That's the trouble with you young fellers today. Nobody wants to do a decent day's work. Now back in my day—"

"I have to get cracking," Lett interrupted, "if we're going to get everything loaded up and out of there today." He knew Jennings well enough that the next subject would be politics. Then the skinny old fart would not stop complaining for hours.

"You tie one on last night?" Jennings asked, cocking one eye at Lett's swollen forehead.

"Why, no," Lett lied. "A can of coffee fell off the shelf and clipped me."

"That's good. I'm a teetotaler myself. Can't abide a drinking man."

"Sir, booze is the Devil's curse to mankind," Lett said.

"Amen," Jennings said. "I'll see you at the Last Chance in one hour." He turned to leave, then shot a frown over his shoulder and growled, "Don't be late."

Once the old man had gone, Lett flipped on the hot plate and started a pot of coffee to boil. He shook some aspirins into his hand without bothering to count and swallowed them dry. A few too many could not do any more damage than Canadian whiskey.

The memories of last night crashed into his tortured skull. *The money! Had it simply been some marvelous dream?*

When he jumped up and dashed to the night stand by his bed his head throbbed like some kid learning to play a base drum was inside it. Lett breathed a sigh of relief when he hefted the fat white envelope.

It had not been a dream. For some wonderful and unfathomable reason the lawyer, Otis Tate, had given him more money than he had ever seen in one place before. Those little kids would be well taken care of now. Lett made a silent promise to see to it that every dollar went for clothes, food and an education. He would never touch a penny for his own benefit. A man, even when his back troubles him, can make his own way.

Delight. Now that Melissa and Avery's support was assured he wondered if somehow he could be able to provide for a wife. God only knows how much he wanted her to himself. For her to never sell her sweet body to anyone again.

God, I got way out of line with you last night, didn't I? I don't know what to say except I'm sorry, but you really do care and I am truly sorry for my words.

Lett rolled up the yellowed curtain and stared through the cracked window pane at Delight's shack. There was no light on inside. He was not surprised. The kids needed their sleep and the morning was young.

He wished fervently now that he had turned down Jennings' offer. Ten dollars, however, was hard to come by. Once the work was done, he would have plenty of time to talk things over with Delight. With any luck at all he just might convince the blond lady, who he had come to love, into leaving with him. Those little kids could use a mother. He knew for certain he would never find any woman who would be as caring to them as Delight. No matter what her past, he wanted her future.

The coffee began perking. Lett turned down the hot plate and after a few minutes poured himself a steaming cup. He soon began to think he might live through the day. In the cupboard he found a can of corned willie, which was what he called corned beef, and a half loaf of bread. Enough for lunch, should his stomach ever allow him the privilege of eating it. He dumped the food into his black metal lunch pail, gulped down one final cup of coffee then hurried off. He knew Jennings was probably already at the mine waiting for him.

Once outside, Lett stopped when he noticed Delight and the kids were up. Melissa must have found something funny for her melodious laugh rang like a silver bell. His heart soared that the melancholy girl was coming out of her doldrums.

He fought down the urge to run and knock on the pallid door. Dave Jennings had ten dollars for him. The kids and Delight, his family, needed him to work as much as possible. He was not going to let them down.

The old Chevy started with a rattle, sputtered a cloud of blue oil smoke, but kept running. Shortly, the last man in Shakespeare with a job headed off for what he knew would be his last shift here. He didn't want to be late for it. Lett knew the day would be a long one.

All his thoughts and his heart were on tonight.

CHAPTER FORTY-NINE

Len Miller jumped to his feet when the long black Cadillac pulled to a stop at Dugan's gas pump. Perhaps, if he was lucky, a tip might be forthcoming. Just last week he had received a whole dollar from a beautiful blond lady who drove a fancy Ford convertible. She looked a lot like Greta Garbo. Len had been too shy to ask her, but later told anyone who would listen that he had actually waited on the famous movie star.

Any cash customers were a welcome change from the usual stream of broke Okies attempting to trade their spare tire, watch or some trinket for a few gallons of gasoline to take them closer to California.

Dan Dugan, Len's boss, had given him strict orders: cash only for gas. "I have to pay for the stuff with cash myself," Dugan had said gruffly. Yet, stacks of tires filled the back room of the station to overflowing and Len knew Dan had a pocket watch for every day of the year. Dan was too softhearted to wait on his own customers. The only way he could stay in business was hire Len to tell folks no when they asked for help.

The driver's side window rolled down. Len walked over. "May I help you, sir?" he asked pleasantly.

A huge bloated face with sagging jowls and deep-set piggish eyes turned toward him. "Yeah," the man said in a surprisingly shrill voice. "Fill it up with the best you have. Then check the oil and clean the bugs off the windshield."

The driver's ham-sized hand clutching a crisp green sawbuck

poked through the window. When Len took the money he noticed every one of the man's fingers, including his thumb, was adorned with what appeared to be diamond rings.

"Yes, sir," Len said fawningly, certain he was in the presence of a famous movie actor. "And if you need anything else, just ask."

"Yeah, information," the driver said, cocking his bulbous head toward the shaded backseat.

Len could make out a man's figure there, but didn't dare lower his head for a closer look.

The fat man continued, "The boss will let you keep the change if you'll tell us the truth about a man we know is around here."

Len swallowed. "I always tell the truth, sir."

The man behind the wheel flipped open his jacket to show off a chrome revolver tucked neatly into a black leather shoulder holster. "Then you have nothing to worry about." His voice reminded Len of a rattlesnake hiss. "As long as you keep your trap shut."

With a full tank of gasoline and spotless windshield the huge Cadillac rolled from Dugan's gas station onto the main street of Lordsburg. The fat driver with no neck rolled his head around like an owl to face the backseat passenger. He wore a sickly grin when he said, "Well, Mister Casey, it looks like we've finally cornered Sam Ransom."

CHAPTER FIFTY

The fiery orb had completed its path across a cloudless desert sky and hid itself behind the hills to the west when Lett Halsy drove back into Shakespeare.

Long, dark shadows lay heavy on the little town, unbroken by campfires or lights shooting through open windows of unpainted houses. The sole building that still fought back the night was Delight's shack in back of the now-silent Roxy Jay Saloon.

As Lett had expected, Bulldog, Epp and McTavish were gone, chasing dreams of jobs. Silently he mouthed, "Good luck my friends." He was not surprised everyone else, except Delight and the kids, had left along with them.

Lett thought, *I own what had been a going business here and I'm going to have to walk away and leave it to the tax man. When the Last Chance Mine died, so did the town.*

He pulled the rattling old Chevy to a dusty stop in front of the batwing doors to the saloon and shut off the engine. Stone silence greeted him.

Lett sat in the car for a while. He was more tired than he could remember. Every bone and muscle in his body ached, all except his head. That hadn't hurt since the aspirins had kicked in early this morning.

Jennings, it turned out, was determined to leave nothing but memories at the Last Chance. The old skinflint even loaded up the guardhouse and gate and hauled them away.

"The stuff ain't never been used, so I might as well take

'em," Jennings had wheezed. "If I leave 'em here some thief will steal 'em."

Only the coming darkness had spared the office building from being taken apart board by board. The white-haired peddler made no pretense. "Didn't really tell that Ransom feller I'd take the buildings. Reckon he won't have need of 'em though. He told me he was done with mining and has some big business deal workin' back east somewhere. Said he'd be hitting the road right soon."

The very thought of having that little weasel out of his life and away from Delight buoyed Lett's spirits immensely. He climbed slowly from his car, stood straight and arched his back. It still hurt badly as ever, but at least he was moving around again.

Inside the Roxy Jay, the clicking of Lett's worn hobnail boots on the plank wood floor echoed eerily, like water dripping inside an empty tomb. The shiny, long mahogany bar and its back mirror looked larger than he had remembered. It was a shame he had to leave such beautiful things behind. There were no other choices, however. He had obligations to others.

More than anything he wanted to wrap his tired arms around Delight's trim waist, look deeply into her blue eyes and ask the lady to be his wife. Yet, he felt afraid.

What if she says no, he mulled for the thousandth time. *I have nothing to offer. The lawyer's money will help, but once that is gone, what? My back is telling me in no uncertain terms I'm no longer a young man.*

Lett knew he was hesitating, trying to build courage. He needed to take a bath and clean up before going to see Delight. He was so gamey, even Wesley the dog would probably let out a yelp and run for fresh air if he came in smelling like he did now.

From inside his pocket Lett fished out two nickels. He shuffled over to the player piano, wound the spring and started to drop the coins into the slot when a pitiful whine stopped him.

"Hello Wesley, I was just thinking about you," Lett said to the mutt that was standing in the open back door. "I have something in the car you might like."

He walked outside and returned carrying his lunch box. "I only ate half of my corned willie. Believe me, you're welcome to the rest of it. This stuff was left over from the war or I miss my guess. It's for you to decide if it's better than rattlesnake."

Lett found a plate behind the bar, opened the black lunch box, dumped the corned beef onto the plate and set it on the floor in front of the dog. Wesley snubbed the offering, looked over his shoulder to Delight's shack and whined.

"You've got better sense than I thought," Lett said with a chuckle. "I only ate a few bites myself so I could live through the day."

The mutt backed outside, keeping his eyes focused on Lett and whining continuously. Lett swallowed hard when he remembered this was how Wesley had acted when he had led him to Elmore Wyman's body.

"What is it boy?" he asked with alarm, following the dog outside into the desert twilight. Lett relaxed when he heard the happy sounds of children's laughter and the radio drifting through the open windows of Delight's shack. He still had some courage to work up and a bath to take so he turned to his own cabin.

Wesley, however, was not about to take no for an answer. He ran to Lett, latched his teeth onto his pant leg and began pulling him toward the closed door.

Lett grumbled. "All right, I'll tell everyone I'm back. *Then* get cleaned up, you little pest."

The moment Lett walked onto Delight's porch, headed for the door, Wesley relaxed his grip then set on his haunches, looking eminently pleased with himself.

The sun-bleached door swung wide on his second knock. Lett stared incredulously at the plump middle-aged Mexican woman who had opened it. She was a total stranger.

"*Si Señor?*" she asked pleasantly. Then, switching to poor English, she said, "You must be the Meester Hallsee who own thees place."

"Uh yes, I am," Lett stammered looking over the lady's shoulder for Delight. The cabin was very small. It took but seconds for him to see only Melissa, Avery and the Mexican woman were there. "Where is the lady who lives here; Delight— where's Delight?" he nearly yelled at the smiling Mexican.

"Señor Hallsee, I do not know thees lady Deelight. My name is Carla Ortega. The lady who live here pay me to watch the leetle ones after she go. She tell me her name is Sara and give me money."

Melissa's blond head poked around Carla's voluminous dress. She rolled sad eyes at Lett and said, "She left this afternoon while you were at work. The man she went away with had the biggest red car you ever did see. It was so shiny and pretty. Carla has been really good to us, but Delight cooked better. Dinner tonight burned my mouth."

Sam Ransom, that bastard! Lett thought, as his heart fell from his chest to land somewhere around his socks. He was making a valiant attempt to compose himself when Carla spoke.

"The lady Sara. She give me thees for you."

From the dining-room table where Lett had planned to propose to Delight this very night, Carla picked up a white envelope and handed it to him. His name was inked on the outside with Delight's flowing penmanship. A hint of her perfume glided by on the breeze.

"I—I'd better go get myself cleaned up," he stuttered, clutching the envelope tightly to keep his hand from shaking. "I'll read it later." To Melissa and Avery he said, "You kids start getting your things packed up. We can't stay here much longer."

"But *Señor*, the lady Sara give me money to watch the leetle ones for many days," Carla said with concern.

Lett knew what she was worried about. "Ma'am," he said, "you can keep whatever money she gave you."

"Oh, *gracias Señor*," Carla said with obvious relief. "These times, they are not good."

"No," Lett agreed wholeheartedly, "they aren't," then turned and trudged to his cabin through the gathering night.

A single bare lightbulb dangled by a frayed cord over the kitchen table. Lett clicked it on and blinked from the sudden harsh glare. He prepared a pot of coffee and placed it on the hot plate to boil.

Sadness and fatigue caused him to sigh when he plopped down into the chair. Wesley came and laid his head over Lett's boot. He had been too tired to take them off.

Lett reached down and petted the dog's bristly head, keeping his eyes on the unopened letter from Delight. He felt as if he were at his wife and son's funerals once again. Opening that envelope would be like revealing the contents of a coffin.

There was no denying the fact Delight had left with Sam Ransom. He had been a total fool to delude himself into believing a lady like her could ever become the wife of a simple working man with two kids to support. She needed flashy cars and lots of money, things he could never offer.

Lett grabbed up the envelope planning to rip it to shreds, unread. A sudden yelp from Wesley stopped him.

"What is it fleabag?" he asked. "Now that you quit eating snakes for a living, I guess you're educated enough to read?"

The dog's answer was a firm whine.

"Just because you ain't been wrong yet, I'll read it. Then

maybe you'll give me some peace and quiet," Lett grumbled while cutting the envelope open with his pocket knife. He unfolded the note and cocked it into the light.

Wesley reared up on the table and pressed his cold nose against Lett's cheek. The man tried to talk to the dog, but could only sob as he read.

My Dearest Lett,

Thank you for giving me a taste of what it is like to have a home and family. The time we spent together will be treasured memories forever. Melissa and Avery are the children I would loved to have had, but never will.

My darling, (words I thought I would never pen), I wish only the best for you and the kids. A leopard can no more change its spots than I can change my past. Mine will follow me like a shadow the rest of my life. I love you too much to cause you hurt.

Long ago I bought a home for when I retired. I'm headed there, catching a ride with Ransom. I only deserve men like him.

In this whole world I love only one man—you. Now because I do love you, I must leave. My darling take care of yourself and those precious children.

You will be in my heart always. I shall never love another.

All my love,
Sara Jane Parker

Lett Halsy's eyes were misty and his lower lip trembled. He realized he *had* been a total fool because he had taken too much time to come forth with his real feelings. Now it was too late to do anything to rectify the situation.

A moment later Lett Halsy took the letter and folded it in two, ripped it, folded it again and ripped it into even smaller pieces. He did not need to keep it. The words written on it would forever remain burned into his heart.

CHAPTER FIFTY-ONE

There was no putting it off any longer, the time had come to leave Shakespeare. Lett sipped on a steaming cup of coffee while he stared through the window at the distant hills and worried how to best take care of those kids without Delight's help.

Hell, he could not even decide which way to point the car once they hit the highway in Lordsburg. Most headed for California. Len Miller, on the other hand, had told him quite a few people were heading east, saying things in California were worse than the place they had left.

A decent night's sleep would have helped. Lett had tossed and turned fitfully throughout the long dark hours. His body ached from moving heavy machinery and his heart ached from losing the woman he loved.

Sara Jane Parker, Lett thought. *Such a pretty name. If I had only spoken three little words before it was too late, the lady I knew as Delight would be here by my side. Dear God, how I want and need her. Why is it so difficult for a man to tell a woman he loves her?*

No matter. Delight/Sara was gone from his life forever. Right now she was probably sitting close beside Sam Ransom in his fancy car, speeding down some highway, her blond hair flying loose in the wind.

Lett shook himself from his bitter thoughts, poured a fresh cup of coffee and walked outside to inspect his car. The clock had yet to strike six, but the thermometer on the porch read nearly ninety degrees.

While he puttered checking the oil, water and tires he agonized on their destination. The warm desert climate agreed with his rheumatism. Perhaps Arizona held as much promise as California. Anywhere there were operating mines he at least had a chance of finding a job. The hard work of underground mining would only be more difficult for him if he had to fight the cold, too.

Arizona it would be. Tombstone, Wickenburg or even Oatman. It all depended on where he found employment. Any town that held work was a wonderful place to live and raise kids.

Buoyed by his decision, be it right or wrong, Lett started packing his belongings into the Chevy. He left plenty of room for the kids, their clothes and toys.

The three thousand dollars Otis Tate had given him he wrapped in oil cloth and stowed underneath the driver's seat. *It's probably safer there than in some bank,* he mused.

Carefully he counted his traveling money. The total came to two-hundred-thirty dollars and twenty-eight cents. *Before that's gone, my man, you'd better have a job. You can't touch the kids' money.*

The door to Delight's old shack swung wide. Carla, dressed in a flannel nightgown, filled the opening. She flashed him a toothy grin and announced. "Meester Hallsee I have feexed some breakfast."

For the first time in a long while food sounded good. Lett walked to his cabin, scrubbed the grime from his hands with a bar of yellow lye soap, then went to join the kids to eat before leaving.

Melissa and Avery were seated at the table, staring wide-eyed at their plates of food, wearing an expression that reminded Lett of a cow looking at a strange calf.

"I'm not hungry," Avery said flatly.

Melissa joined in. "Me neither," she said, gingerly sliding her plate to the center of the table with one finger.

Lett couldn't help but grin when he figured out the problem. He stuck a fork into a pile of what appeared to be green and red peppers mixed with a little egg and took a small, cautious bite. It felt like he had stuck the lit end of a cigarette into his mouth. "A tad spicy," he wheezed, reaching for a glass of water.

Avery said, "I blew an' blew on mine, but it's still hot."

Carla stuck her hands on her hips and shook her head in disbelief. "Maybe I put in too many jalapeños."

Lett rolled his eyes at the Mexican woman and thought, *There was a man named Bulldog I wish you could have met. You two would have hit it right off.*

"I am *mucho* sorry, *Señor,*" Carla said in obvious distress. "I did not think about the leetle ones not liking jalapeños."

Or the big ones, Lett thought. He smiled and said good-naturedly, "Reckon they take a little getting used to. That's all right ma'am, we'll stop in Lordsburg and have pancakes."

Melissa and Avery beamed with happiness.

Lett added, "You kids get all of your stuff into the car. We won't be coming back."

"Where are we going?" Melissa asked.

"Arizona," Lett said. "There's work in the mines there. It might take us a while to find it though. We'll have to be very careful with our money."

Melissa slid back from the table and jumped to the floor. "We can camp out like daddy did. It's not bad once you get used to it." She glared at Carla. "And *I'll* do all of the cooking."

While Avery scoured the cabin for lost toys and Melissa packed clothes, Lett took one last walk through the Roxy Jay. In the kitchen he found only two large cans of prunes remained. Obviously even McTavish had deemed them too dangerous for consumption; they were swollen and leaking.

Into an empty wooden dynamite box he put pans, a skillet,

plates, bowls and silverware to sustain their camping. There were salt, pepper and a few spices in his cabin he would add later.

He glanced longingly at the player piano. It was beautiful and he hated to just leave it, but there was no choice. Then a thought struck him. Ever since he had come to own the place people had been dropping nickels into the thing. Never once had he even thought of where they had gone.

Lett ran to the piano and slid it from the wall. There was not even a locked box for the nickels. The device simply dropped them into a five-gallon metal bucket that set into a hole in the floor. The bucket was filled to overflowing. Counting all of those coins would take hours. It would give the kids something to do. There was a lot of money in that bucket. And they needed every nickel of it.

A sudden gust of wind from a passing dust devil rattled the swinging doors. Lett walked over planning to shut and lock the solid doors that folded from inside the bar to cover the swinging ones. He stopped and grinned at his folly. *This is a one-way trip. It doesn't matter what happens to the place.*

There were far more important concerns. Nickels to be loaded, miles to be driven and children to be raised. The last part would be the hardest. He *would* do it. Somehow. Someway.

The drive to Lordsburg and the Vanderbilt Café was only two miles. In that short distance Avery had to go to the bathroom and Wesley, who the kids insisted on bringing along, upchucked on the floor mat.

Silver City is only an hour away, Lett thought desperately. *They have mines. If God's not too mad at me for throwing rocks at him, I might get a job there.*

Naming the Vanderbilt Café in Lordsburg after a ritzy New York hotel was a local bad joke. Everything from oysters to pancakes were cooked on a huge cast-iron griddle that spanned the entire back of the building. The cooktop started the day on the clean side, so pancakes ordered early in the morning stood a fair chance of tasting like they were supposed to. Lett hoped the cook had sense enough to keep those flapjacks away from any jalapeños.

Avery made a dash for the bathroom while Lett and Melissa slid into one of the high-backed booths that lined both walls.

Myrna, a skinny, silver-haired lady who had been a waitress at the Vanderbilt ever since Lett had first eaten there, brought him a cup of coffee and glasses of water for Melissa and Avery. She slid three grease-stained menus onto the table then stood looking at Lett as if trying to decide whether or not to speak.

"Thanks for the coffee," Lett said. "I really need it."

"Mister Halsy," Myrna said in a near whisper, "could I see you—alone?"

Lett's brow furrowed in puzzlement as to what she could possibly want. He shrugged his shoulders and told Melissa as he slid from the booth, "I'll be right back. Tell Avery I'll order a big stack of pancakes for everyone."

Myrna smiled at Melissa. "And I'll heat up the syrup for them too."

Once Myrna and Lett were out of Melissa's hearing, she grabbed his hand and said, "That blond—woman—who rented the crib from you—"

"Delight," Lett interjected.

"Yeah, her," Myrna said, nodding toward the farthest booth that had two battered suitcases sitting in the aisle next to it, "she's been there all night. I tried to get her to see a doctor or at least Len Miller. She's waiting for the bus, but someone's beat her up real bad. Maybe you can talk some sense—"

Myrna didn't have time to finish her sentence before Lett bolted away, heading for Delight.

CHAPTER FIFTY-TWO

Lett stopped short of the booth and swallowed, trying hard to collect his thoughts. He simply could not believe his good fortune in finding Delight. If Carla had not used jalapeño peppers too liberally, he and the kids would be driving for Arizona now.

He stepped around the suitcases and slid into the booth across from the blonde who kept her face to the wall.

"Howdy Miss Sara," he said. "Could an old friend buy you a cup of coffee?"

Lett couldn't stop a grimace when Delight slowly turned to face him. Her right eye was swollen closed. An ugly purple bruise covered her cheek.

"Oh Lett, I'm sorry you had to see me like this," she whispered huskily.

That was when Lett saw angry red welts alongside her throat. "Did Sam Ransom do this to you?" he asked, his voice cold as tempered steel. "I'll kill the bastard!"

She shook her head. "No, it wasn't him. We were ran off the road by a big black car just outside of town, some goon started pounding on Sam with a pair of brass knuckles. I—I tried to protect him."

"Where is the guy that did this?" Lett's rage was building, "He'll eat those knucks."

Sara reached across the table and placed her soft hand over Lett's clenched fist. "They're long gone. All of this happened early last night," she said calmly. "There was an older man who seemed to be the boss. He made the thug stop hitting me. After the goon beat Sam unconscious they let me get my luggage out of Sam's car. Then they brought me into town and dropped me off. The old guy said he was sorry I got in the way, that they only wanted Sam Ransom."

Lett's fist relaxed and he stroked Sara's hand. "I'm glad they finally got together. It's just too bad you had to be there for the reunion. Right now I think we'd better get you to a doctor."

A tear streamed from Sara's open eye making a mocha line from her makeup that matched the color of the tepid coffee in her cup. "I've had worse than this happen to me. Oh Lett, I thought I'd never see you again."

He smiled. "I'm glad you were wrong about that. I'd planned to ask you to marry me last night." Lett took a handkerchief from his shirt pocket and dabbed carefully at her moist cheek. "Now I'm going to ask you before you get another chance to get away from me. Sara Jane Parker, please be my wife."

Sara turned her head to the wall. "My darling, you know that wouldn't be fair to you and those poor kids. I can't change the past."

Lett slipped from his seat, walked over and set next to Sara. He stroked her long blond tresses with his calloused fingers, trying to comfort her.

"Everyone leaves their past behind them," he said softly. "It's called growing older. All we have is our tomorrows and I want to spend mine with you. I love you, Sara."

Great sobs racked Sara's body like waves crashing in from an ocean. Lett was afraid he might accidentally hurt her wounded body so he scooted away. Her grip was surprisingly strong when she reached and rolled his shoulders toward her. Sara laid her unbruised cheek on Lett's chest, fixed her open eye at him and tried to smile.

"When I'm with you," she said, "I do believe in miracles. I don't deserve you, Lett Halsy, but yes, I will marry you."

"Then we'll rustle up a preacher over in Arizona," Lett said happily. "I expect they have at least one and that's all we need."

Calming now, Sara took a sip of cold coffee and said, "Lett, I own a house on the ocean, over in Rockport, Texas. It sits on an acre of land. There's lots of room for kids to play. I know there are no gold mines in Texas, but I've managed to save a little money. With this Depression on and some time to think things over together, I'll bet we can do as well there as in Arizona."

Lett shrugged his muscular shoulders. "I've never seen the ocean. And I've never been to Texas, but as long as we're together, I'll be happy."

Sara tried to smile. "You haven't called me Delight anymore."

"I reckon she's best left in Shakespeare. Sara and Lett Halsy are going to Texas and leaving her behind."

"I *do* love you," Sara said, snuggling closer.

"Are you going to be my new mommy?" a happy voice chirped at the end of the table.

Lett and Sara looked into Melissa's smiling face. "Yes honey," Lett beamed, "we're getting married."

"I'm glad," Melissa said to Lett. "She cooks really good and is lots of fun. Avery and I like her a lot." She looked closely at Sara's swollen eye and said, "My first daddy had a shiner like that once. If we stop and buy a beefsteak and you hold it on your eye, it'll heal right up."

"We'll do just that," Lett said. "By the time we get to Texas, Sara will be just fine."

"I know that," Melissa squealed. "I've been listening. We're going to the ocean. I think that's great."

Lett and Sara watched while Melissa ran after Myrna who was carrying huge plates of pancakes to the table where Avery was anxiously awaiting them.

"What do you think," Lett asked, "should we join the rest of our family for breakfast?"

"First things first," Sara said hoarsely. She placed her soft hand behind Lett's head and drew him close, carefully keeping her swollen eye and cheek clear, Sara kissed Lett full on the lips. She winked at him. "We'll have to practice on this after I heal up."

"It may take a lot of years to get it right," Lett said with a smile.

"That's fine by me." Sara finally noticed the angry red welt on Lett's forehead and asked, "What in the world happened to you, and don't tell me you ran into a door?"

Lett chuckled. "No, God beaned me with a rock, trying to drive some sense into my thick skull. I think it took."

"Lett Halsy," she said with mock irritation in her husky voice. "I was always worried I'd be lonely and bored in my old age. Somehow, being married to you, I don't think that's going to be a problem."

Lett grasped her hand gently. "Then I'd reckon we'd best have breakfast with *our* kids then find us a preacher on the way to Texas. By the way," he added firmly, "you're *not* old, you're beautiful."

Sara Jane Parker could only smile with her heart as she slid from the wood booth to begin the first day of her new life.

CHAPTER FIFTY-THREE

Sara Jane Parker changed her name for the final time that very afternoon when she became Sara Jane Halsy. They were joined in a small Presbyterian church on a tree-lined street in Las Cruces, New Mexico.

The rotund preacher had cast a curious eye at the battered couple, but was kind enough to say nothing about their wounds.

While the minister said the vows that bound a man to a woman, tears streamed down Sara's cheeks. To Lett's relief, Melissa sobbed from happiness. She was coming out of the emotional shell she had built.

Avery shuffled his feet in boredom, while Wesley's barking kept time with the music the preacher's wife played on the pump organ. The mutt had treed the parson's cat seconds after they had pulled up at the church.

Soon, the newlyweds would be watching their adopted children frolicking with Wesley on the warm sandy beaches of Rockport, Texas.

Sara took special care to keep her smallest suitcase within close reach.

Sara Jane Halsy, a housewife and mother, would never have recognized Sam Ransom's money case for what it was. Nor, hurt and bleeding, would she have had the presence of mind to stealthily slide it—along with the thirty-four thousand dollars it contained—in with her luggage.

But a feisty little lady named Delight would have.

ABOUT THE AUTHOR

Born in the shadow of Pike's Peak in Colorado, **Ken Hodgson** has enjoyed many various and interesting careers. He has worked in a state mental hospital, been a prospector and a gold and uranium miner, and owned an air-compressor business. A former newspaper columnist, Ken has written hundreds of magazine newspaper stories and articles along with over a dozen published novels. Ken is an active member of Mystery Writers of America, Western Writers of America, and International Thriller Writers. He splits his time between San Angelo, Texas, and Tucumcari, New Mexico, where he lives on small ranches with his wife, Rita, and totally spoiled cats, Sasha and Ulysses.